Big Cat

Jack Churchill

Big Cat

Published by The Aeolian Press, 2013
www.4winds-productions.com/theaeolianpress

Cover photo © Martin Belderson
Book layout, art and design © Martin Belderson, 2013

ISBN: 978-0-9576251-1-2

The Aeolian Press

DEDICATION

To my long-suffering family

— CONTENTS —

ACKNOWLEDGMENTS

First, my uncle and aunt, Bob and Carol, for allowing me to discover the hidden wilds of Surrey when I was a kid. They also provided superb proof-reading and editorial advice, as did my partner, Catherine, and my parents, John and Elizabeth.

- 1 -

- Early Spring -

- The North Downs, Surrey, England -

THE UPWARD SWING OF THE CROWBAR IN LYNTON Creswell's hand came to an abrupt stop. His face contorted in disbelief. 'You're doing what?' he said, in a voice thick with rage.

The watching crowd fell silent. In the hush, all that could be heard were the whines of the crippled bull terrier. In Creswell's world, a losing dog was a dead dog, and he only owned winners.

Her heart pounding, Rosie fought to keep her voice composed. 'I said; Rosie Flinn, dog warden, and you're under arrest. This... you...' She gulped down a breath. 'This dogfight contravenes the Animal Welfare Act, 2006 and—'

Creswell twisted his bulk to face her. Rosie retreated a step. His bulging stomach might not be intimidating, but the broad span of his shoulders and corded muscles in his neck were.

'—and the Dangerous Dog Act, 1991.' There was now a tremor of uncertainty in her voice.

Outrage had driven Rosie to this remote barn, to steal up to it, and attempt to save the life of the wounded bitch.

Fear quickened her heart. It thudded hard and fast as the realisation struck that her rash intervention had created a confrontation it was unwise to be part of, especially for a mother of two with no backup and no coherent plan of what to do next.

Lynton glanced right and left at his brothers, Pat and Terry. Neither possessed his hulking body mass but Rosie suspected their combined IQ was even lower than their big brother's. In the harsh shadows cast by the barn's single overhead lamp, the three men looked like Neanderthal throwbacks. Piggy eyes stared at Rosie as they tried to comprehend this bewildering turn of events.

'She a copper?' said Terry.

He clutched the collar of the winning dog. Eager to finish off its opponent, the snarling pit-bull lunged at the wounded terrier. He yanked it back, but Rosie noticed his fingers, smeared with dog blood, struggled to keep their grip on the collar's slippery leather.

'Don't recognise her; she ain't local,' said Pat. 'Here, are you a copper? You got to tell us if you are. It's the law.'

Rosie's children, Lizzie and Peter, went to the same primary school as Lynton Creswell's son, Shad. At bedtime two hours earlier, Lizzie blurted out what Shad had boasted about in the playground earlier that day. His Dad and uncles were going to kill some dogs tonight. The news had stoked Rosie's fury to its highest heat. The brothers were not exactly criminal masterminds and it had not taken a major feat of detective work for her to discover the fight's location. On hearing the terrier's agonised yelps, she had charged into the barn.

'I'm a dog warden,' repeated Rosie. 'What you are doing is illegal, and I will certainly call the police.' She felt in her coat pockets for her mobile phone. Oh damn, where was it?

'She ain't The Filth,' said Terry, 'just a council nosey-parker. She can't arrest us.'

Smack. The thick metal of the crowbar slapped into Lynton's open hand. Smack. The metal struck his palm again. Smack. Metal to palm.

Rosie trembled. She did not need psychic powers to read Lynton's mind. The dimmest light bulb outshone his mental capacity, but that did not give her any kind of advantage. Persuasion and the fear of consequence were concepts alien to impulse driven creatures like the Creswells. Rosie became acutely aware of the thick odours of blood, of dog excrement, of fear, in the barn, and of a new scent, excitement. The mob drew closer to her. This is not, she told herself, a good time to discover you aren't much of a hero. A hero would face these morons down. A hero would, um, be better prepared. A hero might even call the police first.

One man, curly-haired and fresh-faced, stepped forward.

'Get lost. Right now,' he said.

Oh no, not him too? An irrational sense of betrayal made Rosie's heart pound even faster. Seconds earlier, watching from her hiding place, she had been convinced he was about to intervene and, before a word escaped his open mouth, that certainty triggered her into action. Better that she should intervene in her official capacity than some member of the public, she thought. A large part of her decision was also because he looked like an adult version of her six year-old son, Peter. The aggression he now directed at her only deepened her dismay.

'You've no business here,' said his mate, a nasty-looking character in biker's leathers.

'Why don'tcha go and fine someone 'cos their dog crapped on the pavement?' said a woman whose ample figure was improbably crowded into tight Lycra top and leggings. 'Go on, piss off.'

She gave Rosie a shove, forcing the dog warden backwards and towards the open barn doors. Her two burly escorts chortled. Somehow, their mockery felt more threatening than the storm of four-letter abuse Rosie had been expecting. Dogfighting fans were not renowned for their mastery of the social graces.

But Rosie was nothing if not stubborn. The more she felt threatened, the more mulish she became.

'Give me that dog immediately,' she said indicating the wounded bull terrier. 'She needs urgent treatment. I'm not leaving without her.'

'Don't think so,' Lynton said. 'That dog's dead, only it don't know it yet.' He took a step towards her. 'Thing is, what do we do with you?'

Terry swung his pit bull around to face her.

The powerful animal's white teeth, exposed in rictus snarl, gleamed in the bright light. Rosie eyed with alarm the tenuous grip of his fingers on the dog.

'How about dog versus dog warden?' Terry said.

'Always wanted to watch someone up against a fighting dog like Tyson,' said Pat.

Rosie couldn't help herself. She knew she'd make things worse but she had to say it anyway. 'Tyson? How original. What a stupid name. Which one of you morons came up with that?'

This caused a temporary halt in the brothers' advance. They looked at each other as if to decide who would assume responsibility and, therefore, take the most offence. Trouble was, they really could not recall who had picked the dog's name.

'Don't matter,' Lynton said after several seconds passed. 'Got a question for you, dog warden. You gonna be dog meat or dog...?' His voice trailed away as he failed to come up with a witty quip.

Rosie noticed both Curly Hair and Lycra Top talking into mobile phones. Oh, great, she thought, now there's going to be live commentary of me being mauled by a pit bull. It occurred to her, finally, that the prudent thing to do might be to get out of the barn and to do so quickly. She spun around, but Pat was faster off the mark. In three long strides, he placed himself between Rosie and the open door. She attempted to feint right and step left, but he read the move with ease and he pinned her tight against his chest with an arm around her neck. Many in the watching crowd whooped and applauded.

'Where do you want her, big bruv?' Pat said between grunts as Rosie wriggled in his grip.

'You stink,' she said. Pat had the rank, queasy reek of a 'Big Mac with fries' addict.

'Oh, enough of this farce. Amateur hour is over,' said a commanding woman's voice. 'Steve, do you want to do your thing?'

Pat and Rosie stopped their wrestling. They both stared in shock at Lycra Top. She no longer sounded like the bored airhead who had spoken moments earlier.

'Suppose I'd better,' said Curly Hair. He held high an ID card. 'Inspector Steve Ashworth, RSPCA. And this time you actually are under arrest. All of you.'

'Yeah, yeah. You don't have the right to arrest us, no more than this girlie. You ain't the police,' Lynton Creswell said with a sneer.

'No, that would be me,' said Lycra Top, 'and I'm with him.'

One of her escorts said, 'Now, now, now!' into his phone.

The glare of approaching headlights and flicker of blue flashing lights bounced off the barn doors as three police vans and a dog unit sped down the farm track.

Lynton, as ever, reacted without thought.

'Take 'em down, lads,' he said.

Crowbar raised once more, he charged at Lycra Top.

Rosie never managed to work out how the woman accomplished the impressive feat of concealing an extendable police baton in her skin-tight clothing, but she had. Its metal shaft snickered as she flicked it to full length. In two sharp, efficient blows, the crowbar was out of Lynton's grasp and he was down on his knees grunting in pain whilst holding a broken wrist.

Both of Lycra Top's companions produced similar weapons. One of them pulled out a pair of handcuffs.

It was then that Terry Creswell released Tyson.

Five minutes later, Steve Ashworth reached high and held out a hand to Rosie.

'Here, let me help you down.'

Rosie had no notion of how she accomplished her panic-driven scramble up into the rafters, and was just as certain she had no idea how to climb back down again.

'I think I'll get you a ladder,' Ashworth said.

As Rosie descended, she surveyed the carnage. Lynton Creswell's unbroken wrist was cuffed to the axle of an aged tractor. Terry Creswell was being treated by one of the police detectives for a nasty bite on his forearm. Lycra Top and the second detective were using a police medical kit to attempt to staunch the numerous dog bites inflicted on Pat Creswell. The sizeable chunk torn from his left buttock presented a troublesome challenge. They had no dressing big enough to cover the wound. The pit bull, its bloodlust already high and driven into frenzied aggression by the large number of targets presented to it, had run amok. It first savaged Terry, then half a dozen of the onlookers until, finding Pat's meaty odour irresistible, it latched onto him.

Tyson, now muzzled and penned in one corner of the barn, was trapped after Ashworth's biker friend, also a RSPCA undercover officer, pulled a net from a concealed jacket pocket. Flung over the dog, it gave them traction as he, Ashworth, the three detectives, plus two uniformed officers, tried to wrench the attack dog from its grip on Pat's rear end. Flesh gave way before dog jaw. The pit bull was torn free with a good pound of hamburger-flavoured buttock held tight in his locked teeth.

Rosie's feet touched the barn floor.

'Thank you,' she said to Ashworth.

The uniformed officers had bundled the dogfighting fans outside and into two of the police vans. Exposed to the night air, the building felt cold. The only sounds were Pat Creswell's keening wails and the whimpers of the semi-conscious wounded bitch. The leather-clad RSPCA man stroked the dog's head as he assessed her wounds.

'Steve, she's got at least two broken legs, has God only knows how many lacerations, and she's lost a huge amount of blood,' he said. He peeled off his jacket and carefully wrapped her in it. 'I'd better get her to the surgeon right now.' With tender care, he lifted the dog. 'Suze, can I take one of your vans and a driver? We need to travel blues and twos.'

Lycra Top looked up. 'Feel free; just ask one of the lads outside. Any argument, send him to me.'

'You get going, Neil,' said Ashworth. 'I'll phone ahead.' He walked outside to make the call.

The dog warden was left to contemplate her actions. Rosie's anger had long subsided, as had the adrenaline surge from the struggle with Pat Creswell. It was replaced by a dull realisation of the likely outcome of the mad, passionate fury that had overwhelmed her. She shivered. She felt as if someone had chucked a bucket of icy water over her.

'You cold?' said Ashworth from the doorway. 'Can I get you a coat?'

Rosie shook her head.

An ambulance for Pat Creswell arrived. They watched as he was loaded face down onto a stretcher, his bloody buttocks exposed to the air.

Balanced on her high heels, Lycra Top crouched to search the straw-covered barn floor with her hands.

'Ha, got it,' she said in triumph. She held aloft the missing chunk of flesh. 'He can be at one with his bum again.'

As she dropped the bloody gobbet into a clear plastic evidence bag then gave it to the paramedics, she glanced over at Ashworth and Rosie. 'Steve, you need to have words with her. Better all-round than if I do it.' She turned away.

'Impressive isn't she?' Ashworth said in a discreet tone.

'Who is she?' said Rosie, equally quietly. 'I wouldn't want to cross her.'

'Her name is Detective Sergeant Susie Derrington and, yes, she is quite a handful.'

There was something odd, unexpected, in the way Ashworth said it. Rosie looked at him. He smiled and held up his left hand. A gold wedding band glinted.

'Yep, she's my missus,' he said. 'Won't let me go undercover without her being in attendance. Very useful she is too.'

Oh well, thought Rosie, another one that got away.

'You should get home,' Ashworth said. 'Let me walk you to your car. We'll be in touch to arrange a time and date to take your statement.'

The sky was clear, but only a few stars could be seen through the combined orange glow cast by suburban London twenty miles to the north and Croydon away to the east.

Ashworth inhaled the chilly air. 'Snow's on its way,' he said.

'How can you tell?' said Rosie.

'Not a country girl are you?'

'Strictly a Londoner until I moved here a couple of years ago.'

'You can smell the snow on the air. Must be something to do with humidity, I suppose. You can sense it coming once you've worked outdoors long enough.' Ashworth paused. 'Listen, Suze is right. When I said earlier, keep your nose out, I meant it. If we hadn't been there, well, I'd rather not think about what they could have done to you.'

Rosie tugged with her fingernails at a splinter in the palm of her left hand. She'd picked it up when taking refuge on the rafter. Pinpricks of pain in her inner thighs made her certain she'd got a couple more lodged in her flesh. Not that she was going to inspect the damage until she got to the privacy of a bathroom with a lock on the door.

'You just can't barge in like that,' Ashworth said. 'I, we, the RSPCA, have a Royal Charter, and the police always back us up. They have to; it's their job and it's my job, but you, you're just a...' He endeavoured but failed to come up with a polite turn of phrase.

'Just a dog warden?' said Rosie.

The edge in her voice made him hold up the palms of both hands as he tried to placate her.

'What you did was great. Incredibly brave. Admirable. But Suze and her lads would have arrested them anyway.'

'I didn't know that.'

The splinter came free. Rosie winced at the searing stab of pain. She sucked the wound.

'No you didn't,' Ashworth said, 'and you could have screwed up months of undercover work.'

'I'm sorry,' Rosie said with genuine contrition.

They reached her car, an ageing blue Daewoo saloon, part of the flotsam left to Rosie after the wreck of her marriage. Dreading a long lecture, she opened the driver's door and climbed inside.

Ashworth crouched to speak to her at eye level.

'Next time you hear of something like this, call us first.'

'Sure.' Rosie hesitated then asked the question uppermost in her mind. 'Are you going to report me for this?'

Ashworth smiled again. 'Me? No. Neil won't either. No way. But Suze, well, I just don't know.' He took a deep breath and sighed. 'She has strong views about interfering busybodies who get in the way of police officers performing their duties.'

'Oh God, I knew it.' This was something senior management at her employer, Mid-Surrey County Council, would not take lightly.

'Hey, don't worry.' Ashworth grinned at her. 'I didn't say she would do anything. Mid-Surrey Police got a good bust here tonight, a great one, in fact. Lots of arrests; dog rescues. There'll be loads of positive publicity and, better still, Suze got to beat up one of the Creswells. That's a career highlight in itself. She'll be okay. Just don't do it again. Suze gives no-one a second chance, not even me.'

'Okay, sorry.'

'One final thing. How did you hear about tonight's dogfight? What brought you here all fired up?'

When Rosie finished her tale, Ashworth mulled over what he'd heard. His fingers drummed on the car doorframe. It was several seconds before he spoke again.

'Tell me, have you considered what will happen once the Creswell brothers are bailed?' he said.

'You mean they won't be in prison?'

'Eventually, yes. Definitely. But, until they go to trial, they'll be on bail. Probably out by tomorrow morning. And you live locally, don't you?'

'What if they find out my address?' The awful realisation of the danger she'd placed Lizzie and Peter in made Rosie feel sick. Regret piled upon regret.

Ashworth's fingers continued their drum tattoo. Finally, he said, 'If you like, I'll have a word with Suze. She'll let the Creswells know they're not to go near you. Suze will hate you for life, but, when she leans on someone, even morons like the Creswells pay attention.'

It was a bargain Rosie was more than willing to strike.

'Yes, please,' she said, at the same time certain she and the kids would move back to her Mum's. For a while. Purely temporary. Maybe for a month. Or two. Or three.

'Deal,' said Ashworth. He looked up at the sky again and breathed deep. 'Definitely snow on the way.'

Torch beams flashed in erratic directions as the four drunk men lurched along the path. Each blamed the others for not keeping the torchlight true to their course. They slipped, stumbled, and barged one another as much from inebriation as from unseen roots and snagging branches. Second in line, Oakshott tripped and grabbed the back of Zaharkin's hunting jacket.

'Careful, *hooy morzhovy*, you bloody idiot,' said the Russian. 'Have you never been in a wood at night before?'

The Englishman's reply betrayed the amount of alcohol he had consumed. 'Sorry, so sorry Alexei. Just not used to it. I mean, how can you drink so much vodka and live? That stuff's way too strong for the likes of me.'

This was not the impression his two partners wanted to make on their billionaire host.

'Don't be so pathetic, Oakers. If Zaharkin thinks we're weak, he won't do business with us,' Beacon said, his voiced pitched low to prevent the exiled oligarch overhearing them.

Jervis joined in. 'You're an embarrassment, you idiot,' he said. 'Breath deep, clear your head and, for God's sake, get a grip on yourself.' He raised his voice. 'I think milk might be too strong for him, eh, Alexei?'

Zaharkin made no reply. Muttering more Russian oaths under his breath, he lumbered on.

Oakshott slipped once more and stumbled to his knees. His torchlight cut a wild trajectory through the tangled undergrowth. Unseen by the men, the beam of light touched upon black fur in the blackness. Smooth muscles hunched. The movement became a dark shiver in the night: a shudder in the dark. In an instant, it was gone.

Ten weary minutes later, the foursome came to an irregular halt outside an age-worn shack propped against a stand of birch trees. Zaharkin's torchlight highlighted his lined face. His breath steamed in the cold night air. Beneath dark eyebrows, his eyes twinkled but could not hide the hardness within.

'And here, my friends, is our home for the night,' he said. 'My little hunting *dacha*.' Zaharkin's arms swept expansively wide to encompass the lean-to.

Jervis poked a bony finger at its brittle, warped shingles. 'This it?' he said. 'It's a bit of a dump, Alexei.'

The sneer, delivered in an educated Home Counties accent, was achieved effortlessly, but had no effect on the amiable Russian.

'*Da*, of course. What else, for sure?'

'Well, for starters, maybe a bit more luxury?'

'For God's sake, Zaharkin, we're only three miles from your mansion,' said Beacon. 'Why didn't we stay there?

'In the warmth,' said Oakshott. 'With servants.'

'I promise you hunting Russian-style and so we are here,' said the billionaire. He swayed drunkenly then pushed with his tubby frame against the damp, resistant timber of the door and forced it open. He gestured to the three Brits. 'Enter, my friends. Come in, come in, *tovarisch*.'

Zaharkin lit an oil lamp. Its light flared to reveal two pairs of rough-hewn bunks, a battered table, four dilapidated chairs, and a decrepit samovar perched on a wood-burning stove. Whilst their host bustled about, his guests spoke quietly amongst themselves.

'Not quite what you'd expect of a billionaire's hunting lodge,' said Jervis. He kicked the frail wall.

'Matches the man, in my opinion,' said Beacon.

Now indoors and safe from the wild and dark woods, Oakshott recovered his poise.

'Hardly riding to the hounds is it?' he said as he unrolled the coarse blanket Zaharkin provided as bedding. 'Oh my God, look at this.'

Wedged between bunk frame and mattress was the mummified corpse of a songbird. He picked it up by one wing. Tiny grey feathers drifted to the floor.

'Quick, get rid of it before Alexei sees it,' said Beacon. 'He'll probably shoot it and claim it was an eagle.'

'Or shove it in a bottle of vodka because he thinks it'll improve the flavour,' said Jervis.

Oakshott opened the door then tossed the bird outside. Wary of offending the oligarch, the three friends smothered their laughter.

Zaharkin regarded the three property developers with a baleful eye. In contrast to his weatherworn camouflage clothing and well-used knife, rifle and binoculars, they cut superficially impressive figures. But their tweed hunting outfits had not yet shed the creases left by their outfitter's packaging. New polished leather straps and belts creaked and squeaked from lack of use and their sheathed rifles showed no sign of acquaintance with mud or grass.

He pulled an unlabelled bottle from behind a pile of firewood. It contained a clear, russet-brown liquid. He sighed. Time again to play jovial host to these three idiots.

'Aha, here it is, my boys,' he boomed. 'This will warm you quicker than any fire.'

He scooped four dirty tumblers from a dusty shelf.

Appalled at the sight of yet more vodka, the three Brits gave a collective shudder.

'I mean, is this worth it?' said Oakshott in a whisper.

'It is if we want Zaharkin's cash for Swanmere Phase Two,' said Beacon.

'Bloody bankers. They're the only reason we're here. They've screwed up everything,' Oakshott said.

'Beacon's right,' Jervis muttered in reply. 'This is business. Treat it as such. We need his money, nothing more, nothing less. Don't bugger up this deal. And stop whining.'

Zaharkin scrutinised the interior of one glass. He spat into it then wiped it with a greasy cloth. It was already clean but his guests weren't to know that. He just wanted to enjoy the looks of revulsion on their faces.

'Come, come,' he said as he filled the tumblers to the brim. 'Drink up, Misters Jervis, Oakshott, and Beacon. This vodka, we call it *Okhotnichya*. Hunter's vodka. Appropriate, *da*, yes?'

They smiled at the billionaire. Each took a glass.

'We drink before we hunt,' said Zaharkin. '*Nu budem*! Cheers!'

He knocked back the liquor. His guests attempted the same. Jervis's eyes bulged and his face turned red. Beacon choked but kept his down. Oakshott failed. Coughing uncontrollably, he spewed vodka down his shirtfront. 'Herbs, Jervis, bloody herbs,' he said. 'It's herbal vodka!'

Zaharkin laughed. '*Da*, sure. The best. Made from forest plants. Now drink, Mr. Oakshott. Drink for your health. For the luck of the hunt.'

He refilled Oakshott's glass. His victim looked imploringly at his friends. They glared back at him. Still grumbling, Oakshott lifted the tumbler.

'I mean, herbal vodka?' he said.

Zaharkin raised his own glass in salute.

'Drink, my friend. *Nazdorovye!* We have until dawn. And this does not have dead sparrow in it, yes?'

Beacon groaned inwardly. Zaharkin had heard their bitching. Swanmere Phase Two was surely in peril. The same thought occurred to Oakshott. He knew he had to do his duty. Mentally cursing all things Russian, he swigged down the vodka and held out his glass for a refill.

'Ho, I will make Russian of you yet,' Zaharkin said as he poured.

In the wan pre-dawn light, Oakshott watched snowflakes accumulate on the heads of a clump of daffodils. Despite the arrival of spring, the easterly wind had delivered one last snowfall. The four hunters crouched in a hollow sheltered by a dense thicket of holly bushes. Zaharkin's reluctant companions were pale-faced and hung-over. He was the only one who relished the coming morning.

'Snow? In Surrey? The bastard brought it with him from Siberia,' said Oakshott.

Zaharkin gazed with delight upon the dense treescape now transformed from drear English grey to Siberian white. 'Hah, is true. Mother Russia has come to visit your soft England.'

Oakshott, suffering both from less than an hour's sleep and a stupendous headache, slumped backwards into a snowdrift, then laid his rifle on the ground and leant against Jervis. His uptight friend stiffened and attempted without success to push Oakshott away.

The snowfall ceased. The Russian scanned the steep wooded slopes around them and nodded with satisfaction. He had brought them to the edge of an open glade through which a clear stream gurgled its way down the valley. Zaharkin knew that at least three deer paths intersected in this clearing; he had made many kills here, most of them clean single shots.

For once, his loud voice was hushed.

'Boys, the news is good,' he said. 'Snow is in our favour. Most times, the deer is hard to see. Too many trees are here, there, everywhere,' he gestured at the valley walls, 'but, against snow, deer is easy to shoot. Now dawn has come, it makes for fine shot, you will see.'

Oakshott leant forward and dry-retched between his knees. Zaharkin grimaced with contempt then turned to resume his careful examination of the terrain.

Beacon glanced nervously at the oligarch's broad back. He spoke to Oakshott in a whisper, 'Oakers, if you're going to be sick again, do it some place where Alexei won't see. Pull yourself together.'

'It's alright for you bloody Scots.' Oakshott scooped up a handful of snow and rubbed it on his face. 'You're used to hard liquor and the freezing cold.' He was more than a little annoyed at the near constant nagging by his two partners. It wasn't his fault Zaharkin had made it his personal goal to destroy Oakshott's liver by alcohol poisoning. This was no fun. No fun at all.

Nor was Jervis enjoying himself. The cold wind pinched his features tighter. He succeeded finally in shoving Oakshott upright and away.

'Alexei, are you sure this is legal?' he said. 'I mean, don't we need a licence for hunting? A permit?'

Zaharkin did not bother to turn to face him. 'Who cares about permits? Is my land, yes? When I buy it, I buy deer too. Is my right to hunt my deer. What is problem with this?'

Oakshott stared with loathing at their host. He leant forward to whisper to Beacon, 'The problem is we're reduced to begging from a Russian peasant. And he ruddy well poisoned me with that damn home-made vodka.'

Zaharkin sniffed the wind then gestured the others to be silent. 'Something out there. I can smell it.' He frowned. 'Is odd. Not deer. Not like in Russia.'

Beacon and Jervis looked at each other.

The former mouthed silently the word, 'Smell?'

Jervis nodded and rolled his eyes.

'It's not like Russia because this isn't bloody Russia,' muttered Oakshott. 'This is England.'

Jervis agreed with those sentiments, but would be damned if he'd show it. Not when they were on the brink of securing Zaharkin's millions. 'For once in your life will you shut up?' he said to Oakshott.

Zaharkin loaded his rifle. The snick of the bolt as it slid home startled the threesome out of their bickering.

'Movement. Over there,' said the Russian. He jerked his chin in the direction of the far side of the clearing. Beacon and Jervis joined him to peer over the lip of the hollow.

'What is it, Alexei?' said Beacon.

'There. Is deer. Young buck.'

Seventy paces away, a roe deer stag grazed. Caught in the first rays of the rising sun, its russet brown coat was crusted by a layer of melting snow. Jervis was unimpressed by the creature. He had expected something larger, something more moose-like, not this delicate thing. He shivered. The snow might have ceased, but the cold continued to work its way into his bones.

'Shoot it then we can go home,' he said. 'Please.'

The buck lifted its head erect to scent the wind. It held the exact same pose as Zaharkin a minute ago. It too smelt something unusual, a smell it did not recognise.

'Is not us,' Zaharkin said. 'We are down the wind, it cannot smell us.'

The stag sniffed the air. Its long delicate ears twitched then its flanks tensed as it held itself ready for flight. Zaharkin raises his rifle. He knew the spooked animal might flee at any moment. Now was the time to shoot. He aimed then paused.

'Strange.'

'What?' said Beacon.

'Nothing. I hear nothing, listen.'

Beacon studied the snow-smothered woods. They were silent. Even the gentle shifting of branches by the wind had ceased. Not a bird fluttered or called out. The stag's flanks trembled as the sun slid behind a cloud. Zaharkin shrugged then re-adjusted his aim. Even without sunlight the optics of his telescopic sight showed the creature clearly. He snuggled the rifle butt tight against his shoulder. His finger tightened on the trigger. With no wind and a downhill shot, he could not miss.

Uninterested by the hunt, lost in his misery, Oakshott had his back turned to the trio. He too sniffed the air.

'Smells like someone's pissed himself,' he said in a mutter, then looked down to make sure it wasn't him. It wasn't. Another wave of nausea swept over him, his head pounded, and, in the hope it would all go away, Oakshott closed his eyes. He shifted his weight so that he could find a more restful position between tree root and snow, but no sooner had he begun to relax than the sudden crack of Zaharkin's shot made him jerk upright.

'Jesus!' he said then retched once more.

With a whoop of delight, the Russian lumbered towards his kill. Caught up in the excitement, Jervis and Beacon followed him. With his tormentors gone, Oakshott settled deeper into the soft embrace of the snow. Protected from the cold by the insulation of his thick, waxed jacket, he persuaded himself this was nearly as comfortable as his own bed back in his mansion. Now was his chance to steal a quick nap.

But the strange stench lingered. If anything, it was stronger. Pushing with his elbows against the snow, Oakshott levered himself upright. With the sun gone, the trees fringing the hollow loomed dark above him. Oakshott was a suburbanite. This, the wild, was alien to him. Disorientated by lack of sleep and without his business partners at his side, he'd lost any sense of being anchored in a familiar world. It seemed absurd that he could be so close to the urban sprawl of London, to the opulence of his home in Surrey's Stockbroker Belt, yet be here, in primeval forest. Something indistinct moved in the dark tangle of roots, branches, and leaves facing him. It made no noise and was almost intangible: just a sense of movement where there should be none. Overcome by a sudden sense of dread, Oakshott reached for his rifle. What was it his instructor told him only last week? Dammit, the cold was freezing his brain. What was it? Oh, yes, 'Dead Man's Click. Remember that and you won't be embarrassed. Almost every firearm newbie forgets and looks a fool. Make sure you're not one of 'em.' He looked down for the safety catch. His fingers trembled as he found the little lever and pushed it to 'Off'.

Oakshott's breath now came in short pants. Rifle held at the ready, he stared unblinking and wide-eyed at the tangle of brambles and holly bushes. But he was no woodsman; he did not see the two large, yellow-gold cat's eyes that stared back from the shadowed undergrowth.

Downslope and across the clearing, Zaharkin gutted the carcass. As he worked, steam rose from bloodstained hand and dripping knife blade.

'Bloody good shot, Alexei,' said Beacon.

'Aye, well done, *tovarisch*,' said Jervis.

The oligarch ignored them. He shoved the deer's entrails to one side then cut deeper into its thorax.

'I like watching a billionaire in his natural environment,' Beacon said. 'It's a revelation.'

Jervis snickered in amusement.

Zaharkin's deep laugh echoed across the narrow valley. 'Ha, yes, this is true,' he said. 'I kill and gut my prey in business just like in hunting, here—'

He ripped out the deer's heart and offered it to Beacon. It twitched in Zaharkin's grip.

The Scot's plump face went pale. 'You have got to be joking,' he said.

'What, you not like to get hands dirty, Mr. Beacon?' said Zaharkin. 'Typical British. If I invest in your Swanmere expansion, I will not be afraid, not like your banks. Look…'

Zaharkin squeezed the blood from the heart.

'For Christ's sake, Alexei,' said Jervis.

'There. It has no blood, no more. Just like English property developer, heh?' He laughed again then held the heart out to Jervis. 'How about you? You weak like your friend? Take it, take it.'

His face contorted in disgust, Jervis accepted the still warm organ. Beacon sighed with relief.

The cat moved towards the hapless Oakshott. Hunched low and silent, it stayed hidden deep in the forest's darkness until a glint of light from the pale sky caught its amber eyes.

To be able to pick out the presence of a predator watching you from within a welter of confusing detail is an instinct embedded deep in most creatures, even Oakshott. He saw the eyes, instantly recognised them as belonging to a cat and almost relaxed. Almost. It took a fraction of second to understand that approaching him, indistinct as its form might be, was not a domestic lap cat. The size of a large hound, it exuded a menace and raw power that no dog, not even the fiercest Rottweiler, could match. Thick muscles bulged and stretched beneath sleek black fur.

Quaking with terror, Oakshott scrabbled backwards. The big panther was almost clear of the undergrowth, a mere ten paces away. Oakshott's spine came up hard against a tree root. There was nowhere left to go. He looked down almost in surprise at what he held in his hands. The rifle. His cold-numbed fingers fumbled for the trigger.

'Snifter, Alexei?'

Beacon passed an opened silver hip flask to Zaharkin who inhaled the honey-sweet fumes wafting from it.

'Malt whisky? Oho, good, almost as good as vodka, no?'

He took a swig then returned the flask, complete with bloody fingerprints. Beacon received it disdainfully in his handkerchief. He wiped the silver clean then glanced to his left, where Jervis still stood with deer heart in hand, unsure what to do with his trophy. Plainly, his patrician friend would be no use right now, but with Zaharkin in such a good mood, this might be the right moment to press him for his decision.

'Alexei,' said Beacon, 'a minute ago you mentioned Swanmere Phase Two. Why don't we—'

A terrified, drawn-out scream made them turn in alarm towards the hollow.

A rifle shot cut hard through the still air.

'Oakshott,' said Jervis. 'What's the idiot done now?'

He tossed the stag's heart aside and, with the other two close behind, ran towards the evergreen wall of holly that sheltered Oakshott.

Rifle gripped tight in his hands, Oakshott was rigid with fright. He refused to make eye contact with them, but simply stared at the bushes. Beacon crouched at his side.

'You okay, Oakers? What happened?' he said.

Oakshott looked at him, then stuttered his reply. 'Eyes, yellow eyes. And darkness. Darkness, black, it was black.'

Zaharkin snorted with disgust.

'He is drunk.'

'I missed it,' said Oakshott. 'Oh God, it's still out there. I missed it.'

Both his friends were impressed by the unusual tone of sincerity in his voice. For once, Jervis spoke gently.

'What's out there?' he said.

'Eyes—'

Oakshott vomited long and colourfully.

Off balance, Beacon lurched backwards. 'Jesus, Oakers, mind my boots. They're brand new.'

'Eyes. Cat's eyes,' came the vomit-muffled reply.

Jervis and Zaharkin exchanged sceptical looks.

'Too drunk,' Zaharkin said with certainty. 'Sees pussy cat, he shoots. Weak man.' Disgusted, he turned away and walked back to his kill.

Careful to position himself where any further puke was unlikely to spatter him, Jervis crouched at the side of his distraught friend. 'Come on, old boy, let's get you home.' He hooked a hand under Oakshott's right armpit. 'The Russki's blasted vodka has well and truly done for you.'

With a grunt, Zaharkin slung the dead deer across his shoulders. The effort of carrying such a weight might make him stagger, but he was pleased with the hunt. It was not a trophy beast, for sure, yet a mature buck was a worthy prize. It would show his disrespectful pair of bodyguards that he still had what it took. Valeri and Konstantin had teased him mercilessly about this outing with the British weaklings.

Right on cue, slipping and sliding in the slush and snow, the trio of property developers passed him.

He shook his head in amazement. It baffled Zaharkin that clueless fools like these could even be of the same species as him.

Supported by his friends, Oakshott continued his hyperventilated babble about the encounter with the beast.

'A monster—black—so big—coming for me!'

'Sure, Oakers, monsters in Surrey,' Beacon said. He ventured a worried glance back over his shoulder. Ignorant of the fact that, days ago, Zaharkin had decided to invest in their venture, Beacon was sure they had made a disastrous impression. He had no idea that this hunting trip was simply the bored oligarch's excuse to have some fun at their expense.

'Shooting at someone's pet,' said Jervis. 'What an absolute idiot.'

'You don't believe me? It was right there you bloody stupid—' Oakshott's outrage was choked off by the vomit that rose again in his throat.

Zaharkin scowled at his departing guests then turned to look again at the holly thicket. The sun was out and the dark green bushes carried no hint of menace. And yet, what? A deeper frown creased his face as he shrugged his kill into a more comfortable position. There had been that strange rancid smell. A veteran hunter, he had no doubt it was an animal's scent, yet it was like nothing he had encountered before. Worse stink than a bear. And the weird moment of absolute quiet? He shook his head in puzzlement, but the billionaire had never allowed himself the luxury of introspection and he wasn't going to begin now, not when a deer's damp blood was soaking into the shoulders of his jacket.

'*Chush' sobach'ya*,' Zaharkin said. 'Bullshit.'

He shivered; it was time to go, time for a hearty breakfast and the comforts of home. Zaharkin sniffed the air again, gave a final shake of his head then trudged along behind the three men.

High on the valley slope, crouched behind the thick trunk of an oak seeded long before the Napoleonic Wars, a tall, grey-haired hunter with a weather-beaten face watched them leave. Careful to stay hidden, Bob Coulston had admired Zaharkin's shot, then observed the hunting party's strange back-and-forth pantomime with amusement that became swiftly converted to disquiet. Fragments of Oakshott's strident description of the 'monster' carried up to him. If any of it was true then he was certain events had taken a disastrous turn for the worse.

As soon as Zaharkin stomped out of sight, Coulston broke cover. He approached the hollow with trepidation. His large calibre rifle unslung, he took care to make sure the gun's muzzle pointed wherever his eyes scanned.

Rifle held in right hand and with finger on trigger, Coulston parted the holly leaves, grimacing as their sharp edges pricked his skin of his left hand. He stopped to listen for anything out of the ordinary, but heard only the wind in the trees and the rippling song of a nearby wren. He carefully surveyed his surrounds then he too sniffed the air for a scent he'd recently come to recognise and fear.

Nothing.

Only now, when satisfied there was no immediate danger, did Coulston examine the ground. Zaharkin's prone position was obvious, as was the churned and vomit-flecked snow bank where Oakshott had encountered... what? Coulston swung around to face the undergrowth opposite.

He spoke in the faintest of murmurs. 'So, it came from here.'

Carefully, ever so carefully, Coulston stepped between two bushes and into the thicket. The flutter of the tubby wren as it flew deeper into the undergrowth made him jump with fright.

'Steady, boy, steady. If the bird feels safe, so should you.'

But his words of reassurance rang hollow. He knew the stakes, knew he was in the worst position possible should the big cat lurk nearby. Close-up, his unwieldy rifle gave him scant protection. There would be little warning of an attack and less chance of survival. Coulston's hunter's instincts told him the cat had fled, but why? He feared the worse, but had to know, had to be sure. It was time to calm his racing heartbeat. He took five deep breaths then, crouching low, pushed further into the undergrowth.

A handful of paces in, he found tracks. In a small patch of snow were four paw prints. Big paw prints, approximately the width of his hand, three in snow, and one in mud. Coulston hesitated. Was it mud? It didn't look right.

Even with the sun shining bright, this deep into the murky undergrowth it was hard to make out the detail. He leant forwards. Fascinated by his behaviour, the watching wren burbled its song again. Coulston's left fingers brushed the surface of the dark paw print. He brought his fingertips close to his face. They were red. This was not mud. It was blood.

'Oh, the bloody fool!'

The stupid drunk had achieved the worst of all outcomes; he'd wounded the beast. A tale came to Coulston, a dimly remembered story told by his grandfather, it warned of the one thing deadlier than a big cat: a wounded big cat.

A dark cloud slid across the sun's face and the wren's song stopped suddenly in mid-phrase.

Coulston listened hard. Once more, the woods fell unnaturally still.

Unnerved by the silence and the growing gloom, he no longer made an effort to fight the fear. Adrenaline coursed through his body. The hunter fled the thicket with no pretence at poise or dignity.

Coulston retreated backwards down the slope and towards the open ground along the streambed. He recalled something else his grandfather had said: never turn your back on a big cat. Not if you want to live.

- 2 -

- Four Months Later -

- Animal Pens, Mid-Surrey Council Dog Pound -

ROSIE'S DAY STARTED BADLY. THAT MORNING, AT THE precise moment she was lathered head-to-toe and ready to rinse clean, the shower thermostat packed up. She was not a fan of cold showers. Then there had been getting the kids to school: a chore whose only consolation was that shepherding two argumentative, school-hating children made her job feel easy by comparison. Well almost, because, no sooner did Rosie's workday begin than it nose-dived further. Big Mo attempted to escape. Again. He didn't get very far, but it hardly mattered, his recapture was never an easy affair.

Dressed in padded bodysuit, rubber boots, gauntlets, and visor helmet, Rosie advanced along a narrow corridor set between mesh-framed pens. Frenzied dogs of every shape and size flung themselves against the wires as they alternated between delight at an interlude to the boredom of life in the pound, and fear of the weird, unfamiliar being that shuffled past. The dank concrete floors stank of urine as over-excited canines outdid each other in displays of territorial marking and poor bladder control.

Big Mo growled and the canine pens fell silent. Big Mo was top dog. When he asserted himself, you showed respect. Yet he had little interest in the structured pecking order that brought reassurance to most dogs. He was a loner, and there, perhaps, in that disregard for other dogs, laid his power. He really did not care. His sole interest was to find new ways to escape from whatever or wherever he was homed, housed, or held captive. Give him a cage and he'd find a way out with guile, speed, and the remarkable wire-cutting power of his jaw muscles. Sausages were the motivation for his jailbreaks; in particular, those on display in the window of Peckworth's Family Butchers situated ten miles away in the town of Bankstone.

Rosie wielded a noose attached to an extendable pole. Physical separation of human from dog was important when Big Mo was on the loose.

'Come on you beast, you've got nowhere left to run.'

Growl.

Being the person who had allowed Big Mo to escape, Rosie was the one designated to return him to his cage. She cursed her moment of inattention when hosing out his pen. He'd barged past her in a whirr of scrabbling claws, but had been defeated by the airlock-style double doors recently installed with the sole purpose of thwarting him.

Growl.

'You don't scare me, mate,' Rosie said.

She lunged forwards.

Big Mo seized Rosie's pole. Here, at last, was some entertainment, he decided. Rosie was jerked left, right, up, left again, before losing her balance to stagger with a resounding crash against one of the pens. Her impact triggered a fresh bout of frenzied yaps, barks, and howls.

Gripping the pole, Rosie levered herself to her feet.

'Give up now, mutt,' she said, 'or it'll be the worse for you.'

There was little conviction in her voice.

Growl.

'I mean, look at what you've done to poor Little Mo?'

Rosie pointed to her right. An enormous German Shepherd pressed himself into a corner of the cage he shared with Big Mo. Quivering with fear, he looked piteously at Rosie in an attempt to communicate that he was a good dog, and good dogs didn't deserve to be caged with a canine psychopath.

Growl.

Little Mo whimpered.

'And look what you've done to my sleeve,' said Rosie. 'Look, Big Mo, look.' She thrust forward an arm, its padding shredded. This was too great a temptation for Big Mo. 'Bad boy, bad dog. Oh, crap!'

Again, Rosie was yanked right, left, then off her feet just as Don Burgess, her line manager, opened the inner airlock door.

'Phone, Rosie,' was all he said before Little Mo shimmied past to hide behind his legs. Don turned from looking over his shoulder at the trembling Little Mo to watch the confrontation.

'Oh no, not again,' he said.

Rosie scrambled to her knees, but Big Mo had not given up on the tug-of-war over her sleeve. She spoke between pull and counter-pull. 'I'm fine, Don... just fine... I'll have this... creature under... control in... a... second.'

Growl.

'You've got a phone call. It sounded urgent. Go answer it. I'll handle the brute,' said Don.

Fabric tore as Rosie yanked her arm free. She stood up, panting for breath.

'You sure, Don? It's Big Mo!'

'Go.'

Rosie tossed noose and pole to Don. He watched her leave then turned to face her nemesis.

Growl.

'Y'know, my friend,' he said, 'I sometimes wonder if Rosie is truly cut out for this job.'

Don leant the pole against a cage. Unprotected, he stepped forward, grasped Big Mo by the scruff of his neck, and scooped him up.

Yelp.

Big Mo, a tiny but tubby Jack Russell terrier, licked Don's nose. Still holding the escape artist, Don turned his squirming captive to face Little Mo. The Alsatian regarded them with trepidation.

'You've got to learn to leave the big dogs alone, mate. It's not fair on them,' said Don.

Big Mo twisted his head to lick Don's nose again.

The dog wardens shared an open-plan office with the other essential but despised drudges who worked for Mid-Surrey County Council: pest control; the traffic wardens; park rangers; and Don, whose unlikely but official job designation was Council Astrologer. Except that he was an astronomer by training, not an astrologer. Hired by a former chief executive with a penchant for only making major decisions after consulting her horoscope, Don fell victim to the commonly held confusion between the pseudoscience of astrology and the true science of astronomy. In his case, this distinction eluded the junior Human Resources manager assigned the task of advertising the job description, interviewing, and then contracting him.

Don thought he'd be visiting schools to spread the word about the wonders of the universe but, hey, a job is a job and he was willing to give it a go. He had suspended disbelief, found a garbage-in, garbage-out astrological word generator on the web, and set to work. Unfortunately, it was only a few weeks before his horoscope-of-the-day email suggested to his boss that she should

Hold off on any major changes for now. Money matters are still in flux, and it would be prudent to wait until the dust settles.

28

How could the very stars themselves be wrong? The Chief Exec ignored the urgent advice of her Chief Financial Officer that they should shift the council's entire cash reserve from their Icelandic bank and to the banking haven of Cyprus. The next day, their bank crashed spectacularly and the council lost more than forty million pounds. The councillors dispatched their now ex-Chief Executive to 'fresh challenges far afield': otherwise known in plain English as a huge payoff with attached confidentiality and gagging clauses.

Don, with a watertight contract and his bosses' fear of the resultant tabloid headlines should he be laid off, was untouchable. By dint of being last man standing as wave after wave of lay-offs and voluntary redundancies cleared the way for ever bigger payments into senior council executives' pension pots, he filled many of the lesser posts left vacant. Don became Town Crier, Resident Clown, Head of Corporate Metrics—luckily no-one knew what it meant, so his ignorance of the role was never challenged—and Chief Dog Warden. And it was Don who shielded his most impetuous subordinate from the consequences of her attempt to break up the Creswells' dogfighting ring.

'Morning, everyone,' said Rosie as she hurried inside.

A few pale faces glanced up but no one replied; they lacked the energy to fight the gloom created by their environment. This was the very definition of a sick office. Indeed, it might have been designed deliberately to drive its occupants out onto the streets and parks to patrol, but there is rarely any purpose to the choice of décor in local government buildings. Behind the cluttered visitor's counter was a vast hinterland of drab open plan officedom. It featured brown glass windows, brown carpets, grey walls, and grey furniture. The overhead strip lighting cast pallid green-tinted illumination on the faces of those who slaved at the grubby twenty year-old computer monitors.

In a doomed attempt to raise spirits, a senior councillor, who just happened to own a sign-making company, pushed through a proposal to hang jokey signs from the office ceiling above the location of each minor fiefdom: 'Meter Maids' for the traffic wardens, 'Parkies' for the rangers, and so on. The dog wardens' placard read 'Pooch Patrol' except that the letters 'c' and 'h' had peeled off. After two failed attempts to glue them back on, Don and Rosie gave up. They thought the new title more appropriate.

Rosie did not have a window; she had a partition. Immunised long ago against the concept of being granted any privacy during a telephone call, she spoke loud and clear into the phone.

'Sweetie,' she said, 'we really don't want Mrs. Darbyshire to call the child psychologist again, do we? No. Good. Now pass the phone to your headmistress. Okay. Be good now. Bye. Don't forget your father will collect you today. Mmmwah!' She blew a kiss then listened.

Opened her mouth.

Closed it.

Listened attentively to the irate voice on the other end of the line.

Waited.

Then spoke again. 'No, the kiss was not meant for you, Mrs. Darbyshire. No, I am taking this seriously. I just think it could be seen as merely very creative use of a tennis ball, flour, and glue for a six year old, anyway. No, I am sure Miss Tevel does not agree. No, I am also sure her missing hair will grow back. In time.'

Don arrived and sat on the edge of Rosie's desk. Although he could not hear clearly the other half of the conversation, he could detect the brittle outrage in the head teacher's voice on the other end of the line.

Rosie acknowledged his presence with a weak smile.

'No, I won't,' she said into the phone. 'No, it was a mistake. No, it... Look Mrs. Darbyshire, I really have to go. Send me the cleaning bill.'

She hung up.

Don attempted a sympathetic smile.

'Damn, sometimes I suspect the school staff run a sweepstake on how may times they can get me to say, 'No' in one phone call,' said Rosie.

'I'd have thought it'd be, 'Sorry'.'

'That was last year's word. The year before, it was, 'How much will it cost to repair?''

'Lizzie in trouble again?'

'This time it's Peter.'

Don dropped a stack of message slips on her desk.

'Today's haul,' he said.

Rosie picked up the topmost.

'Another alleged dognapping? Have a heart, Don. Around here some pampered millionaire's mutt chases a rabbit, gets lost in the woods, and the panicky owner rings us. Just as we arrive, it wanders home because it's hungry.'

Don tapped the message pile.

'That's fifteen cats and dogs reported missing around the Hamleys in the last month. Something's up.'

'A mass break-out from Stalug Luft Hamley? You know what these neurotic owners are like. If any of that lot owned me, I'd be digging my own escape tunnel too.'

'I'm not joking,' Don said. 'That's a lot of stray pets. Too many. And it is your job to track them down, like it or not.'

'Not, but I'll do it anyway,' said Rosie. She lifted a zippered clothes hanger from her partition wall. 'If I've got to roam the country lanes of Upper and Lower Hamley, I'd better get my posh frock camouflage on. The 'Ladies Who Lunch' of Hamley won't talk to me otherwise,' she said as, still clad in her padded protectionware, she stomped towards the women's toilet.

'Tell me, when did you last see little Terrence?'

Rosie now wore her official dog warden's jacket, expensive blouse and skirt, sheer tights, elegant make-up, and pearls. Ballpoint pen in one hand, she took a sip of Lapsang Souchon tea from the white china cup held in the other. An open notebook was balanced on one thigh.

Her host, a Mr. Thomas Meredith Anthony Schilling, picked up the framed studio portrait of his cat and placed it on the coffee table in front Rosie. 'It was two days ago,' said the splendidly camp retiree, 'we have never been parted more than two hours, until now. He's only three.'

'May I borrow this?' Rosie said.

'Of course, if you think it would help.'

She studied the grumpy-looking Siamese in the photograph. It wore a red silk bow around its neck. Rosie decided red was definitely not Terrence's colour. She closed her eyes. The day's events had become a bit of a blur. Maybe it was caffeine overload? This was her eleventh, possibly twelfth, cup of tea or coffee? A surreptitious check of the list in the notebook told her that, no, this was number fourteen, and it was still only two–thirty in the afternoon.

Her house calls followed a near-identical pattern. It was a trap no polite visitor in Britain could hope to escape.

First visit, Rosie was offered excellent black coffee, and a photograph of a Chihuahua in a handbag.

Her second call resulted in another dog photograph, but Rosie had to drink weak tea this time, not at all to her taste.

Next house, a cat portrait.

More tea, industrial strength, excellent.

Then another cat photo and tea politely declined on discovering it was adulterated with vanilla essence.

Dog photo. More coffee: instant and milky, yeuch!

Dog.

Coffee.

Toilet break.

Cat.

Weak tea, almost cold, bleah!

The next pet owner launched into an attack on the worthlessness of local government and dog wardens, in particular. He then thrust a photo of Big Mo into her hands. Big Mo? Rosie decided not to mention his whereabouts. Even her nemesis did not deserve such a haughty owner, especially one who put milk in mint tea.

Next up, a cat.

Tea in a mug; slumming it now.

Then a rabbit, nice change for once.

Tea, and an urgent toilet break.

Big dog.

Tea.

Little dog.

Tea with soya milk. Oh, the horror of it!

Medium dog.

Decaf tea. A blessed relief to Rosie's nervous system.

But not to her bladder.

Finally, Terrence.

Rosie sighed. She noticed Terrence's owner watching her with a troubled expression. He seemed on the verge of tears. His desolation sent a wave of guilt coursing through her. What could she say? In truth, apart from ringing all the pet rescue charities and animal hospitals, she did not have a clue where to start. Most of the owners had already done the same and met with no success.

'We'll do what we can, Mr. Schilling. With so many animals missing we're sure to catch these petknappers.' Acutely aware of the hollow tone to her voice, Rosie knew she was convincing no one, least of all herself. 'Now if you'll excuse me, I need to make one more visit then I'll start hunting for clues.'

Unable to control her caffeine-induced tremble, the cup and saucer rattled as she placed them on the coffee table.

Rosie stood up. 'Perhaps you could direct me to the bathroom?' she said.

- 3 -

- One week later -

- Mid-Surrey County Council, Redholt -

DAYS PASSED AND NONE OF THE MISSING ANIMALS turned up. Rosie tried every line of investigation she could think of except the most obvious one: a phone call to Steve Ashworth at the RSPCA. She decided it was an exercise in embarrassment that could wait, possibly forever. The police made it clear they had higher priorities, and visits to local vets produced no extra information. Pleas for assistance on Internet forums only brought hateful responses from online trolls. She even asked Highways Maintenance to report road kills. Nothing remotely resembling a clue emerged.

Rosie did not give up.

Don's corner desk was alongside a window. Its glass might be tinted a shade of brown that made the apple on his desk look bloated and rotted, but it was a definite step up from the cubicle hubs in which everyone else toiled. Not only did he have a window, Don also had walls, two of them, solid and immovable. In the open-plan council office, it was the height of luxury.

'Uh, I hope that's not extra paperwork for me,' he said as Rosie approached carrying a stack of arch-lever files, printouts, and an Ordnance Survey map of central Surrey.

'I was watching TV last night,' she said, 'one of those Scandinavian serial-killer shows. The detective stuck a map on the wall with pins connected to photos of the victims.'

She gave Don's windowless wall a meaningful look. Astrological charts of the zodiac, a legacy of his past existence, were stuck to the wall. Don saw them as a useful reminder of the gullibility of the human race: a fact that sustained him through many meetings with the Council's senior officers.

'Oh no, it's mine,' he said in protest. 'Imagine the precedent it'd set if I let you use it. Besides I like my posters.'

Rosie ignored him, dumped her burden on his desk, and then unfolded the map.

'It was amazing what the detective could deduce from it,' she said. 'Now, which one comes down? The Vedic astrology or the Tarot?'

Don conceded defeat. 'Okay, just don't let your Sarah Lund fantasy stretch to wearing cable knit jumpers to work. It's against the council dress code.' He paused as he considered the choice of posters. 'Ah, okay, you can get rid of the Tarot. It's always creeped me out.'

Once the map was on the wall, Rosie tipped some coloured pins into the palm of her hand then pointed at the stack of files. 'You read out the details and I'll pinpoint them on the map. We'll use different colours: red for a cat.' That was in honour of Terrence. 'And blue for dogs.'

Don selected a white pin.

'Don't forget the rabbit,' he said.

'Okay,' said Rosie pointing to the map, 'this covers from Mickleham in the north to Five Oaks in the south, and from Coldharbour in the east all the way over to Godalming.' She tapped the map. 'Upper and Lower Hamley are almost exact centre, here in the North Downs.'

🐾

Armed with a stack of photocopied montages of the missing pets, Rosie decided to visit every house on the sparse-populated, sunken lanes that fell inside the perimeter of the greatest concentration of missing pets or, as Don called it, 'The Hamley Dead Zone'.

One hot afternoon, her fourth visit of the day was to a large, mock-Jacobean manor house in Lower Hamley. Flanked by manicured lawns, the building's yellow-gray stonework radiated soft strength in the summer sunlight. The edge of the formal garden was crowded by the low wooded hills, their greenery held back by the high stone boundary walls. Driving a small and aged council van equipped with mesh covered rear windows, Rosie turned through wrought-iron gates and onto the house's drive. The van's tyres scrunched on gravel as she parked near the front door.

'What a beauty,' Rosie said.

The house basked in the heat. It was hard to imagine a more welcoming vision of domesticity and she permitted herself a wry smile. Perfect home it might be, but it was very different from the damp, concrete pre-fab council house she shared with her two children and her mother.

'Probably freezing cold in winter, with an ancient boiler liable to blow up. Plus dry rot, wet rot, and Deathwatch Beetle,' she said, desperate to find some way to reduce this residence to her level of domesticity.

She was wrong.

The interior was as beautiful as its facade.

A maid dressed in formal uniform opened the iron-bound oak front door. Startled to encounter someone wearing something she thought was only found in fancy dress catalogues, Rosie was so disconcerted that she mutely thrust her 'Missing' handout at the maid.

'We have no cats or dogs,' said the maid examining the leaflet. Her West African accent was soft and warm. Just like the house, thought Rosie.

'I'm Rosie Flinn, County Dog Warden. May I see the house-owners?' she said. 'Just for a brief word, nothing more.'

Inside the wood-panelled entrance hall, tea chests and cardboard boxes were stacked higher than Rosie's head. The house's owners had only recently moved in.

'Faith, who is it?'

A well-groomed man appeared in the open doorway of the reception room. Startled, the maid, Faith, spun around and, in the cramped space left by the chests, knocked a vase from its stand. Rosie stooped and caught the vase just before it hit the floor.

'Faith, go and unpack the kitchen, please,' said a woman's voice.

Rosie looked up.

A trouser-suited woman stood at the man's side. Dark-haired, plump, and smooth-featured, in their neat clothes they resembled a pair of sleek, well-dressed seals. Rosie shook her head to dispel the bizarre image then restored the vase to its place.

'She came with the place, her brother too,' said the woman. 'We won't be keeping them. They're hopeless, completely—'

'Hopeless,' agreed the man. 'Good catch, by the way.'

'Growing up with two sports-obsessed older brothers I got to be good at throwing and catching,' Rosie said. She smiled at them and touched the badge stitched to her fleece jacket. 'I'm Rosie Flinn, County Dog Warden. Have you just moved in?'

'That's right,' said the man, 'Naomi and Johnno—'

'Dawes,' said Naomi. 'How can we—'

'Help you?' Johnno said.

Did they always finish each other's sentences, wondered Rosie?

'I won't keep you long,' she said. 'I'm investigating the disappearance of some local pets: cats and dogs. Some of your neighbours—'

'Johnno, do we have neighbours?' said Naomi.

'Well, yes, I suppose we do. Somewhere.' Johnno looked through the leaded glass window to inspect with suspicion the terrain beyond their garden.

'Um, do you have pets? If you do, it might be sensible to keep them indoors, just for a while.' Rosie showed them the leaflet. 'Recently there've been a lot of unexplained disappearances.'

'I'm afraid we didn't move here to have neighbours,' Naomi said, 'or—'

'Pets,' agreed Johnno.

Their sentence interruptus act was starting to get on Rosie's nerves.

'Well,' she said, 'if you see or hear anything suspicious or—' From her inside jacket pocket she dug out her business card then handed it to Naomi, who held it as if a contagious disease contaminated it. 'Maybe strange vehicles?' God, now she was doing it to herself she thought, then said, 'Any people out of place, anything odd, give me a call.'

'Oh, I don't think that is very likely,' said Naomi. 'We don't do that sort of thing.'

Rosie felt a sudden urge to escape these strange, glossy, not-quite-normal people. She walked to the open doorway and waved a hand at the hilly landscape beyond. 'But when you're out and about? Riding, walking?'

'We don't do anything like that, either' Naomi said. 'We moved to the countryside to be seen by people who matter. To socialise.'

'Need to develop contacts, y'know,' said Johnno. 'Play the game. And they all live—'

'Around here,' said Naomi as, with the firm pressure of her hand placed in the small of Rosie's back, she guided their visitor through the door.

Nonplussed by the strange encounter, Rosie crossed the wide expanse of gravel to reach the van. She was used to the condescending ways of the super-rich, living in Mid-Surrey you had to be, but it did not mean it was ever a pleasant experience to encounter them. A kneeling man, another African, was weeding the flowerbed next to her vehicle. This must be the brother, thought Rosie. He's older too.

Wiry and smiling, the gardener stood, brushed his hands against his canvas pants. He spoke to Rosie in the same flowing accent as his sister.

'Good afternoon, madam, my name is Henry Olembe.'

It's been a long time since anyone called me 'madam', she thought. Maybe never.

'Er, hello, Rosie Flinn, dog warden,' she said. 'Have you seen any stray cats or dogs around here in the last few weeks? A lot have been reported missing.'

She gave him one of the leaflets. He read it with care then slowly shook his head.

'Sorry, madam, no.'

'Maybe you can call me if you happen to see any strays or maybe strange vehicles? The number is on the flyer.'

Rosie turned to unlock the van.

'It is the *kyaani*. It awoke in the hills and it is hungry,' said Henry.

Rosie stopped. More weirdness? Oh well, this is Surrey.

'I'm sorry?' she said.

Henry returned the leaflet to her.

'In my homeland, in Ghana, there is a spirit of the forest, the *kyaani*. It sleeps until the land, the hills, are in danger. Once it is woken, it does not rest until the danger has passed. It is here too. The *kyaani* has woken.'

Definitely weird, thought Rosie, but, unlike the seal-people, he, at least, was friendly.

Faith walked around the side of the house. She carried a tray with two glasses of water on it.

'And you're suggesting that this spirit, this... what did you call it?' Rosie said.

'*Kyaani*.'

'This *kyaani* holds a grudge against the cats and dogs of Mid-Surrey?'

Henry shrugged.

'It has woken in these hills and it must eat.'

Rosie looked at the images of dogs, cats, and solo rabbit crammed onto her leaflet.

'Right. Well it's certainly showing quite an appetite.'

Faith arrived.

'Thank you for catching the vase, madam,' she said. 'I have water for my brother. Would you like some?'

She offered her glass to Rosie.

Through the stone-mullioned window of their drawing room, Naomi Dawes watched Rosie and the Olembes as they chatted. Behind her, Johnno attempted to connect a Blu-ray player to a widescreen TV.

'Good grief, now the dog woman is talking to the Olembes,' said Naomi.

'Nao, she's only doing her—'

'Job. I know, but still! They've got to go. They're too—'

'Independent.'

'Exactly.'

'Think they'll go quietly?'

'If they want their passports back they will,' said Naomi.

'What shall we get to replace them?'

'Oh, something more respectful. Filipinos? Or Thai?'

'Mmm, you know, I'm hungry. Do you fancy nipping into Guildford for some shopping and an early meal? I'm told a wonderful Vietnamese place has just opened. Who knows, they might also be able to recommend some cousins or the like?'

The late afternoon sun wove shifting dappled patterns through the trees in the hills above the Dawes' estate. The air was hot with the scent of tree resin. Birds flitted high in the canopy, whilst bees, flies, and thousands of unseen insects created the ambient pulsing drone that marks woodland in high summer.

Softly singing a Ghanaian song to herself, Faith Olembe wandered along a path. In the crook of one arm was a wicker basket. No longer in her uniform, she now wore jeans and a blouse. She stepped quietly and with care, picking wild grasses and ferns then twisting and weaving them with her fingers.

Faith stopped. She followed this path frequently, but something up ahead was out of place. On tiptoe, she craned her head to see. An unfamiliar sound, something out of vision had alarmed her. She was on the edge of a wide, circular glade and, reluctant to walk into the open, she stepped behind the nearest tree trunk.

'Dammit! Bloody brambles,' said a voice.

Forty paces away, Rosie emerged from an overgrown track that ran between two barbed wire-topped, chain link fences, which, on reaching the clearing, turned sharply to stretch away in opposite directions. Released from the narrow confine of the track, Rosie was hot, bothered, and unkempt. She'd been forced to fight her way through thorns and nettles all the way up from the main road and was not suitably dressed for the task. Her tights were laddered; her legs scratched.

'With this security around their estates,' she said to herself, 'I can't see how the hell the animals get out.'

With a vigour fuelled by her annoyance, she shook one of the fences. In the distance, a siren wailed.

'Oh, for goodness sake—'

'Are you lost?'

Coulston pushed himself upright. He'd been sitting hidden from sight, his back propped against a fallen tree trunk. Rosie started in surprise, spun around, tripped, and then stumbled backwards into the second fence.

Another, different alarm sounded.

'Don't do that! Who are you? A guard?' Rosie was scared and angry.

Coulston wore his hunting clothes and his rifle was slung on a diagonal across his back.

'Nothing as fancy as that; just a hunter. I reckon Alexei Zaharkin can afford better guards than me,' he said. 'Those are his alarms you triggered.'

Even lowly dog wardens had heard of Zaharkin, and heard the stories about his fierce defence of his privacy. She stepped away from the fence.

Unseen by Rosie, but noted with wry amusement by Coulston, a camera hidden high on a branch above the fence tracked her movement.

The guardroom of the Zaharkin estate was a room in the damp, windowless basement of his stately home. One wall was lined with a bank of monitors, each dedicated to one of the twenty—odd cameras scattered around the boundary of his land. A bodyguard, Konstantin, used the system's control panel to switch the image of Coulston and Rosie to the main central monitor. With a practised flick of the joystick in his hand, he zoomed in with the camera to study their faces. He leant back in his chair and called through the open doorway, 'Valeri, come here. The hunter's back and he's got another girlfriend.'

Wiping gun oil from his hands, the oligarch's second bodyguard entered the room.

'How does he do it,' said Konstantin. He had no liking for local women. His crude English, picked up from Zaharkin himself, seemed to scare them. He belched; wind again. If the boss's chef was anything to go by, these people couldn't cook either. Give him a wholesome Russian *mat'* any time.

Valeri's lips moved as he attempted to decipher the silent conversation on the screen. He scratched the scar that creased his forehead. Courtesy of an Afghan *Dukh* with fortuitously bad aim, it itched whenever he concentrated hard.

'We should install a microphone,' he said. 'I could do with something interesting to listen to around here.'

'Yeah, but all he ever does is talk. No action, real dull,' said Konstantin.

'If we ever spot him on the estate, let's bring him in, have some fun.'

Valeri's version of fun usually involved any one or all of: fists, knives, lead-weighted coshes, and guns.

The pair of them, utterly loyal to Zaharkin, fled into hasty exile with their boss when he double-crossed one fellow oligarch too many. To return to the motherland meant death, so Zaharkin set about enjoying his billionaire lifestyle in England with gusto, but his bodyguards were bored, lonely, and homesick.

'Never seen him on the cameras inside the estate,' said Konstantin. 'Have you?'

'No, only around the perimeter. He must be too frightened to dare come inside.'

They had also grown lazy. Coulston knew the position of every camera and motion detector. He'd even watched them install the devices. There were dozens of dead spots that gave access to the estate.

'Anyway, I'm sorry, I shouldn't have startled you,' said Coulston, 'It's just that you look so...' He shrugged and gestured at her once smart clothes. 'So out of place. Are you actually lost?'

Rosie bristled. She did not like being patronised, especially by strange, disreputable tramps with guns.

'A hunter? Didn't know we had those in Surrey,' she said. 'Isn't your gun's a bit too big for pigeons or rabbits? What do you shoot?'

'You'd be surprised. Nature red in tooth and claw,' said Coulston.

'Bit pompous for a hunter aren't you?'

Coulston laughed. 'Actually, deer.'

'A Bambi killer?'

Instinctively hostile to the idea of shooting docile, harmless animals, Rosie had never heard of anyone hunting deer around here. For God's sake, she thought, this place was practically in London's suburbs.

'It helps keep the numbers down. I do have a licence, you know,' Coulston said.

Although Rosie knew she was never going to approve of him, her deep-ingrained good manners asserted themselves.

'I'm sorry, I didn't mean to be rude. I've had a bad day, Mr...?'

'Coulston, Bob Coulston.'

'Rosie Flinn, County Dog Warden. I'm investigating the disappearance of pets around here. Cats and dogs.'

'A dog warden.'

Coulston said it deadpan. He was enjoying this unexpected encounter. However, Rosie could recognise condescension at a thousand yards.

'That's right.' Her tone was icy. 'So if you hear or see anything?'

She handed him the flyer with the photos of the missing pets. Coulston examined it.

'Miss Flinn, can I ask you something?'

'If you must. And it's Ms.'

'Why are you here? This is quite literally a long way off the beaten track.'

Rosie nodded at the 'Missing' leaflet.

'All those pets. If you plot on a map where they live, they cluster around the Hamleys and the centre of that cluster is right here.' From a pocket, Rosie extracted her map and showed him the locations of the missing pets. Rosie smiled ruefully once she'd finished describing her Scandinavian methodology then said, 'And since I was in the immediate neighbourhood, I thought on a nice day like this it would be a good idea to visit the dead centre of it all. Look for them here, maybe find clues. And this is it, near as I can tell.'

'Very clever,' said Coulston, 'fascinating too.'

'But, obviously, it's not my best ever idea.' Rosie waved a hand at woodland devoid of assorted Chihuahuas, Siamese cats, pooches, guard dogs, and a white rabbit named Percy. Her voice trailed away to silence. Why did you say that out loud to a stranger, she thought. Don't you know how stupid it sounds? Then she rallied. 'So, in answer to your question,' she continued. 'No, I'm not lost, at least I hope not.'

Coulston carefully folded the leaflet and put in a jacket breast pocket.

'Well, I haven't seen stray pets of any description. If I do, I'll be sure to call you,' he said. 'May I?' He held out a hand towards the map.

Rosie surrendered it and, once more, became annoyed, this time with herself. Why on earth was she blabbing to this man? Coulston possessed a gun. He might be a pet-killer. In fact, he was the only person even close to a suspect she had encountered.

'This is it, dead centre, you are absolutely right,' Coulston said and looked up from the map to study the flustered dog warden. He tried to calm the unease he now felt; the certainty that he knew what had happened to the missing pets. How was it possible this dog warden found this spot, of all places? It was, in a way, admirable.

Coulston came to a sudden decision.

'Let me show you something.'

He sensed Rosie's unwillingness.

'It's all right,' he said. 'Honest. I just want to show you the absolute dead centre of your plot. You might find it interesting.' In truth, Coulston felt compelled to look himself. 'It's just over there, in the sunlight.' He indicated the middle of the clearing.

Rosie did not move.

Coulston pointed to the camera. 'Look, up in that tree, we're not alone. You're being watched by Zaharkin's security.'

Rosie turned and saw the lens of the surveillance camera.

Four miles away, Valeri had returned to cleaning his gun, and Konstantin had gone to the toilet to relieve himself and daydream of curvaceous *biksas* and *borscht*.

'You're quite safe from me,' said Coulston. But maybe not from anything else, he thought. A dog warden? Dear God, what next? He pushed through the knee-high bracken that fringed the grass of the bowl-shaped dell. In its centre lay a low, flat rock. Coulston walked to it. Lit by bright sunlight, the brown and green lichens on its surface stood out in high relief.

Rosie took another look at the camera, sighed, and then followed Coulston into the clearing. Half-expecting to discover a charnel house pile of pet skeletons, she was disappointed to find a mere weather-beaten, crudely shaped cube of rock. She kicked it with her right foot.

'So much for theories,' she said.

'Well, yes and no,' said Coulston. 'Do you know where we are? What this place is?'

'No.'

'Take your time. Look around you,' he said as he turned his face up and towards the sky.

Her gaze followed his and she saw the trees.

Nine even-spaced ancient oaks ringed the glade.

Each trunk was at least three of her arm spans in width. The great trees reached into the sky, boughs arching to meet high above where Coulston and Rosie stood. The vast green hall they created stood silent, strong, and primeval.

Rosie gasped then said, 'It's beautiful, incredible,' she said, 'like the nave of a Gothic cathedral.'

'You're not the first to say so,' said Coulston. 'In Old English its name is Ingethanc Weald. This is the heart of England's most ancient forest.'

'I've never heard of it.'

'It's on no map. Local legend has it that this was a druids' grove long before the Romans came. The wights are gone, but the forest's still here, leastways what's left of it.'

'Druids? You mean sacrifices?' Rosie imagination was running wild again. The charnel house images resurfaced in her mind. What had happened to her missing pets?

Coulston laughed. 'No, no-one knows what the druids really got up to; everything you've heard is modern invention or Roman propaganda. And I'm glad it's that way because I love the serenity of the Weald; I've been coming here since I was kid. I wouldn't like to think of anything nasty going on.' He hesitated. 'It's just strange your search should lead you here. There are so many odd stories attached to the Ingethanc, to the Heart.'

It was his turn to kick the rock.

'This lump here is the Queer Stone. It's said in a certain light you can see a face on the surface, twisted in fear and pain. Not that I ever have, mind you, and I come here often enough.'

To Rosie, the rock looked innocuous and bland. She could see no face.

'And another thing,' said Coulston. 'Do you know what kind of rock this is?'

Rosie didn't. She shook her head.

'It's blue dolerite. But the native rock around here is chalk, greensand, sandstone. Nothing like this.'

The name blue dolerite tugged at the edge of Rosie's memory. Its significance came to her in rush: a recollection dredged from a middle-school trip on a rainy day to Salisbury Plain.

'Stonehenge,' she said.

Coulston nodded. 'It's Carn Menyn bluestone from Wales. From the same quarry as the slabs that built Stonehenge.' He stroked the rock. 'Strange, isn't it? More than four thousand years ago, a Bronze Age wight transported this lump of rock three hundred miles and embedded it here.' He shrugged. 'Must have thought it contained great power.'

Despite the afternoon heat, Rosie shivered. She felt a sudden longing for the beige comfort of her office cubicle.

'I'd better go,' she said, still unsure of what to make of this strange man. 'Thanks for the, um, interesting, er, well then, goodbye.'

She set off towards the road.

'I think your route is that way, Ms. Flinn.' Arms crossed, Coulston jerked his head in the opposite direction.

'Really? Oh, of course. Thanks.' Rosie retraced her steps to follow the correct path. 'Goodbye, Mr. Coulston.'

'Do you want me to guide you to the road?'

'I'll be fine,' Rosie said. 'Just fine.'

She hesitated at the nettle-infested mouth of the track.

'Why don't more people know about this?' she said. 'This Inge-thingy, the Heart, it should be famous.'

'Have you seen Stonehenge recently?' said Coulston. 'What they've done to it? Fenced it off. Car parks. Concrete everywhere. Tourist tat on sale.' He shook his head in disgust. 'Better to keep the knowledge strictly local.'

Rosie smiled. 'Well, I won't tell anyone.'

Coulston watched Rosie wend her way down the track. When she was out of sight, he spoke again. 'Hello, Faith,' he said.

'Friend Robert.'

Faith stepped from behind her tree. Whilst waiting for Rosie to leave, she had woven the grass stalks into a charm the size of the palm of her hand.

'You heard what the dog warden said? About the missing pets?' said Coulston.

'She was at the house. She is a good person. I like her. Strong. She cares about those animals.'

'Glad to hear it,' he said. 'These new people, the Dawes, are they treating you well?'

Faith shook her head.

'They will bring us much trouble, I fear.'

'I'm sorry.'

Faith smiled.

'We will endure,' she said. 'Here, for you.'

49

She offered him the finished charm. It was in the shape of an eye, but with the iris as a vertical slit. Coulston gently lifted it from her hand.

'A cat's eye,' he said.

'That is so,' Faith said with a nod. 'You will not be attacked if you wear it.' She reclaimed the charm then tied it to the collar of his hunting jacket. It hung behind his neck. 'The *kyaani* will not strike from behind when other eyes are on it.'

Coulston decided not to tell her that big cats have round irises not slits. Recalling the terror of that snowy dawn four months ago, he decided he might need all the help he could get. He was certain the big cat had spied on him from hiding many times, but he himself had never even glimpsed it.

'Thank you. Hope it works,' he said.

'Why did you show this place, The Heart, to the woman?' The Olembes held the grove in deep veneration and understood Coulston's determination to keep its secrets.

'She asked me the same question. I don't know. Because she made the effort to come up here? Because she told me about the pets? I'm not sure,' he said. 'Maybe because I just feel the need to explain. To try, anyway.'

'But why challenge people who do not understand?' Faith said. She adhered to the principle of live-and-let-live.

'Why?' A wave of anger washed through his body. 'Because they're clueless. They live in this country, but they're like varnish on the surface; they've lost their connection to the land. People like the dog warden just annoy me.' But, even as he said it, he knew it wasn't true. There was a determination about her that he recognized and respected.

'Her name is Rosie. She told me so. And I think the dog lady now understands a little.'

'I think she does too.' He paused and re-adjusted the rifle strap across his chest. 'Tell your brother I will come tonight. We need to talk; I need his advice.'

Faith nodded. 'Henry will await you after the sun has set.'

'We're soon going to need more than charms,' he said. 'What happens when it runs out of pets? It's wounded; it needs to eat. It'll look for easier, bigger prey. Around here there's one very easy option for a black panther to take.'

'Then it will no longer be safe for you to hunt unaided. We will help.' She turned and walked back down the path. 'Stay out of the shadows, brother Robert.'

'Walk in the sunlight, Faith,' he called after her.

Now alone, Coulston scanned the foliage and sniffed the air. He unslung the rifle then stepped into the undergrowth and out of sight.

A wind blew through the trees of the druid grove. In the branches, high above where Coulston, Rosie, and Faith had talked, dangled scores of charms near identical to Faith's cat's eye. They spun on the breeze. Some, still green, looked new. Others, decades old, were weather-beaten and decrepit. A few, dark-stained with age, were fashioned from waxen horsehair and twists of bronze.

Hair awry and clothing dishevelled, Rosie marched across the office to where Don worked at his desk.

'Look at you,' he said. 'Must have been one hell of a bush someone pulled you through backwards.'

She flung her dog warden's fleecy at him. And missed.

'Don't start.' She slumped into a chair, too fatigued to retrieve the jacket.

'Finally had enough of the Hamley social set?' said Don. 'Find any vanished pets?'

'No, but I had a strange encounter with a hunter, name of Bob Coulston. He hangs around the woods over there, carries a big gun, shoots deer.' Rosie inspected the scratches on her legs. 'Claimed he knew nothing about my pets.'

Don smiled. Early on in the hunt, he'd noticed how quickly the missing animals became personally attached to Rosie.

'Him? You suspect he's your dognapper? I don't think so.'

'You've heard of him?' Rosie said in surprise.

'I'm amazed you haven't. The Mid-Surrey Advertiser has run stories on him for years. He's the county's very own big cat hunter; tracks sightings of the Surrey Puma.'

'Oh great, first I get tales of a vengeful forest spirit from an African gardener, then I'm shown some sacrificial druid grove, next it's a forty year-old urban legend about an escaped big cat!' Rosie had vague recollections of news stories about sightings of the mythical big cat appearing on TV since she was a little girl.

'Rural legend not urban,' corrected Don the Council Astrologer. 'Plenty of people, reliable steady people, claim they've seen it.'

He reached across to the nearest filing cabinet, pulled open the lowermost drawer then began to flick through the folders it held.

'In here are the more interesting records kept by our dog warden predecessors.' He cocked an eyebrow at Rosie. 'During what few quiet moments I have, I find them an entertaining read. Some truly crazy times are memorialised in here. Ah, this is it.'

From the drawer he extracted a bulging dossier held together with yellowing Sellotape.

'In the Sixties and Seventies it seems the dog wardens were very interested in the Surrey Puma.' Don hefted the file in his hands. 'But that's not much of a surprise since the consensus was it escaped from some rich man's exotic menagerie, and so the dog wardens got involved, very reluctantly.' He held the folder out to Rosie. 'Here, have a read. There's four decades of news clippings. Your mate Bob Coulston's in there too.'

She refused to accept it.

'Oh, come on, Don,' she said. 'You're not taking this seriously? Don't you realise how old it would have to be? If it survived this long, it must be nearly senile. Probably couldn't catch a sick hedgehog let alone a healthy pet.'

'True, but if it didn't kill your missing pets then what's making them vanish? Here, I have this for you too.' He pulled three reports from the pile of paperwork on his desk and passed them to her. 'More pets. Another cat and two dogs: a pair of Dobermans.'

Rosie tried to stare him down but failed.

Don tossed the battered folder into her lap.

'Read it, please,' he said. There was an edge of anxiety to his voice. 'A Doberman's hardly easy meat.'

That night, Rosie hefted the still-unread dossier in her hands. She had a choice: nit-comb Lizzy and Peter's hair, or read a load of old, yellowing newspaper clippings about a bunch of attention-seeking nut-jobs like Coulston.

She chose the nits.

- 4 -

- Evening -

- The Jervis residence, Lower Hamley -

GRUNTING WITH THE EFFORT, JERVIS ATTEMPTED TO ease himself from the deep bucket seat of his Aston Martin. He'd recently developed a nasty twinge in his lower back, and it struck again as he raised his knees to swivel from the car. It felt as if someone had stuck in a skewer and twisted hard. Left hand gripped firm on the steering wheel, he pulled then pushed his arm straight.

'God, ow, ow, ow. Bloody car.'

It was an undignified struggle but, with a heave, he escaped the vehicle's embrace.

Jervis liked to display his status symbols: the Aston Martin; a box at the Royal Opera; Michelin star meals at The Fat Duck in Bray; a hospitality suite at Twickenham; the Royal Enclosure at Ascot; and Jansis, his trophy wife. Living with or making use of those same status symbols was a different matter. He feared the back pain induced by low-riding cars, despised opera in all its varieties, shuddered with horror when presented with elaborate meals that came with attached headphones, loathed beer-swilling rugby fans, was a famously unlucky punter, and, unfortunately for Jansis, detested his wife.

Pausing to let the ache subside, Jervis leant against the car's bodywork and regarded his house. Created by some famous Scandinavian architects whose names he could never remember, it was multilevel, all glass angles and white concrete: a look reminiscent of a poorly shuffled deck of cards. It sat incongruously before a backdrop of dark, overbearing woodland. He hated it. Naturally.

'What the hell is this?'

Jervis might abhor his home but that was his normal state of existence. What enraged him was untidiness. A folded sheet of paper hung at a discordant angle from the letterbox, trapped there by the fierce spring of its flap.

He pulled the paper free.

It was leaflet: 'Have You Seen These Missing Pets?' Below, laid out in a grid, were mug shots of some strays and a telephone number to call.

'Bloody dog wardens,' he said.

He screwed up the flyer, was about to throw it away then remembered how annoyed litter made him. And now he was irritated about being annoyed. Still clutching the ball of paper, Jervis unlocked his front door. Inside, the ground floor was open-plan, its decor stark, modernist and bleak.

'Darling? Are you there, darling?'

Jervis wanted her to be at home. He needed someone on whom he could take out his anger. He walked to the living room area. One wall was lined with shelves that stretched, Scandinavian style, to the ceiling. They contained few books, but, in a concession to colour, framed photographs occupied every available surface. Most showed Jervis posing with a handsome blonde woman of the same age: wedding; holidays, garden parties, and the ribbon-cutting opening of his upmarket mall.

'Where is the silly bitch? Oh—'

He noticed a yellow Post-It note stuck to the surface of the glass-topped dining table.

'Gone to London, shopping, dinner at Gino's, back by nine.'

Jervis crumpled the message in his fist.

'But drunk by five, no doubt,' he said.

A swift toss sent the Post-It to join Rosie's leaflet in the waste paper basket, but the sudden action triggered another back spasm. He winced as the stabbing pain struck again.

'Better do something about it before it gets much worse, Jervie old boy,' he said to himself.

With one hand held to the small of his back, he straightened with caution. Late evening sunlight cast mottled shadows over the house's paved terrace and swimming pool. The light from reflected ripples on the water's surface caught his attention.

'Ah, I know just the thing,' he said.

Bright underwater lights clicked on. They made the swimming pool's water glow electric blue in the dusk. Wisps of steam curled from its surface.

Jervis slid open the patio doors and stepped outside. He had changed into swimming trunks and dressing gown. A towel hung around his neck. In one hand, he carried a tumbler of whisky; the other held his mobile phone to his ear. Still in throbbing pain, he hobbled with tender caution across the patio.

'Come on, answer, you silly cow.'

No reply.

Jervis ended the call and stopped at the pool's edge.

He tutted. Even his favourite rubber ring was in the wrong place. Jervis limped slowly around to where the bulging tyre inner tube nudged against the far side of the pool. He stooped to place his Scotch in the attached drink holder then shoved the ring into the water. It parted the steam before it, leaving curling wisps of vapour in its wake.

Five laps then a relaxing swig of whisky should do the trick, Jervis decided. Jaws clenched as he fought the back pain. He stood unsteadily then paused, nose wrinkled in disgust.

'What is that stench?' he said.

The woods sat silent in the soft evening light. Nothing stirred save in the dark trees beyond the patio where a black shadow slunk, belly to the ground.

The big cat's roar started low, almost beneath the register of human hearing then built in intensity until it trembled the ice cubes in Jervis's drink.

He turned around to look for the origin of the terrifying sound, and saw the amber eyes. In the few seconds it took for his mind to confront the reality of a full-grown black panther stalking him, the big cat was already on the neat, short grass of his lawn.

'Oh bollocks, Oakshott was right.'

An adrenaline rush hit him, but the property tycoon did not panic; he stayed cool. Fighting his thumping heart and the tunnel-like vision adrenaline brings, he wrenched his ultra-focused gaze from the approaching big cat and glanced right then left. The pool was between him and the safety of the house.

'Don't run, Jervie-boy,' he said in a mutter.

He knew instinctively the panther would pounce if he turned and dashed for the patio doors. Mobile phone still held in one hand, he snatched up a poolside rake with the other.

Another roar. Jervis felt it in his bones and his eyes were drawn irresistibly to the cat. The predator paused to glare at the terrified man. In those tiny fragments of a second, Jervis noticed three things. First, the panther was not a uniform black. Sunlight played across its fur and revealed dark spots in a brown-black coat. Second, the appalling broad width of its shoulders and head.

This was no rangy, dog-like creature, but a killing machine. Finally, how uncomfortable and exposed he felt standing there in dressing gown and swimming trunks.

The panther's tail lashed, once, twice. It was about to leap. Jervis hurled the rake at the cat. He missed and his survival instincts took over. Mobile held high above his head, he leapt into the swimming pool and scrambled aboard the inflatable ring. Cats hate water, he thought, they can't swim. Thrashing his feet, Jervis steered to the middle of the pool. Steam rose thick around him. He punched numbers into the phone. Stay here and you'll be safe, he told himself. He leant forward. Through the cloud of steam, he could see the indistinct silhouette of the big cat as it paced around the pool.

It took only two rings before Jervis was connected to the emergency operator.

'Which service do you require: police, ambulance or fire?' said a polite woman's voice.

Jervis's words came fast, almost in a babble. 'Oh, Thank God. Police. There's a wild animal, a panther, I don't know how got here, it must be an escapee, a zoo maybe—'

Behind him, obscured by the steam, the panther slid into the water. Big cats can swim. In fact, big cats love to swim.

Jervis attempted to explain what had happened to the confused operator. 'I'm in my swimming pool, in my rubber ring.'

Ripples rocked the inner tube. Focused on assuring the operator he was not drunk, Jervis did not notice.

'I think I'm safe,' he said, 'but it was stalking me, it leapt at me.'

Two ear tips protruded above the surface. Like parallel shark fins, they parted the steam as they arrowed towards Jervis.

The emergency operator had heard many wild stories in her time, some of them true. Better let the police handle this, she decided. 'Connecting you,' she said.

The cat's ears dipped beneath the water.

There was a faint click and Jervis was put through to the police.

'Address and name, sir?'

Jervis opened his mouth to answer but, instead, was wrenched down through the middle of the ring. He tried to brace his arms and legs against its rubber walls, but the effort was futile. The brute force of the sudden attack pulled him underwater. His hands and feet jerked high before they vanished from sight and the mobile phone was flung up, high in the air. Spinning slowly, it started to fall as his agonised screams abruptly became a confusion of bubbling.

'Sir? Sir? Are you there?' said the police operator.

Splash. The phone plunged into the water. It twisted and tumbled in violent eddies as skeins of red blood swirled around it. A dressing gown-clad arm pulled in a swimming motion but was yanked back. The phone clunked onto the bottom of the pool. A fresh gout of blood turned the water dark red.

The mobile continued to transmit the sound of underwater thrashing and gurgling to the appalled police operator until, finally, water seeped in and shorted its battery.

- 5 -

- Early Morning -

- The House of Rosie's Mother, South London -

DOWNSTAIRS, THE PHONE RANG LONG AND INSISTENT. Rosie snuggled deeper down beneath the duvet. Not that she had a choice; it was the only direction available. Peter was jammed in tight on one side, Lizzy on the other. Some time in the early hours, they had crept in beside her. It amazed Rosie how much bed space two sprawling children could take up. Between them, they left her a tiny corridor of mattress. She didn't mind, she loved it.

The phone continued to ring. Let it be, Rosie decided. Her mother would do the same because she did not answer phone calls before breakfast in the firm belief that such an event was always the harbinger of bad news. And she could certainly do without that before her first cup of tea, thank you very much.

But still the phone rang.

Thump. A little body was out of the bed and running downstairs. Lizzy was gone before Rosie could stop her. She just cannot resist the excitement of a phone conversation, thought Rosie, but then, for Lizzy, almost

61

every aspect of life, no matter how mundane, was intensely fascinating.

The ringing of the phone stopped. Rosie strained to hear the conversation.

'Hello?' Lizzy said. 'My mum? Yes, yes she is, hold on please.'

Rosie's heart sank. She slid her feet from underneath the duvet and onto the cold floor.

'Mum,' bawled Lizzy, 'there's someone on the phone for you. From work.'

'Coming,' Rosie yelled back as she shrugged on her dressing gown. What time was it? Five forty–five? This had better be good.

'Mum, it's Uncle Don!'

Rosie tightened the dressing gown's belt and cast an envious glance at Peter. He was still asleep. Snoring. Lucky sod, wish it were me, she thought.

'Hello?' Rosie said in the croakiest fake voice she could muster. Until she knew more, it seemed wise to prepare the ground for a malady-based excuse.

'Rosie, that you?' Don said.

'It's me,' she said, her voice creaking like a door from a Hammer Horror movie.

'My God, you sound ill. Do you need a doctor?'

'No, no, nothing like that,' Perceiving she might have overdone it, Rosie eased off on the effect a little. 'Just tired. Don't you know what time it is?'

'Big Mo's escaped,' said Don.

'Again. When? How?'

'The cleaners phoned me. One of them didn't read the warning signs and wedged open both airlock doors. He was free before they could do a thing. Little Mo's gone too.'

'How long ago?' said Rosie, certain she knew the pair's destination.

'Must be at least an hour. It took the cleaners that long to summon up the gumption to call me.'

'Well, Big Mo averages about five miles an hour.'

'At least.'

'So, if they follow their usual M.O.—'

'You definitely watch too much crime drama on TV,' said Don. 'Look, we've already got two Mo's, let's not add a third. It's way too early for me to cope with confusion of any kind.'

'Then they're almost halfway there.'

'Where? Oh, of course. The pork sausages.'

'The pork sausages,' agreed Rosie. 'I need to get dressed and get going. Bankstone's a fair way from here, but I can probably be there before them. I'll call ahead; the butcher gave me his number last time they raided him.'

'Good, but Rosie...'

'What?' She didn't like the change in tone of Don's voice.

'You know we can't keep Big Mo forever,' he said. 'Much as we both like him, the time is fast approaching when we'll have to make a tough decision. And about Little Mo, too.'

Rosie hung up the phone.

It rained, but it was more than mere rainfall, it poured with the relentless intensity that usually signals the end of any hope of sunshine in the foreseeable future.

'You learn a lot about dog psychology in our line of work,' said Nigel Peckworth. 'And Rule Number One is: they're greedy beggars and you can use that against them.'

'I think Big Mo might be a greater challenge than most dogs,' said Rosie. 'He's some kind of jail-breaking, sausage-stealing genius.'

'And we can use can use that against him too,' Nigel said. 'I know what I'm doing, trust me.'

Standing beneath the awning of Peckworth & Sons Family Butchers, they watched Bankstone High Street come to early morning life. Large trucks, their hazard lights flashing, made goods deliveries, whilst a sparse trickle of shop workers scurried along the pavement, heads down against the rain.

'Six generations of pork butchers in my family and proud of it,' said Nigel. 'It adds up to more than two centuries of meat vendor against dog. We know what we're up against. And no dog gets a free second helping of my saveloys, especially those two.'

The memory of their last raid and of the devastation they'd wrought still rankled.

'Won't Big Mo see us out here?' said Rosie.

'Of course,' said Nigel. 'But we've got to put the dog under pressure, got to force his hand. It's why I asked you to park around the back. He'll see your van, smell it, and suspect a trap.'

'And that's good because?'

'Because at the rear there're at least four different routes of entry: the chiller and storeroom; the kitchens; the meat preparation area; and the office. Now we cannot cover all of them, but he dare not risk passing your van, just in case you're inside it, ready cut off his escape. So we force him around to the front where there's only one entrance: the shop door.'

'But Big Mo will smell us, see us first,' Rosie said. 'He'll never—'

'Oh, he will. Remember, we've got greed on our side. And we've got sausages.'

They both looked at the link of six pork sausages lying just inside the open door.

'Still, you might be right.' Nigel said. 'Just to be on the safe side let's move to that shop door across the way.' They splashed across the road and took shelter in the dry doorway of a wine merchant.

'Er, sorry about this, Nigel,' said Rosie in a whisper. 'I'm sure you know what you're doing, six generations of experience and all, but they're very quick, those two. Big Mo'll be gone before I can cross the road and net him.'

In her hands, she held a throw net, its mesh strong enough to defeat a wolfhound.

'Rule Number One will give us all the time we need. Greed trumps everything, you'll see,' Nigel's full attention was fixed on the alleyway at the side of his shop. 'Are you sure you can take care of the Alsatian?'

'Little Mo? Oh, he's fine,' Rosie said. 'No problem there.'

'Um, good, good,' said Nigel. He wasn't so sure; he had vivid memories of Little Mo's large canine teeth. 'Well, the important thing is we appear relaxed and don't make eye contact with the little buggers when they turn up.'

'Okay,' said Rosie, 'but aren't we standing too far away?'

'Don't worry. Rule One works every time.'

They stood and waited in silence.

A council street-sweeper truck ground past them, amber lights flashing, its little brushes whirring fast as they beat the pavement. Their motion reminded Rosie of the little terrier's legs when he achieved top speed.

'Nigel,' she said.

'Yes?'

'What's Rule Number Two?'

'Don't know. Never had to go beyond Rule Number One.'

His answer made no sense to Rosie, but she was willing to concede that he possessed by far the greater expertise. She dug her hands into the pockets of her fleece jacket and leant against the shop's locked door to wait.

Nigel saw them first. Rosie noticed him stiffen then force himself into a relaxed posture. He spoke to her out of the side of his mouth, 'Don't stare. I can see them. They're in the alley.'

Not staring was harder than Rosie expected.

She forced herself to look away, but the strain of doing so whilst still trying to watch the alleyway in her peripheral vision made her eyeballs hurt. Her eyes began to water.

The pork butcher noticed Rosie's discomfort. 'Look at your feet,' he said, 'then look at the middle of the road just to the left of the alley, but no further. You'll see them perfectly well.'

She followed his advice and was just in time to witness Big and Little Mo stick their heads around the corner and, noses twitching, take in the aroma wafting from the butcher's shop. The synchronicity of their action reminded Rosie of two corny, old-time music hall comedians in a black-and-white movie.

Big Mo examined the street for threats. He saw and identified Rosie and Nigel immediately. Ordinarily he would have fled, but Rule Number One kicked in. His powerful sense of smell told him sausages were near. Very near. He simply could not resist their allure and, followed by his giant sidekick, the terrier sidled alongside the brickwork beneath the shop's window. They walked in the slow motion, stiff-legged gait assumed by dogs who wish they were invisible, are not, but pretend to be so.

The sausages were now visible. Big Mo's eyes flicked constantly between the glorious sight in front of him and the ominous presence of both butcher and dog warden across the street.

Rosie was poised to intercept.

'Do we go?' she whispered.

Nigel pressed himself further into the door's alcove.

'Wait just a little longer,' he said.

Big Mo noted the tension in the humans' posture and knew this was the critical moment. To feed or to flee? He compared the distance to the pork sausages with that which the two humans would have to travel to intercept him. Once more, the inexorable power of Rule Number One came into force. He made the only decision a sausage-craving alpha dog can make. Big Mo accelerated sausage-ward, Little Mo at his heels.

'No need to rush,' said Nigel.

He ambled across the street. Rosie, who had expected the whole thing to be much more fast-paced, followed.

As the Jack Russell seized one end of the sausage link, his eyes were on the humans. This would be easy. He pulled. The sausages stretched horizontal and stopped. Big Mo pulled again. And pulled once more. But the sausages refused to come with him. Rosie could see the whites of Big Mo's eyes; they were fixed on the net she carried. His breath came fast and he wheezed as he tugged with all his might. He knew what was about to happen but, as long as he had sausages in his jaws, he could not admit defeat, could not retreat.

Little Mo came to the rescue. Paws planted in a defiant stance, hackles raised, the big German Shepherd stood in the doorway, lips curled to reveal his sharp white teeth.

The sight made Nigel quail. On the dogs' last raid, Little Mo successfully held off the butcher and his two apprentices before the pair made their escape.

'Miss Flinn?' he said.

'It's Ms.,' then, in her most commanding voice, Rosie said; 'Bad dog, oh you bad boy, Little Mo. Lie down, right now.'

If Big Mo was an alpha dog, Little Mo was a zeta. He cowered immediately. He didn't want to hear that kind of language from the woman who fed him. Ears flat, tail between his legs, Little Mo lay down.

The terrier knew it was over, but he still wanted those delicious tubes of offal. He pulled and pulled and pulled, but the sausages would not yield. Their links elongated but did not rupture. Watching his determination and desperation Rosie now understood why there was no need for any rule beyond Number One. Even as she tossed the net over Big Mo, he continued to wrench and worry at the bait.

Once Rosie had the struggling escapee entangled, Nigel undid the thin steel hawser that secured the sausages to the frame of the sturdy display cabinet.

'Rubber-skinned sausages. An invention of my Dad's, works every time,' he said, waving the links in the air.

The dogs' eyes followed the swing of the meaty temptations that had trapped them.

'Greed trumps all,' said Nigel.

As Rosie drove, she sang:

'Hey little dawgee where you gone?
Hey little dawgee where you hide?'

She didn't know the rest of the words to the song, so she contented herself with repeating the opening lines over and over again. Her two sodden captives in the van's cage howled along with her. Yet this morning's success did not sooth Rosie's sense of guilt about the still-missing pets. Rather than drive the straight route to the dog pound in Redholt, she set off on a twenty-mile detour through the lanes of Upper and Lower Hamley.

'Hey little dawgee where you gone?
Hey little dawgee where you hide?'

There were homes she wanted to visit before the morning commute began, places she'd leafleted yesterday, but where no one answered the door.

'Just got to make some quick house calls, boys,' she said.
'Hey little—'

Rosie signalled left. Made the turn, took the corner fast and—

'What the hell?'

She braked hard and her unwieldy van aquaplaned on the road. Before Rosie could regain control, the wheels threw up a sheet of spray. She skidded to a halt alongside an astonished and very wet policeman.

Police cars, vans, and an ambulance blocked the lane. None had their emergency lights flashing. Police tape stretched across an open gateway.

Rosie wound down her window.

'I'm desperately sorry, officer.'

The constable opened his mouth to speak then closed it again. Like so many officers before him, he found her smile and eyes irresistible. All thoughts of issuing a ticket for reckless driving vanished. It was a tactic that had saved Rosie, not the world's greatest driver by any means, many hundreds of pounds in fines and charmed a magistrate's bench out of a probable driving ban.

'What's going on, constable?' she said.

Water dripping in large languorous drops from the brim of his helmet, the policeman leant one arm on the van's roof and bent to speak to her. Rosie's captives barked furiously. Startled, he turned his head to squint at the van's interior. Teeth gnashing, the dogs flung themselves against the wire cage. They hated coppers.

He stepped back a pace.

'I'm afraid the road is closed, miss.'

'I'm the dog warden—'

'I can see that,' he said. 'It says so in big letters on the side of your van. And we can all hear it too. Did someone call you as a joke?'

Rosie was puzzled. 'Joke? No, I'm searching for some stray cats and dogs, fifteen of them. Look, I can show you, here—'

She gave him her 'Missing Pet' flyer.

'I distributed these around here yesterday. I thought I'd make follow-up visits to the houses where no-one answered.' Rosie leant forward to peer through the windscreen. She could see a brutally modern house at the end of a short driveway. 'What happened here? This was one of them.'

The police constable turned his back to the rain and read the leaflet.

'I think you'll need more than a rope on a pole to catch what did this,' he said.

'Did what? An animal?' she said. 'Who lives here?'

Three crime scene technicians appeared from behind a large Forensic Service van. They carried bulky holdalls and wore masks, white disposable plastic overalls, plus shoe covers. Rosie watched them walk up the driveway. A second uniformed officer guarded the front door which she opened to let them enter.

Rosie's policeman tossed the now sodden leaflet onto her lap.

'If you're not here on official business, I can't tell you anything right now, miss,' he said. 'So if you'll just turn around. And if we see any strays we'll let you know, although in this rain...' He shrugged then stepped away from Rosie's van.

'Thanks for nothing,' she muttered.

Rosie crunched the gear stick into reverse, looked over her shoulder, revved the engine, snuck one last peek up the driveway, and released the clutch. A horn blared and Rosie slammed on the brakes. The two dogs scrabbled hard to keep their balance. Two enormous headlights filled the view through her rear view mirror.

'Where the hell did that come from?' she said.

A TV satellite uplink truck blocked the lane. Five times the length of Rosie's van and more than twice its width, it dwarfed all the amassed police vehicles.

'Christ, how the hell did they find out so quick?' said the policeman. One arm raised, palm held flat, he walked towards the truck. 'Back-up, you can't park here.'

He tried to shoo the truck away but, with a wheeze of air brakes, a second TV satellite rig from a different network, pulled up behind the first. Then a third arrived. The trucks were so broad they blocked the narrow lane. In her wing mirror Rosie watched the policeman try to marshal both the trucks and the camera crews who emerged from them. A uniformed sergeant and two other constables clambered reluctantly from the warmth of their dry patrol car and went to help him.

Rosie was boxed in.

'Wonderful, no escape. That's just brilliant,' she said.

Beyond the police tape, there was movement at the front door. Rosie set her windscreen wipers to full speed so she could see the action more clearly. A handful of people emerged from the house.

'What on Earth is he doing here?'

Coulston, wearing a raincoat over a dark formal suit, conferred with two similarly dressed men and a woman on the wide marble doorstep. As he spoke, he peeled bloodstained gloves from his hands.

'Big cat hunter, my arse,' said Rosie.

Big and Little Mo barked their agreement.

From their appearance and demeanour Rosie concluded the foursome were detectives. 'The bastard was just stringing me along.'

Rage overwhelmed common sense. Rosie shouldered open her door.

Coulston, with his back to the gate, did not see Rosie duck unchallenged under the police tape and stomp up the drive. Once in earshot, she heard him say:

'—suggest you contact Zaharkin immediately. Also the other partners: Beacon and Oakshott.'

Rosie did not have a clear understanding of why she was so angry. The product of a melange of embarrassment, chagrin, irritation at Coulston's condescension, and a general sense of confusion, she gave it full irrational vent.

'Hey, you, deer hunter, I want to see your licence,' she said in a shout.

Startled by her arrival, Coulston was too amazed to speak. It was only then that Rosie recognised the female detective. She had never seen the now conservatively dressed woman in daylight, nor in anything but Lycra and high heels. Rosie, about to let loose another vituperative blast at Coulston, hesitated, her mouth went dry.

'Christ, it's the bloody dog warden,' said Suze Derrington.

The other detectives laughed in disbelief.

'Sergeant, you know Miss Flinn?' said Coulston.

That's Ms. to you, mate, thought Rosie.

'Sir, she's an interfering meddler,' Derrington said, a red tide of anger rising in her face.

Sir, thought Rosie? Oh no, you've done it again.

'She almost bollixed up an undercover op we did with the RSPCA back in the spring,' said Derrington. She gave her colleagues a forceful account, strewn with four letter words, of Rosie's ill-considered single-handed attempt to arrest the Creswell brothers.

'And here she is again,' Derrington concluded, now nose-to-nose with Rosie, 'butting in where she has no business.'

Rosie wished she had as fine a skin complexion as Sergeant Derrington. Up close, it was very impressive.

Coulston eased an arm, then his shoulder, between the two, forcing them apart.

'Sergeant, perhaps it might be better if I dealt with the dog warden; this is wasting valuable time.'

His action forced Derrington to take a pace backwards.

'Don't move,' Coulston said to Rosie, 'I need to finish my business with these detectives.' He turned back to them. 'I'd recommend Oakshott first, he's based at the Swanmere Phase Two site,' he said. 'See if he'll tell you the truth.'

Derrington nodded. 'Come on,' she said to her team, 'let's get out of here before the media circus gets going.' As she stalked away, her parting shot to Rosie made it clear she had no confidence in Coulston taking the correct action. It was an ominous message. 'I warned you, dog warden. Now you'll have to pay the price.'

Coulston turned to face Rosie. 'Miss Flinn, what are you doing here?' His voice betrayed his frustration and disappointment.

'It's Ms., I told you so already,' said Rosie. 'Why didn't you say you were a policeman? You are a policeman aren't you?'

Coulston extracted his warrant card from his coat and showed it to her.

'Inspector. Detective Inspector,' he said.

She examined his ID. 'Boy, did you have a bad hair day when they took the photo. Hey, you're not Mid-Surrey Police. What's a London copper doing here?'

'Just advising. Just leaving.'

He walked down the drive.

Rosie scurried to catch up.

'Advising on what?' she said.

'There's been a serious incident. And it is none of your business.'

The pompous tone in his voice fuelled Rosie's annoyance. She pointed at the mass of trucks. 'The policeman down there said there's been an animal attack.'

Coulston stopped, looked at her, his face now expressionless.

'Oh, come on, not big cats?' she said. 'The Surrey Puma? Phfft! I heard all about you and your nutty theory.'

Coulston glared at her.

'Theory no longer. Far from it. Unfortunately,' he said.

'If someone's been attacked, bitten, it is my business. I've got two stray Dobies and a Rottie roaming these woods. How do you know they weren't responsible?'

Coulston glanced down at the bloodied latex gloves he still held between forefinger and thumb. 'No dog did this, believe me. This goes beyond a few bites.'

'Well, if it was an escaped animal then it's my jurisdiction, my case. We've got the files to prove it. I'm the dog warden.' Rosie was really losing it. She knew her argument could hardly be called well thought out, but she voiced it anyway.

Coulston shook his head. Heavy drops of accumulated rain sprayed from his hair.

'Cut it out, Ms. Flinn. It is not your 'case'; you have no 'jurisdiction'. Can I give you some advice?'

'No. But I'm sure you're going to anyway.'

'Stay out of the woods. Stay indoors.'

Rosie refused to be so easily deterred. 'So what did happen here?'

Coulston looked over her shoulder. Beyond the gate, camera crews and reporters jostled each other as they set up their cameras and tripods. 'I'm sure it won't be long before you know but, in the meantime, just let us do our job,' he said as he waved over a uniformed constable. 'We'll start by getting your van free of this unholy mess.'

- 6 -

- Late Morning -

- Zaharkin's Mansion, Upper Hamley -

'DA, DA, OF COURSE, THANK YOU, IT WAS MOST distressing, really.' Zaharkin drummed his fingers on the plum-red leather of his desktop as he spoke into the telephone. 'Jervis will be missed by very many people.' But not by me, he thought. 'Now to business, which is why I ring you. I want to check how the profits from Swanmere Phase Two are divided between remaining partners. Oh, you do not say? You anticipate my call, very good, and so?'

Feet together, shoulders hunched, he listened to the distorted voice of his senior corporate lawyer.

'Yes?' Zaharkin said. 'Divided equally between surviving partners. At least another ten million?'

His feet did a little dance of glee on the Persian rug that carpeted his study.

'This makes me very happy,' he said, then remembering the recent tragic event, changed his tone. 'On such a sad day, of course. Thank you.'

He hung up. Through the window opposite his desk, Zaharkin had a scenic view across his lawns to a small lake and, beyond it, to the woods in which he had hunted with the Swanmere partners. It is absurd that a big cat could be out there, he thought, and then laughed. At last, the smug English were getting a taste of what the rest of the world had to live with.

The billionaire walked to the window and surveyed the soft, tree-lined contours of the rolling North Downs. Who were his neighbours? He had to think hard; he so rarely met any of them. Oh yes, a KGB traitor hidden here for thirty years by MI6, but whose presence was an open secret. Then there was a fellow oligarch with no manners and no sense of humour, at least not when it came to being on the receiving end of Zaharkin's practical jokes. The Saudi prince was fun. He flew in once a month to entertain high-class prostitutes and drink himself into a stupor. Who else? Ah, the new ones, a couple, two wealthy City types. Probably stinking hypocrites like most rich English. Loot the nation of its wealth, wreck the economy, then blame the poor and make them pay the bill. Such breath-taking hypocrisy enraged Zaharkin, himself an expert practitioner of the art.

Well, let the cat eat them all, he decided. He'd make sure he was safe.

Towel around her neck, Rosie bustled along the concrete walkway towards Big and Little Mo's enclosure. She carried her dog-catching pole, and a tray on which lay some large lozenges. The dogs heard her coming and, suspicious of her intentions, howled. When Rosie reached their pen, the terrier ceased his din and trotted forward, nose down, his concentration focused entirely on the door, ready for the moment it opened. He knew these humans' reactions were slower than his and, despite the morning's disappointment, he was ready for a re-match. Give Big Mo an inch and he'd take it as an open invitation for escape and a further appointment with some pork sausages, but preferably not rubber ones.

'You aren't going to give me any trouble are you?' said Rosie.

After the victory at the butcher's shop, she was determined to push home her advantage. As she spoke, the pills rattled on the tray. Big Mo knew what was about to occur and didn't like it. The Jack Russell abandoned the door and leapt high to grip the wire mesh in his jaws, teeth bared, lips curled in a snarl.

'Now that is just unnecessary,' Rosie said.

She placed the tray on the floor and picked up a pair of blue disposable latex gloves.

'Rosie? Where are you?' Don's voice echoed along the concrete corridor.

'In here,' she said.

Don appeared in the walkway. He looked worried.

'Listen, I've just had the Chief Exec on the phone,' he said.

'The big man himself. What did he want?'

'Now this is not my idea, right?' Don hesitated. 'Not my fault but—'

'But what?'

Uncertain how to handle this, Don scratched his head.

'It seems you got in an argument with the police at the scene of this alleged big cat killing today,' he said.

'Not deliberately,' said Rosie. She nodded at the two dogs. 'I'd just picked up these two over in Bankstone, I was heading back here.'

'Not deliberately? You made a fifteen-mile detour to get there. And even if—'

'Don, it was a coincidence, nothing more. And it was a twenty mile detour.'

'But did you tell the police—'

Rosie did not let him finish. 'Coulston, your big cat hunter, was there. Turns out he's a detective inspector. Even worse, that awful Sergeant Derrington, the one I told you about, remember? She threatened me.'

77

'Rosie, will you just let me finish a sentence? Did you tell the police that catching this big cat was our job?'

'Yes. No. Yes.' Rosie suddenly saw where this was headed. 'Don, I didn't realise it was a big cat. When the police said animal attack, I thought it was a feral dog or something. One of ours: the missing Rottweiler. I only saw the news on the TV when I got back here. Frankly, I still find it hard to believe.'

'They found paw prints, claw marks. Good grief, Rosie, the man was disembowelled.'

Rosie's teeth clenched; her jaw muscles tightened.

Don knew she was never going to admit he was right and she was wrong. 'They've called in the Army,' he said. 'That's how serious, how dangerous this is. Listen, you've got the police all stirred up. Just keep out of their way.'

Rosie snapped on one of the gloves. Teeth still gripping the wire mesh, Big Mo's eyes followed the movement.

'Or what?' said Rosie.

'The police spoke to the Council Leader, and now he's talking about disciplinary hearings. You don't want it on your record that you interfered in a police investigation.'

Snap. The second glove was pulled on.

'That Susie or Suze Derrington or whatever the hell she's called has got it in for me.'

'It wasn't her. It was your friend from yesterday.'

'Coulston did it? The pig.' But Rosie's anger subsided as the implication sank in that her job was at risk. She smiled weakly at him. 'Message understood, Don. I'm just looking for those missing pets, nothing more, and I'm not going to let it spoil my day because, first—'

Rosie picked up one of the lozenges and stooped so she was eye-to-eye with the terrier.

'First, I have to give Little Mo his suppository.'

Smiling, she showed the lozenge, held between finger and thumb, to Little Mo. The dog's eyes widened in fear. He gulped. Don winced.

'Listen, once you've finished, you're taking the rest of the day off. I've signed you out already,' he said. 'In fact, take a few days off. Keep out of sight, let this all blow over.'

Two hours later, Rosie parked her battered Daewoo on the outer edge of a vast parking lot crammed with thousands of cars. Bored witless by the prospect of domestic bliss at home with her mother, and annoyed with herself for being chronically unable to follow good advice, she had decided to check out the one snippet of information gleaned from Coulston's conversation with the detectives.

Beyond the cars were the gleaming white walls of Swanmere Mall. The monolith was designed to keep the elements out and shoppers in. It worked. Hordes of sodden consumers scurried through the unrelenting rain to reach its many entrances. This was Oakshott, Jervis, and Beacon's domain: the retail development that made their names and their fortunes. It was not the mall that brought Rosie here. Parked facing away from it, she gazed at a wide expanse of ochre-yellow mud set against a backdrop of woodland and hills. Earthmovers and landscrapers churned deep ruts as they crisscrossed the cleared ground. A large sign stood on the edge of the wasteland. It read:

Swanmere Phase Two
LUXURY APARTMENTS AND HOUSES
A gated community
Delivering security and peace of mind

As she watched a bulldozer excavate the stump of a once great tree, Rosie thought of the over-arching green hall of the Weald.

'Bastards,' she said. And that reminded her of Coulston. 'Bastard,' she added.

The dark woods came to the right-hand edge of the car park's tarmac. Low overhanging branches brushed the roof of her car. The sky darkened. Thunder rumbled.

Rosie watched ton upon ton of mud being shoved back and forth by the earthmovers. She puffed her checks, blew out her breath. It was never as dull as this in those Danish crime shows. Her eyes strayed to the bulky file that lay unopened on the passenger seat. Don's clippings. Oh well, why not?

She pulled the dossier onto her lap and began to read. The press cuttings were arranged chronologically, with the newest on top. Coulston featured heavily in the most recent, observed Rosie, who also noted he was always referred to by his police rank. Dammit, if only I'd read these when Don gave them to me, she thought, I might have saved myself some embarrassment. Not that it mattered much, if the quotes attributed to him were anything to go by, he'd been a pompous nutter for a long time.

As she worked back through the folder, something struck Rosie. Most of the people who reported big cat sightings were just like her: ordinary folk in ordinary jobs who stumbled across something extraordinary. What they said appeared to be consistent and authentic. They did not come across as fantasists. Rosie was suddenly worried. What if Coulston was right about the big cat?

A lightning flash made her look up. It was immediately followed by a thunderclap. The storm was getting closer.

Her stomach rumbled as if in response to the thunder.

Rain pelted hard against the windscreen.

Imitating Don, she spoke to herself; 'Rosie, what the hell are you doing here? I told you to stay at home.' She closed the folder and put it aside. It was time for some lunch. She twisted around to pluck a clear plastic lunch box from where it sat between two empty child seats. 'Well, Don,' she said. 'I can't do my work because the army is in the hills shooting foxes, badgers and weasels, anything but a big cat, and, if I tried to do my job, they'd probably shoot me too.'

Her fingers struggled to open the box's greasy clips.

'But Rosie, why come here?' She was proud of her Don

impersonation, especially the air of benign exasperation he used whenever he spoke to her.

'Well, I'm bored, it's Friday, my Mum's collecting the kids from school, I don't like being threatened, and I overheard Coulston talking about Swanmere. So, yes, you've got me, I'm being nosy.'

She popped open the lid. Inside, mangled sandwiches mingled with chocolate cake.

'Ham and mustard and chocolate icing. Yumm. I've got to stop Lizzie making me a packed lunch.'

She plucked an apple from the mess. Smeared in butter and icing it slipped from her fingers, bounced to the floor then came to rest beneath the brake pedal.

'Yep, that's me,' she said. 'Nosy and bored and generally pissed off.'

Rosie contorted herself to bend her head under the steering wheel. She reached for the fruit. Thunder rumbled again; it was nearly overhead.

The car rocked as something heavy thudded onto the bonnet. Startled, Rosie jerked upwards and bashed the back of her head on the underside of the dashboard.

'Ow. Shit. Damn. Ow.'

Rubbing the tender spot, she eased herself upright. Then stiffened with fright.

The panther crouched on the bonnet. Amber eyes stared at Rosie. Sleek, beautiful, and powerful, the big cat bared its teeth. Fangs gleamed in the pale light of the storm. Lightning flashed again, reflecting off the cat's wet flanks. The panther craned forward to examine her; its whiskers touched the rain-flecked glass of the windscreen.

Rosie pressed herself back into the seat.

Another thunderbolt cracked the sky, and the cat was gone. It sprang onto the roof then pushed itself off the rear of the car and bounded into the trees.

As she turned her head to follow its movement, Rosie glimpsed the panther one final time then it was gone.

Now facing forwards, she sat rigid with shock.

'No-one is going to believe me. I need proof.'

She jerked into action. Her small, silver-coloured, holiday-snap style camera was in the well between the front seats. Rosie grabbed it then opened her door.

The rain had already washed away most of the muddy paw prints left on the bonnet by the panther.

'Oh crap.'

Rosie reeled off her entire repertoire of four-letter words then remembered to check the car's roof. Under the protection of the trees, the cat's prints were much clearer.

Rosie powered on the camera and, by bracing her feet awkwardly between door and car seat, she stretched to snap a photograph. The rain lashed down even harder. The prints began to dribble and run.

'No, no. This cannot be happening,' said Rosie in despair.

An idea occurred to her. She reached into the car and grabbed the sandwich box. Tossing its contents aside, she slammed it over the best of the surviving paw prints.

'There,' she said in triumph.

Lifting the upturned box, she snapped two more photos.

The thunder growled long, low and deep. It dawned on Rosie that she stood with her back to the woods, those same woods in which lurked a panther. She scrambled into her seat and slammed the door shut.

'Rosie, you're a divorced mother of two. What the hell were you thinking?' she said to herself. If Don wasn't there to say it to her, she would. Trembling with the aftershock of her encounter, Rosie shook her dripping head and closed her eyes. A sharp tap on the passenger window startled her, and a small yip of fear escaped her lips.

Coulston and Henry Olembe peered in at her.

For a few seconds she gaped open-mouthed at them then lunged across the passenger seat and shoved open the door. 'Get in, get in! The panther's here.'

'Hello, Rosie Flinn, dog warden,' said the Ghanaian.

'You're that gardener, Henry,' Rosie said as she pushed herself upright.

'That is correct. A plastic box was on top of your car. Here.'

Sighing, Rosie accepted the box. Henry scrambled in to sit beside her in the passenger seat. He carried a short spear and, as he forced the weapon into the car's restricted interior space, its steel blade tinked against the inside of the rear window. Henry gave up; it was never going to fit. He opened the passenger door a crack and let the tip of the spear stick out.

Coulston wedged himself between the child seats in the rear, his rifle balanced across his knees.

'I suppose I shouldn't be surprised to find you here,' he said.

'Didn't you hear me? Your bloody panther's out there!'

She stabbed a finger at the trees beside them. Coulston raised an eyebrow.

'That so? A big cat? Well, it comes as a real shock to me. Just as well we came prepared.'

Rosie regarded Coulston's rifle and Henry's spear.

'So you're here officially?' she said.

'God, no. The local plods find it hard to take advice from the Met, let alone the fact that the brass sees me as a bit of an eccentric. I thought it best to just get on; do what we can until they decide different.'

'It will kill again,' said Henry. 'There is no doubt in my mind.'

Coulston leant forward and patted Henry's upper arm. 'Henry tracked it here from Jervis's house,' he said. 'In the rain. Very impressive.'

'Thank you, brother Robert.'

The policeman's attention switched to Rosie. 'Describe it to me. Don't miss a detail.' When she finished, he said, 'So, not a Doberman then?'

'Okay, okay. I was wrong,' said Rosie. 'I apologise; but you didn't have to go over my head and complain.'

'Seems to me it's you who's decided to ignore some perfectly good advice,' said Coulston.

'You might have cost me my job.'

'Did you think a panther's caught as easily as a stray poodle? I was trying to do you a favour.'

Irritated, she pushed Henry's spear shaft away from her face. 'How do you two know each other?' she said. 'Got some kind of master-slave thing going here?'

Henry laughed. So did Coulston. Scornfully.

'Hardly. I need Henry more than he needs me. You saw the panther.'

Rosie nodded. The awful memory of the big cat on the bonnet, staring at her, fearless, triggered a shudder of horror.

'Well, who do you think can hunt a big cat? Them?' Coulston pointed over his shoulder at the bustling shoppers. 'Look at them. Half of them own 4x4s but have never driven off-road in their lives. The only nature they come into contact with is on TV wildlife shows.'

'But the Army—'

Coulston cut her off. 'The Army knows how to shoot straight, but they're not hunters. This panther is only seen when it wants to be. They don't have a hope. But Henry grew up in the highlands of Ghana, in the forests, and understands these woods. He can read them better than any Englishman I know.'

'Friend Robert, you honour me,' said Henry.

'It's true,' said Coulston. 'And he knows first-hand about melanistic leopards, panthers to you and me, and how dangerous they are.'

'Sadly, it is true. I have seen many deaths. But what we hunt is more than a panther: it is the *kyaani*.'

'Your forest spirit. You mentioned that already,' said Rosie. 'So why did a *kyaani* come all the way from Ghana to Surrey?'

'It lives in all forests. It is the forest.'

Rosie swivelled in her seat to face Coulston.

'Come on, you're not buying into this avenging spirit stuff?' she said.

'Look, put aside what Henry thinks,' said Coulston. 'This animal's a killer. You know I've been tracking the Surrey Puma for years?'

Rosie nodded.

'And my grandfather before me, more than fifty years between us. People call it the Surrey Puma, but pumas never have a black coat; they're tan-coloured. The Native Americans call them the Ghost Cat. This is a real animal all right, flesh and blood, but it's a panther. It's a completely different species.'

'So where's it come from?' said Rosie.

'Probably escaped from some rich man's illegal private zoo. But, and I know it sounds crazy, what Henry says also makes some kind of sense.' Again, Coulston waved a hand towards the crammed parking lot. 'Do you know what was here before the developers moved in?'

Rosie had a faint memory of controversy and scandal over how the planning regulations had been steamrollered by the developers' machinations.

'Some kind of pond wasn't it?' she said.

'More than a pond, it was the Swanmere. I lived around here as a kid. I fished in it, swam in it. Chased dragonflies. Got chased by swans a few times. Then along come Jervis and company. They bulldozed it, built that—' He jerked his chin at the mall. 'They replaced the reed beds with retail units. If there is a spirit which exacts vengeance for the desecration of nature then here is where I would have it set to work.'

Rosie snorted with disgust. 'Come on, you don't believe in this stuff, not really.'

'You're awful quick to dismiss anything out of the ordinary,' said Coulston. He hesitated. How much should he tell her? Not the full story, not yet, he decided. 'There might just be some kind of weird link between the developers and the big cat.' He leant forward between the front seats. He'd seen some activity on the building site. 'Do you know why the panther chose this moment to be here of all places? In daylight? Don't you know who that is over there?'

Rosie saw a tall, thin businessman in a yellow hard hat leave the Phase Two Portakabin offices. A younger man, obviously an underling, escorted him, and he held high an umbrella to protect his boss from the rain. The pair walked towards a row of parked cars.

Rosie shrugged. 'No," she said.

'That's Colin Oakshott,' said Coulston. 'One of the dead man's partners.'

They watched Oakshott drive away in a bright red E-Type Jaguar.

'And he owns a Jag,' said Coulston then laughed. 'How wildly inappropriate.'

'So it wants revenge,' said Rosie. She was fascinated but felt completely out of her depth. 'Henry's right?'

The African nodded in affirmation.

'Maybe so,' said Coulston, 'but I prefer a more prosaic explanation.' Oh well, why not tell her, he thought. Right now, the more people who know, the better. 'You see, Mister Oakshott wounded the panther three month's ago.'

He told Rosie the tale of that snowy dawn and the bloody paw print.

'It's been hunting easy prey ever since. And yet—'

Rosie was horrified. 'My missing pets?'

'The *kyaani* hunted these men before they ever shot at it,' said Henry in a tone of absolute certainty.

'But why stalk the developers? Unless you accept what Henry says.' Coulston leant back against the seat and closed his eyes. 'I don't know what to think.'

The rain stopped. The thunderstorm had long since rolled away. The sun found a gap in the clouds and shone with sudden, bright intensity. The sunlight illuminated the car's interior. Rosie noticed how tired both men looked. Henry glanced through his window and up at the sky.

'Robert, the darkness has passed,' he said.

Coulston massaged his face. 'We'd better be going. Any chance of a lift?'

Rosie braked to a halt outside a small, quaint timber and thatch cottage on the edge of Redholt.

'This place is yours?' she said to Coulston. She wasn't sure what she had expected, but this did not match her image of where the rugged detective inspector would live.

'I grew up here,' he said.

The two men exited the car. Coulston leant in through Henry's open door to speak to Rosie.

'Have I persuaded you?' he said.

'Yes,' said Rosie, 'but I'm not sure about what.'

Coulston laughed. 'Join the gang,' he said. His face became serious once more. 'I meant, have I persuaded you to leave the hunt to the experts?'

Stubborn as ever, Rosie refused to answer him directly. 'Tell me, if you think Henry's wrong,' she said, 'then how is it possible for a panther to live here? In England?'

Coulston looked at his watch. 'If you can spare half an hour I can show you something that help explain.'

'What? In this house?'

'No, over there.' He pointed down the lane to where a stubby stone spire rose above the woods.

'Henry?'

With a rattle of its loose handle, Johnno Dawes pulled open the door of the garden shed.

'Are you in here?' In search of a pair of wellington boots, he hesitated on the threshold. 'Hello?'

There was no reply, so he went inside.

The rain-damped shed reeked of potting compost, mineral oil, and old leather. Johnno, conditioned since childhood to respect a gardener's domain and fearful of being caught here uninvited, leant across the crude workbench and ducked his head to peer through the grimy windowpane. He saw no one but, in looking through the glass, he pushed aside the woven grass eye that hung mid-frame from a slender thread.

'Where the hell has the man got to?'

Johnno was annoyed. He needed those bloody wellingtons. He'd last seen Henry this morning at the bottom of the drive climbing into a car driven by an equally scruffy man, another gardener no doubt. Though how a gardener could afford a BMW was beyond him. It really was too much, Johnno decided. The least he and Naomi could expect was a full day's work from the man. What were they paying the Olembes for, if not that?

Blast it, where had the wretched man hidden the boots? It was the local golf club's celebrity tournament tomorrow and Johnno wanted to be prepared should it rain. The event was one of the big occasions of the Mid-Surrey social calendar. Hamley Golf Club was no mere municipal course open to the public. Locals liked to say it was so exclusive, even the positions of toilet attendant passed from father to son and mother to daughter like family retainers at a stately home. Save for a few media personalities, its members were drawn from the select worlds of banking, insurance, finance, and City of London law firms. There was not a black face to be seen on its fairways. Johnno and Naomi were desperate to attend. To secure an invitation they had exploited the contacts in their address book with ruthless efficiency. It had been touch-and-go; the couple were handicapped by the fact they were newcomers. Their eventual success left them frazzled and exhausted, but delighted.

Johnno's jaw muscles tightened. Here they were, working themselves to the bone, and their gardener vanishes, without a by-your-leave.

He stepped away from the window and, in doing so, his knee nudged a rake propped against the bench. Falling sideways, it struck an array of spades, forks, and other implements stacked in one corner. They, in turn, clattered to the floor. Annoyed by his clumsiness, Johnno bent to collect the fallen implements.

'What on earth?'

Amongst the gardening tools was a long spear. It had a broad leaf-like blade and its razor-sharp edge gleamed in the shed's half-light. Johnno placed it to one side, shoved the remainder back in their corner then froze in his posture, one hand hovering over the confusion of shafts. Dear God, there was another one. Johnno extracted a second, shorter spear. This was a design he did recognise. *Zulu Dawn* and *Zulu* were two of his favourite movies and fancied himself quite the military buff. It was an *assegai*, its narrow iron blade almost one-third the length of the shaft. He had a brief, bloody vision of the weapon being used by the Zulu *impis* with deadly effectiveness against the British redcoats. It was swiftly followed by a more vivid image of himself being hacked to death by Henry whilst Faith looked and laughed.

The blood of the men who fought to the death against the Zulu charge ran thin in Johnno's veins.

Terrified, he fled.

In the kitchen, Faith chopped onions for the casserole she was preparing for the Dawes' dinner.

Johnno rushed in, saw her, muttered some words under his breath then, composing his wild-eyed countenance, said, 'Er, Faith, do you know where our wellington boots are? I can't find my favourite pair.'

'Of course, Mr. Dawes, I unpacked them yesterday. They are in the garage behind your car.'

Johnno made no acknowledgement; instead, he walked through the kitchen, calling out Naomi's name as he disappeared from view. Faith watched him go then, with a shake of her head, returned to her task. She could not be sure, but what she thought he'd mumbled was, 'We'll be murdered in our beds.'

Five minutes later, Naomi entered, having left her gibbering husband in the drawing room.

'Faith, do you know where Henry is?'

She watched the maid briskly quarter a chicken with the meat cleaver.

'Madam?'

'Where is your brother?'

'He is with the police.'

Naomi found her gaze drawn to the bloody cleaver in Faith's hand.

'May I ask why?' she said.

'Oh, he is helping them with an enquiry.'

It was unfortunate that Faith did not know that in Britain this was media code for: he is a suspect, but the police don't have enough evidence to arrest him. She then made it worse by trying to clarify his role.

'The killing this morning, they asked for his assistance.'

To her credit, Naomi did little more than blanch whilst performing some very nimble thinking.

'Faith, there is no need to cook,' she said. 'Johnno and I will be out this evening, we're staying the night with friends.' What she had swiftly decided, but did not say, was they would check into a hotel and not return to this house until the Olembes were gone, ideally shackled safely in the cells of an Immigration Service detention center.

'It's a Norman design, rebuilt from the Saxon original,' said Coulston as he and Henry eased open the thick wooden door of the parish church. 'Over eight hundred years old.'

The door moved quietly on its iron hinges.

Coulston ushered Rosie inside.

Weak, cloud-filtered sunlight shone through the stained glass window above the altar. Right and left were parallel rows of simple wooden pews. In the periphery of her vision, Rosie sensed quick movement to her right. A scuttling grey mouse paused to regard the three intruders then darted into a crack between two of the wall's stone blocks.

She sniffed the air. It carried the aroma of an ancient parish church: a mixture of the pollen from wilted cut flowers, the fumes from beeswax polish, and mildew spore.

Henry sat on the nearest pew. Rosie joined him. It had been a long day. She watched Coulston walk down the aisle towards the church's plain stone altar then turn left into the small north transept. He knelt on the wide stone slabs of the floor.

'Over here,' his voice, although barely above a whisper, carried clearly.

'Go,' said Henry. 'You must see this. It is important.'

Embedded in the floor beside Coulston was a large engraved sheet of brass. It was a memorial of the type that was in high fashion amongst medieval nobility in the Thirteenth and Fourteenth Centuries. It portrayed the life-size image of a knight in chain mail, armour, surcoat, and with a long-sword at his side.

'Meet Sir Roger Norton,' said Coulston, 'grandson of one of Richard the Lionheart's squires who was imprisoned with the king in Austria and awarded this manor after King Richard's return to England.'

'So what?' said Rosie. She wanted to call her Mum, check she'd collected the kids.

'Look down here,' said Coulston, 'Behind his feet.'

The detail on the timeworn brass was hard to make out. Rosie crouched to examine the area he was pointing at. 'It's very faint. What is it?'

'The borders of the plaque show chattels: Sir Roger's most precious belongings. Often a lord of the manor is pictured with his hounds at his feet, but not in this case. Here, I'll show you.' From his trouser pocket, Coulston pulled out a small torch and shone it obliquely across the metal. Now no longer indistinct, Rosie could see, drawn in simple, clean, dynamic lines, what was unmistakeably a big cat, its fangs bared, claws extended.

'A panther,' Rosie said in amazement.

'Absolutely.' Coulston's fingers traced the outline of the big cat's torso. 'And, look, it's not even spotted like an ordinary leopard.'

'Is this genuine? When was this made?'

'Sir Roger was buried here six hundred and fifty years ago. The memorial shows scenes of a typical nobleman's life, save for the panther, of course. So there's no reason to doubt its authenticity.'

She studied the cat. 'It's so like the one I saw today.'

'Lucky you,' said Coulston. There was envy in his voice.

Rosie attempted to rationalise the idea that big cats had been in Britain in the Thirteenth Century. 'But was he a crusader? Could this be a heraldic symbol, or a scene from his life somewhere in the Middle East?'

'In heraldry, leopards and lions are drawn in a much more mannered fashion than this. And Sir Roger never went on a crusade. Perhaps his grandfather's experience taught the family a lesson they took to heart. He lived his entire life here. Look at it; the artist who drew this had seen a panther in the flesh, there's nothing stylised about it. And there are medieval chroniclers, monks, who wrote about Norton and his great cats, how he trained them, how feared they were.'

'Cats? More than one?'

'Oh yes, the chronicles are quite clear about it.' Coulston stood, easing joints stiff from kneeling on the cold stone.

'So where did he get them?' Rosie said, still examining the brass plaque.

'Not so hard, even then. They probably shipped them by sea, just as people have imported exotic pets by jet since the Sixties. Medieval records report all sorts of animals turning up in Europe. An Indian sultan even sent a rhinoceros to the King of Portugal.'

Rosie thought again of the panther and the thin glass that had separated them. She shivered.

'So you're saying they've been here for centuries? Breeding? How could they stay hidden?'

Coulston stood, held his palms up as if in surrender. 'It's unlikely. To be honest, I have no idea, only that there have clearly always been rich idiots who kept dangerous animals as pets. There is no evidence Norton bred them, and Henry, of course, interprets this differently, but...' He hesitated. Having been mocked many times over many years, Coulston found it hard to tell this story to a stranger. Now was not the time to be indecisive, he reminded himself. He needed as many allies as possible. 'Have you ever heard of The Black Dog?' he said.

Rosie shook her head.

'It's a mythical creature, supernatural,' he said. They both glanced across to where Henry sat and dozed on the pew. 'There are legends of it all over these islands. Bigger than a deerhound, ghost-like in the way it appears then vanishes again, it has huge white fangs, and leaps like a cat. Sound familiar? The first tales of the Black Dog appear around the time Sir Roger was alive.'

Unwilling to talk too loud, he stepped closer to Rosie.

'In folklore, it's also a harbinger of death,' Coulston said. 'And do you know the name of the most famous Black Dog, a legend used in fiction, made into a book and many, many films?'

Rosie needed no further clues; she was an avid reader of the Sherlock Holmes mysteries.

'The Hound of the Baskervilles,' she said.

- 7 -

- Night -

- Whitecombe Station, Surrey -

'OAKERS, I HAVEN'T GOT TIME FOR THIS... NO, I KNOW you think you hurt it; but it changes nothing, nothing at all. We don't go to the police.' Beacon spoke into his mobile phone as he strolled at the rear of a crowd of fellow commuters. They had disembarked from the 19:08 London Waterloo to Portsmouth service. Eager to get home and escape the rain, they splashed through the gate beside the Victorian-era brick building that contained Whitecombe Station's shuttered ticket office and part-lit waiting room.

'We tell no-one you shot at it. No one!' As he listened to his partner's agitated voice, Beacon's fingers tightened around the phone. He imagined it was Oakshott's throat in his grip. The thought brought a smile to his face. 'What? Offer a reward?' He placed a hand over the phone's mouthpiece. 'Bloody fool,' he said with venomous intent.

Beacon held the phone away from his ear as he waited for Oakshott to finish yet another self-serving rant.

He paused beneath the eaves of the ticket office. Headlights illuminated him as the car park emptied.

'Look,' he said after thirty seconds passed, 'I didn't believe you when you freaked out on that hunt and I apologise. Again. Now, I've talked to Alexei Zaharkin and he's got his armed guards on red alert. They're ex-*Spesnatz*... Yes, the Russian SAS. If you're so frightened, why don't you do the same? Use one of those mercenary outfits in London? Personally, I think it's all bollocks... Yes, yes, I know you did. In that case, lie low, have a stiff drink, have lots of stiff drinks, play in your golf tournament tomorrow... No... No, I'm not being patronising. Hello? Hello?'

He looked at his phone, saw the signal was lost and pressed the disconnect key. 'What a prat,' he said.

The station was at the southern exit of a deep cleft cut through the hills by the railway. A short lane led to the main road and the commuters' cars queued its length, flooding the car park with the impatient red glare of their brake lights.

Beacon's car, a large, black Mercedes 4x4, was in the farthest corner. He walked towards it, weaving his way around the last of the exiting cars. His phone chirruped. An incoming call. Without thinking, Beacon answered it.

'Hello? Yes, this is he... What? The BBC? How did you get my number...? An interview?' He stopped, still a long way short of the Mercedes. 'Oh, very well then, as long as you're quick... Yes, I'll hold.'

Oh, brilliant, he thought, not only had the wretched BBC tracked him down, they had put him on hold. Beacon hated it when that happened; he considered himself too important to be made to wait.

'Perfect end to a perfect day,' he muttered to himself.

In a radio studio, thirty miles away in Central London, Radio 5 Live talk show host, Sarah Thornton, received a finger-point cue from her producer and spoke into the fat, tubular studio microphone. 'On the line we have

Dawlish Beacon, friend and business partner of the victim. Mister Beacon, our thoughts and sympathy are with you, and all of Miles Jervis's friends and family at this time.'

In the now deserted car park, Beacon's upper lip curled into a sneer. He knew how to play this particular mealy-mouthed game.

'Thank you. It is, um, a most distressing time.' He liked the tremble he put into the 'um'. It showed the listeners he was vulnerable and upset about his friend's death. Beacon smirked, this would garner him sympathy by the bucketload.

'This event is causing near panic in Surrey,' said Thornton. 'Do you know if there have been more sightings of the beast?'

'Well, it's all a bit confusing. We still don't know if there really is an escaped big cat on the loose. The police have confirmed nothing.'

Beacon studied the skyline as he talked. In the trees on the far side of the railway line, the distant lights of a large private boarding school glimmered and twinkled. Two hundred paces in the other direction, beyond a deserted scaffolding yard, a single light shone above the door lintel of a tiny railwayman's cottage.

'And the Army said today there is no sign, no tracks. Does that worry you?' said the distorted voice on the phone.

'I prefer to leave speculation to the experts.'

He turned, and strode towards his car again.

'But what precautions will you be taking?' said Thornton.

Beacon stopped walking. The Mercedes sat isolated beneath the car park's solitary streetlamp. He frowned. The squat 4x4 looked suddenly like a feral black beast ready to pounce. The bowls of the car's headlamps reflected and focused the streetlight's sodium yellow glow. They gave the appearance of two cat's eyes staring at him. Overcome by sudden irrational terror, he gasped.

In the warm, bright but shabby studio, Thornton's head jerked back. Frowning, she made eye contact with her producer. This was not how interviews usually proceeded.

'Mr. Beacon? Dawlish Beacon? I think we may have lost the line,' said Thornton to her listeners.

The producer shrugged. The moment the line went quiet, he'd checked the connection. It had not been broken.

Heart pounding, Beacon made a decision. He pivoted around then walked towards the station's waiting room. He felt stupid for being so fearful, but he just wanted the security of standing indoors, to be somewhere lit, to be safe.

'Oh, uh, sorry about that.' he said into his phone. 'I just had, um, a temporary...' Unwilling to explain what had occurred, his voice trailed off for a moment then he said, 'Would you mind repeating the question?'

'Ha, I thought for a moment the big cat might have got you,' said Thornton.

'No. That was my friend, Miles Jervis.' Take that, you shallow piece of turd, thought Beacon.

Sarah Thornton winced. Through the soundproofed window that separated her studio from the production booth, she could see her producer place his hands over his face in despair. It was now her turn to rally.

'I am so sorry,' she said, 'that was in incredibly bad taste. I asked about any precautions you might be taking?'

Wooden benches lined the walls of the bleak, scruffy waiting room. More than a century of passengers' tobacco smoke stained the joists spanning the dark void beneath the steepled roof. A single low wattage light bulb hung from the central rafter. Beacon pushed the door open, walked in then checked behind to make sure it was closed tight. The dingy room smelt of disinfectant and old age. Beacon's nose wrinkled at the odour.

'I really don't know what we should be doing,' he told Thornton. 'I don't know enough about what happened to

Miles. I suppose all we can do is the usual, not go anywhere isolated, lock doors, that sort of thing.'

Through the grubby window, Beacon scrutinised the car park. The Mercedes no longer appeared so menacing. He shook his head in amused disbelief that he, of all people, could react like... well, like Oakshott. And yet he did feel relieved to be in the safety of the waiting room. Better still, the scare gave him another opportunity to get one over on this awful BBC type. He smiled maliciously as he spoke.

'I mean, even your question spooked me a little as I was walking to my car,' he said.

'I am really not doing very well here,' said Thornton. 'I am so sorry.' Crestfallen, she could not recall an interview ever become so speedily derailed.

'We're all more than a little on edge.'

Phew, back on track thought Thornton. 'Why don't you tell us a about Miles. The kind of man he was?'

'Strong. Very strong. That's why this is such a shock. He is, was, the last person you'd expect to fall victim to anything.' Beacon paused, gulped dramatically. He grinned. Perfect delivery, old boy, he thought then said, 'Let alone something as bizarre, as tragic, as this.'

Above and behind him, in the darkest corner of the eaves, a black shape stirred. A lithe body uncoiled.

'And I understand you were at school with him?' said Thornton.

The panther, its shape strangely soft and indistinct in the dense shadow, crept along a high rafter.

'We were all old boys of Radley School,' said Beacon still looking out of the window, 'Jervis, myself and Colin Oakshott, our other partner—'

The panther came closer, its form now harder, more defined.

'Then Miles joined the Coldstream Guards. I wasn't tall enough, so—'

The panther growled. Long, rumbling but impossible to confuse with thunder, the sound was so intense that both presenter and producer lifted the headphones from their ears.

Slowly, fearful of what he knew he would see, Beacon looked up. The panther glowered back at him.

'Oh no, no. How did it get in here?' he said with a wail. The big cat leapt. Claws flashed towards him. White fangs seized his skull and jaws crunched.

Mouth agape, Sarah Thornton listened to Beacon's screams. Then the producer snapped out of his shock. My God, we're broadcasting this live to the nation, he thought, and yanked down the faders on his mixing desk. He had a brief vision of a contract termination letter arriving in the post.

Thornton, a seasoned radio professional, was immediately suspicious. This bore the hallmark of a sick hoax. She made a mental note find out how, from whom, and from where they had got hold of this phone number.

'Er, well, sadly one of the hazards of live radio is that we are sometimes the victim of pranks,' she said. 'That, I suspect, was a particularly distasteful one. Some people will do anything to get on the radio.' She shuffled the pages of her script. 'And now, here's Connor with the weather,' she said brightly.

- 8 -

- Night -

- Coulston's cottage, Redholt -

THE FRONT DOOR SHUDDERED UNDER AN ONSLAUGHT of blows. The hall light snapped on and Bob Coulston shuffled into view. He wore dressing gown and pyjamas but no slippers. The knocking stopped and the ringing began. His visitor had discovered the doorbell, and, once it was pressed, it did not appear they wanted to remove their finger from its push-button.

Outside, Rosie stood on the doorstep. She abandoned the bell and again hammered with her fist on the door.

'Come on, come on. God, I hope he's in.'

The door opened.

'You,' said Coulston.

'Me. Have you heard the news? I thought you should know.' Rosie spoke at machine-gun pace.

'I suspected it would be a mistake to let you know where I lived. What do you want?'

Rosie could not keep still. Her breath came in pants. 'Didn't you hear? It was live on the radio. I came to see what you're going to do about it.'

'What radio? Heard what?' said the bewildered detective.

'Another of the Swanmere partners, Dawlish Beacon, he was killed. Live on the BBC. By the big cat. At Whitecombe Station.'

'On the radio?'

'I mean, he was being interviewed on the phone when it attacked. I heard it all. They thought it was a hoax, but I didn't. I knew. It was horrible.' The pace of Rosie's delivery slowed as she thought about what Beacon must have gone through. 'I didn't have your number, so I came to tell you.'

'Christ, I'd better get dressed,' said Coulston. 'Come in.'

Determined not to reveal her satisfaction at this opportunity to peek into Coulston's inner life, Rosie stepped inside.

'Go to bed a bit early don't you?' she said as he closed the door behind them.

'Policemen don't work nine to five. I sleep when I can.'

Coulston ushered her into the cottage's living room. With a click of a switch, he turned on the overhead light. Rosie, who was ahead of him, gasped.

Across the room, a spotted wild cat snarled at her, eye to eye. It was small, barely larger than a large domestic tomcat, and it was stuffed. Posed inside a domed glass case on the top of an antique bureau, the dead cat crouched on a tree branch.

'Meet Telford,' said Coulston. He crossed the room and tapped the glass in front of the cat's nose. 'A car ran her over one rainy night in Shropshire five years ago.'

Rosie stepped close to get a good look.

'Is it a leopard?' she said. 'Surely it's too small?'

'Asian Jungle Cat,' he said. 'A nocturnal hunter. They eat frogs, rats, lizards.'

'What was it doing in Shropshire?' As Rosie spoke, she took in the rest of the room. Books about big cats filled a tall, broad bookcase, and filing cabinets lined one wall.

'Why is there a panther in Surrey? It's the same question, same answer. Someone imports them, they escape, and, in Telford's case, if the car had not hit her, she'd still be out there,' said Coulston, 'in the wild.'

On the wall facing the room's picture window was a huge map of Britain. Coloured pins dotted it. Enlargements of fuzzy, out-of-focus snapshots of cats filled the wall space around its edges. Aha, thought Rosie, this is something I know all about. She walked over to study them. These could be big cats, or small ones, thought Rosie; there was nothing in the images by which to judge the size of the animals. Many of the photos were faded with age; some were even black and white.

'You've been at this for years. Did you collect all this yourself?' she said.

Coulston laughed. 'No, blame my Grandad. I inherited it all. The books, the research, and the obsession. He started this back in the Fifties. Got into it big-time. He was a Royal Engineer, served in The Malayan Emergency, in tiger country. Built bridges in the mountains and learnt his big cat lore from the hill tribes. Said he and his mates used to find leopard footprints around their tents every morning. They almost never saw them, never knew when they were close by. One day, it was a tiger's tracks. His heart almost stopped. The pugs, the paws prints, were huge, twice the size of a leopard.'

He spread his long fingers wide to show Rosie.

'The tiger had been inches from him; only the tent's canvas separated them. He spent the rest of his time on that job hoping it wouldn't leap on his back. But he also took it seriously, learnt all he could about big cats. A decade later, when the whole Surrey Puma hunt started, suddenly there was a big cat on his doorstep. He loved it. He was on its trail, tracking down local eye-witnesses, not the crazies, but the kind who would never speak to reporters, steady folk.'

'So he thought it was all true?' said Rosie.

'All true? No, some so-called witnesses were real loonies, but he believed the rest told the truth. My Dad thought he was barmy, the way sons always do. Of course, Grandad was my hero, so I used to go out tracking the beast with him.'

Rosie moved across the room to inspect Telford again.

'You said it's a jungle cat. How could it survive in Britain? It's so cold and wet here.'

'What do fashionable wealthy women wear outdoors in the winter?'

'Fur. But that's not... Oh, oh yeah.' Rosie fell silent; she got his point.

Coulston was at the map. He pointed out details to her. 'The blue pins are pumas; confirmed sightings. Red are the leopards and panthers. Yellow are other species like lynx and ocelot. Green pins are the unconfirmed sightings. White are the suspected hoaxes.'

There were concentrations of coloured pins in the Scottish Highlands, Central and North Wales, the West Country, Oxfordshire, and Surrey.

'So many,' said Rosie. 'If only a fraction of them are genuine, wouldn't they be a threat to us? I've never heard of a big cat attack before, but this is a man-eater. It's killed two grown men.'

'It didn't eat Jervis,' said Coulston. 'In the wild, attacks are very rare. Even tigers co-exist with humans, but only on their own terms. If you take exception to them killing your dogs or some of your livestock, then things change. In Siberia, tigers hunt down the poachers who try to trap them. Killing a cub is like signing your own death warrant.'

'Is it the same with panthers? You said a man wounded it and now two of his friends have been killed.'

And I was there too, thought Coulston. Out loud he said, 'Oakshott? I don't know, I can find no record of a leopard ever doing anything like this, only tigers.'

Coulston contemplated his library of books.

'But it would explain a lot, Henry's *kyaani* included,' he said.

Rosie returned to the map.

'So if they're not meant to be a threat to us, then what do they eat? Surely, this many would kill lots of... I don't know, sheep. The farmers would be up in arms,' she said.

Coulston crossed his arms and smiled. This one was easy. 'How many deer do you think there are in Britain?'

'I don't know. Forty, fifty thousand?'

'Thirteen million. That's government figures. It's more than the human populations of Wales, Scotland, and Northern Ireland combined. The big cats have got food, woods and forests to shelter them, and a human population of mostly city dwellers whose closest acquaintance to the countryside is when they drive through it on the motorway.'

'But even so, around London there's what, fifteen, twenty million people? Why haven't more people seen it like I did?' Rosie said.

Coulston placed a fingertip on their location. 'You'd be amazed. Southeast England is one of the most densely populated tracts of land on the planet, but it's still mostly unoccupied, and it's full of invaders, exotic species from abroad. There are bullfrogs, wallabies, parakeets, all sorts of creatures in Surrey, plus hundreds of thousands of deer. Almost no one ever notices them. You should come out with Henry and myself sometime. It would open your eyes.'

They heard a mobile phone ring-tone kick into life in the hallway.

I'm sure that's Marc Bolan's voice, thought Rosie. 'Isn't that T.Rex?' she said. 'That's your phone's ring-tone?' She laughed with delight at the absurdity of it.

Coulston looked embarrassed. '*Big Black Cat*. I'd better answer it.' He left the room.

Rosie continued to study the map and noticed Mid-Surrey didn't even have the greatest number of sightings. She could hear Coulston's muffled voice then he hung up. Re-entering the room, he said; 'It's official now. I'm on the case again and, get this, the surviving Swanmere partner, our friend Oakshott—'

'The Jaguar driver?'

'The same. He's offered a bounty. Five hundred thousand pounds. Tomorrow, the hills are going to be swarming with drunk morons armed with guns.' Coulston looked down at his dressing gown. 'I'd better get dressed.'

'And I'd better go,' said Rosie.

They walked into the hall.

'You're not going to give up, are you? I can't persuade you?' he said.

The tone of resignation in Coulston's voice made Rosie smile. Then she recalled that moment of terror in the car. She knew she should think of the kids, be sensible, be ordinary. She always did so, always played safe. Well almost. Well, no, not really, hardly ever, in fact. Her heart thumped loud as she thought of those great amber eyes. She wanted to see the beast again.

'Would you? If you'd seen what I saw today?' she said.

He shook his head. 'Remember, I've never even seen it and I've been tracking it for years. Listen, you got closer than anyone else to this panther and survived. Surely that's enough?'

Now Rosie shook her head. Coulston's mobile phone rang again. He ignored it.

'Just don't do anything stupid,' he said. 'Agreed? And I mean it about going into the hills. Do not go without me or Henry for company.'

'What me? Likely story.'

Coulston closed the front door behind her. As he opened his phone to check his voicemail, his face took on a grim countenance. The previous call had brought shocking news. It was official: the beast was a man-eater. Not only was Beacon's corpse part-devoured, his skull had been cracked open by the panther's jaws.

- 9 -

- Dawn -

- South London -

AFTER THE UPHEAVAL CREATED YESTERDAY BY DON'S early morning phone call, Rosie's Mum insisted her daughter keep the handset on the bedside table. It was a smart move.

'Friend Rosie? This is Faith Olembe. You helped my brother and Robert Coulston yesterday.'

Over the telephone, Faith's whispered voice, soft and fluid, brought evocative memories of warmer times, of green fertile shores, African skies laden with distant thunderheads, and white sands skirting azure seas. Rosie, phone cupped in her hand, lay in her warm bed cosseted by the recollections. Then she recalled where those memories came from. The honeymoon in The Gabon. The liar. The betrayer. The cheat. Abandonment. Her present state of crushing loneliness. Rosie was harsher in her reply than she intended.

'What do you want? How did you get this number?'

'Will you meet us?' Faith said with more than a little trepidation. 'We, Henry and I, go to track the *kyaani*,' she said. 'Friend Robert suggested you might like to join us.

He is very busy right now. He gave me your telephone number and requested I call you.'

Rosie sat up. 'What time is it?'

She noticed something missing. Two somethings. No Pete or Lizzie. For once, the children had stayed in their own beds, but now this call threatened to scuttle any chance of a Saturday morning lie-in.

'I believe it is five o'clock,' said Faith.

Rosie swung her legs out of the childfree bed, walked to the window then drew the curtains wide. Outside, the blue pre-dawn light spread its soft glow over the serried roofs that extended to the far horizon in a sharp-ridged sea of red tiles. It was a monotonous landscape broken only by scattered lone sycamore trees and the vertiginous cliff-like faces of distant tower blocks.

'Henry and I shall go to where it killed last night. The railway station. We shall follow it until we find it and then...'

'Go on,' said Rosie.

'Then we shall see what fate may befall us. Will you come with us?'

How can I possibly resist? Rosie was about to voice the sarcastic thought, but the dreary panoramic view of suburbia made her hesitate. A stream of thoughts flowed unbidden through Rosie's mind. How different her world was now from this place and the childhood she'd spent here. She remembered how alive she'd felt during the search for the missing pets, the moment of wonder at the Heart of the Weald, and, above all, the panther. Rosie could still recall every detail of yesterday's encounter. The broad flat head. The soft, pink edge to its black nostrils. The black fur made sleek by the downpour. A single raindrop collecting on the end of one whisker. She had survived what few others did; seen what few others ever would.

'Friend Rosie, are you there?' said Faith's distant voice.

'Oh.' Rosie looked down at the phone held cradled at her waist. She raised it quickly. 'Sorry, I was miles away. Yes, of course I'll help.'

'Robert is working with the police, but he does not think they will do what is necessary, not quickly enough. He wants us to track it. He will join us when he can.'

'Um, okay.' Some of her determination drained away. She preferred the idea of Bob being with them and liked the reassuring presence of his large calibre gun even more. Rosie knew she was right to be afraid. She'd looked into those yellow-gold eyes and felt the visceral fear of the big cat that is embedded deep in the human psyche. She tried to ignore the doubts gnawing at the edge of her self-confidence, but it was not easy.

Faith sensed her hesitation. 'My sister, have no fear, we will be armed. Henry has faced a great many dangers in a great many forests. We shall start as soon as you get to the station.'

'The station? At Whitecombe?'

'Just so.'

'Well, okay then, tell Henry I'm on my way.'

Rosie disconnected the call and sat on the bed. Downstairs, mugs clinked as her mother made a pot of tea. Once again, doubt assailed Rosie. She had two young children. Why did she feel this impulse to place herself in danger? Was it strength or weakness? She shook her head as if to physically dispel the confusion she felt. Rosie knew these thoughts were irrelevant. She was going to go on the trail of the big cat and nothing would stop her.

Golden light flooded the bedroom as the sun rose. Masked by a shred of cloud, for a fleeting moment it looked like an enormous cat's eye. Faith and Henry would have interpreted it as a great omen. Rosie never saw it; she was downstairs busy negotiating childcare with her Mum.

'Come on, come on, got to pull yourself together for this,' Oakshott muttered. He'd been talking to himself a lot recently. Without Jervis's bile and Beacon's sneers to motivate him, he had to do the job himself.

The morning was sunny. It was eight o'clock and, despite the relatively early hour, spectators and competitors crowded the lawns around the First Tee and the stone-built, ivy clad clubhouse. A banner was strung between two trees. It read:

The Hamley Celebrity Charity Golf Challenge and Ball

Oakshott had considered the obvious course of action, but he could not go into hiding, not when he was scheduled to the first to tee-off at his golf club's premiere networking event. The fear of what had happened to his friends, of what Oakshott knew, deep down, would happen to him if the big cat stalked him, was a lesser priority than the pull of duty, of social obligation, and the opportunity to mingle with his fellow plutocrats. He loved the golf club. His need to be seen in the right places, mingling with the movers and shakers, to be in charge, was pathological and easily assuaged by frequent visits to its fairways.

With the burden of this self-imposed pressure upon him, Oakshott rationalised away his fears. Stiff upper lip of the Englishman, he'd told himself earlier as, in his bathroom, and with trembling hand, he attempted to shave.

His appointment as Honorary Vice Treasurer of the golf club brought its share of responsibilities. In truth, he was as deluded in this as in so many other matters. His money had bought the position and eased the weight of what few responsibilities came with the post because, as he was fond of saying, money was all you needed and all that mattered.

Oakshott fiddled with the straps of his gloves and tried to ignore the stares of those around him. Standing apart from his fellow members, and acutely aware of his unwanted notoriety, he overheard some of the conversational fragments that escaped the crowd's buzz of anticipatory chatter.

'Oh, the poor man,' said an attractive woman in a floral print dress.

Hmm, pretty young filly, very beddable, thought Oakshott.

'Looks dreadful,' said her father, who also happened to be Oakshott's chief rival for the post of Honorary Treasurer.

You wait your turn; I'll get you for that, was Oakshott's silent riposte.

'I would look dreadful too, and so would you if you'd just had your closest friends killed.' This was the Club Secretary's contribution.

Spot on, old boy. Oakshott permitted himself a smile. I'll buy you a stiff one in the bar later on.

'Offered a huge reward, so I heard,' said Naomi Dawes to the Club Secretary.

Yes, and it'd better be worth it.

'Extraordinary courage,' threw in Johnno.

I don't know who you are, but you're my kind of man, despite those dreadful yellow wellies you're wearing.

'It's what made England so great, built our empire,' said Naomi.

The old stiff upper lip ploy, it's working, Oakers, it's working, he thought. A tremor of pleasure eased, for a moment, his queasiness.

Oakshott assumed all this interest from his fellow members was because of the panther and its eviscerations of Jervis and Beacon. He was only partially correct. Not everyone knew who he was, but they still stared. The numerous shaving cuts made by his unsteady hand made him look as if the cat had already been at his throat.

'Ready for the off, boss?' Perry, a teenage caddy, carried Oakshott's clubs. With the boy's pimples and Oakshott's bloody throat, they were not poster boys for the sport of golf.

The event's professional commentator, earning more today than he would in a month's work at the BBC, tugged at the lime green bib he wore. It was a tight fit on his portly frame and he hated its constriction. Nor did he like the words NON-MEMBER emblazoned across its front and rear. It felt demeaning. Everyone knew this was an exclusive club; they didn't have to hammer it home. The commentator was in lugubrious voice as he spoke into his hand-held radio microphone. By the time his distorted monotone burst from the speakers rigged around the course, he sounded more Dalek than human.

'First pair to tee off, local business leader Colin Oakshott.'

To scattered applause, Oakshott waved one hand. Quite a few people pointed at him. Most simply stared in silence.

'And his playing partner, king of comedy, star presenter of *Rock N'Roll*, ITV's celebrity rhythmic gymnastics show, and our Club President, Mr. Tommy Belfast.'

There was a boisterous cheer from the crowd as the veteran British comedian, debonair, white haired, moustachioed and in his eighties, walked onto the green. He held high his golf club to acknowledge the greeting.

Right hand thrust out, Tommy strode towards Oakshott.

'Dear chap, I heard the terrible news. I have to say I think it shows remarkable grit, fortitude, pluck to...' Tommy paused for the requisite number of seconds demanded by social convention, threw in a gulp for good measure then continued; 'Well, let's just say I thought I'd be without a partner today.'

They shook hands.

'Have to honour commitments y'know?' Oakshott said whilst affecting his best laconic manner. 'Not the done thing to bail out. I am the Honorary Vice Treasurer here, you know.' He had called in half a dozen favours to get the Club Committee to allocate Tommy as his partner, but the ever-present fear of the big cat banished the thrill. He just wanted to get this over and done with as quickly as possible. He placed his ball on the tee.

'Best of British luck, eh?' Tommy said.

Oakshott made no reply.

'Stiff upper, good man, quite right too,' said Tommy. 'I heard the newspapers have put up a bounty for this killer cat. Half a million to the one who bags it.'

Oakshott took the driver proffered by Perry.

'Typical tabloids,' he said. 'Got it wrong again. It's my half million, not theirs. Least I could do. Before it kills someone else.'

Tommy moved alongside to whisper, 'Hope you don't mind me asking, but do you think we're in danger? Should I be worried?'

'Wouldn't know about that,' Oakshott said in the most forthright voice he could achieve. 'I'm here to play golf.' God, why won't this aged creature leave me alone, he thought.

But Tommy, a veteran of the stage and small screen for six decades, could spot an off-key performance when he saw one. He leant close to whisper in sympathy. 'Safety in numbers, eh? Good idea.'

'I'm here to play golf,' Oakshott said. His words came out curt and hard. 'For charity.'

'Er, yes, right, sorry.' Tommy decided to leave the poor man to his grief.

'Shall we get started?'

'Right-ho.'

Thwack. Oakshott's ball hooked left and into the rough. 'Oh, bollocks,' he said. His jaws clenched in anger. This was not how he'd imagined the round would start.

The comedian patted him on the back. 'Don't worry, you've a lot on your mind.'

Tommy Belfast's ball flew straight and true up the middle of the fairway. He faced the adoring crowd.

'Not bad for an old 'un.'

They cheered his corny TV catchphrase.

Knuckles white on the shaft of his driver, Oakshott knew he was outclassed as a golfer and as the centre of attention. 'What an appalling nightmare this is going to be,' he muttered.

The station forecourt at Whitecombe looked very different in daylight. Oakshott's huge, well-publicised reward had brought the county's underclass blinking into the unfamiliar early morning sunlight. Eager bounty hunters, arriving in their 4x4s, pickups and grubby white vans, occupied every parking space, jammed the lanes between, and choked the access road.

The waiting room itself was cordoned off with police tape. A forensic team was at work. They had no shortage of samples to take, especially blood. And they had an audience too. Scores of unshaven, beer-guzzling men jostled to gape at the activity inside. This uninvited and unwanted audience wore an eclectic mix of camouflage gear, work clothes, and hats. The only unifying factor was that they were all armed. Even so, their weapons ranged from antique, ill-maintained shotguns to state-of-the-art hunting rifles with scopes.

Rosie pushed her way through the throng. As she did so, like Oakshott, she overheard fragments of conversation. None of it inspired confidence in the speakers' competence.

'—already spent the million, leastways me wife has.'

'The reward's half a million, dipshit.'

'Don't call me a dipshit, you... you dipshit.'

Rosie paused. She thought she recognised those voices and their limited vocabulary.

'See this gun? It were me Grampa's. Hey, you!'

Lynton Creswell. It had to be him. Rosie looked over her shoulder just as his beer-bellied shape lunged at her. She twisted away from his outstretched hands and darted into the crowd.

'Pat, Terry, it's the bitch dog warden what squealed on us. Grab her.'

Her slender form gave Rosie the advantage over Lynton whose attempt to barge through a mass of men of similar build to himself met belligerent resistance. She pressed on into the maze of vehicles. Once she was satisfied Lynton had lost her, Rosie leant against the side of a gold-painted RV to gather her breath. The vehicle was so long it spanned two opposing parking spaces and the lane between. She watched horrified, ready to flee again, as a Stetson-clad hunter showed his rifle to his mates. Even to Rosie's untrained eye, it was obvious he was holding it for the first time.

'What does this do?' he said.

Finger on trigger, his thumb flicked a small lever on the rifle's casing.

Bang! The gun discharged. Everyone in the car park ducked. Mercifully, the weapon was pointing upwards when it went off and the culprit, despite standing in a blue cloud of gun smoke, attempted an insouciant stance that said, who me?

'Mate, that would be, um, the safety catch,' said one of his friends.

'Yeah, whotsit do?' said the genius with the gun.

'There she is. Hey, come here.'

Rosie recognised Terry Creswell's rat-like features and ran. As she tore through the crowd, she heard more snippets of less-than-inspiring discussion.

'—what if it's no bigger than a house cat? Would they pay up then?'

'One step ahead of you there, mate. Got a dead one inside me van, just in case. Was the neighbour's. Pissed on me flowerbeds one time too many.'

Rosie pushed deeper into the mob.

'—gotta 'ave a drink, mate. You can't shoot straight with that thing, anyhow.'

Deeper still.

'—set up the deckchairs for me barbie.'

'—never used a scope before. Can't be too hard, can it?'

A hand settled on Rosie's shoulder. God, no, how had the Creswells found her? Ready to take-on the dog killers she whirled around.

'Friend Rosie,' said Henry Olembe, 'you came.'

Rosie felt weak at the knees. She could not have experienced a greater sense of relief than at the sight of his solemn face. Brother and sister stood pressed against the side of a huge Japanese 4x4. They were dressed simply. Faith carried only a long, slender cloth-wrapped bundle and her wicker basket.

'I came,' Rosie said. 'but why are we here? In this madhouse?' She did not attempt to hide her annoyance.

'Oh, not again.' Oakshott eyed the large thicket of trees that stood to one side of the ninth hole's fairway. 'Maybe I should forfeit this hole, I'll never find the ball in there.'

Tommy, busy signing autographs, looked up.

'Come on, old chap,' he said, 'Now's not the time to give up. I'm surprised at you. Thought you were made of sterner stuff than this. At least take a look to see if you can find it.' He raised his voice as he again addressed his fans. 'Not half bad is he?' They cheered in recognition of another of his hoary old game show catchphrases. Tommy, ever the entertainer, delivered the mocking second half of the line; 'And not half good, either.' They roared with laughter. To Oakshott he said; 'Give me a minute to take my shot and we'll come on down and help you look.'

Oakshott muttered foul curses. He snatched his club from Perry's hand. The laughter and cheers of the onlookers pursued Oakshott down the fairway. His jaw and fists were clenched tight in fury as he stomped towards the trees.

'Don't tell me you're after this bounty as well?' Rosie said.

Henry smiled and spread his hands wide.

'Well, I suppose you need it more than most of these

118

idiots.' Rosie was barged by two wrestling drunks. 'And at least you know what you're doing.'

Henry smiled again.

'Brother, do not be so cruel,' said Faith. 'When Robert called us, he thought you would be here anyway. He said—'

Rosie's hiss of annoyance cut her off. 'So Coulston thought I'd need baby-sitting? Thanks but no thanks. I can manage to—Urk!'

A hand gripped her arm. She was jerked around.

'You cost me my dogs, bitch,' said Lynton Creswell.

'Friend, you have no business here,' said Henry.

'I'm not your friend and this is my business, Sambo,' Creswell said. He rested one hand on the butt of his holstered pistol.

Henry's hands, previously empty, now held a short spear.

Where the hell did that come from, thought Rosie?

'Yeah, so?' Creswell was unimpressed. He started to draw his gun, but the spear slashed the air so fast Rosie only heard the zipping noise the blade made; she never saw it move.

Zip. Henry cut away the gun belt, which fell to the floor.

Zip. Followed swiftly by Lynton Creswell's trousers.

Zip. Henry made another cut and the dogfighter's shirt was slit open. The spear tip rested at the man's throat. Not a drop of blood had been spilt. Rosie wriggled free of Creswell's now-unresisting grip.

'Come, Rosie, we must go,' said Faith.

She took Rosie by the hand and they ran into the wood at the car park's edge.

'You are a fortunate man,' Henry said. There was death in his eyes and in his voice. 'Next time, you will not be so lucky.'

Creswell, fearful that the steel might slit open his windpipe, held his breath. Henry waited several seconds. He watched the bigger man's face turn purple then, in one graceful motion, whisked the spear away and followed Rosie and his sister into the trees.

Creswell breathed again. It was like watching a balloon deflate. He looked down. A pool of his urine spread slowly on the tarmac at his feet.

Oakshott thrashed the ferns with his club. Ten paces to his left, Perry, did the same. In the dense green foliage of the copse, it was impossible to see anything on the ground other than what was immediately at their feet.

'Bloody ball, bloody golf, bloody waste of time, bloody Beacon, bloody Jervis, bloody hell!' The golf ball was right there, in front of him, hiding in a nest of brown, withered bracken. 'Over here, I've found it,' he said to Perry.

He bent to flatten the area around the ball. As he did so, a huff of hot breath wafted over his bowed head. Oakshott waved his free hand in front of his face.

'Jesus, what is it about caddies and bad breath?'

'Pardon, Mr. Oakshott?' Perry said, struggling, half a dozen paces away as he tugged the heavy golf bag free from the brambles that entangled it. He looked towards his patron and the rattle of clubs stopped suddenly.

'Oh. Oh my God. Oh no,' said Perry, his voice rising to a squeak.

The low rumble of a growl made Oakshott look up. He stared into a pair of amber eyes. The panther bared its fangs and hissed. All Oakshott could think was how remarkably few teeth a big cat has. Size is everything.

Back on the fairway, Tommy continued to sign autographs and exchange banter with a crowd of thirty or so admirers. He concentrated hard on the narration of a rambling anecdote whilst autographing a photograph for a fan.

'—and then he said; but my bottom won't fit in that, and I said—'

Perry ran yelling from the trees.

'What? What's that boy saying?'

'The panther, the monster, it's attacking. Get away.

Run!' screamed Perry as he tore past.

The crowd, already made nervous by both the recent killings and Oakshott's presence, panicked. They scattered. In mere seconds only Tommy and his own caddy remained standing on the fairway.

The octogenarian comedian was irked by the loss of his captive audience. 'Where's everyone gone?'

Again, he was answered by a distant shriek from Perry. 'The black panther! Run for your lives!'

Away in the trees, Oakshott screamed. At last, Tommy's thought process caught up with this startling change to his morning round of golf. He swivelled around to face these new cries.

'That poor man,' he said as he turned back to take in the sight of the now-distant and fast-fleeing spectators. 'We have to do something.'

With a clatter of wood and metal, Tommy's caddy abandoned the golf bag and took to his heels.

'What the f——' For the first time in several decades the equable comedian was about to use a swear word, but another bubbling scream interrupted him. He picked up the nearest golf club. 'Never let it be said I let a fellow golfer down.'

He strode towards the copse. Now at a safe distance, some of his fear-struck fans paused to gather breath and watch Tommy's lone rescue mission.

Oakshott stumbled between two trees. Disorientated, he had lost all his bearings. His right arm hung limp; the shirt sleeve shredded and bloody. Hoping against hope that he had evaded it, he looked over his shoulder. The panther was to his front. It lunged at him.

Warned by the crackle of bracken as the cat charged, he dodged backwards and managed to avoid the killing blow. But the panther's claws slashed him in his right leg. Oakshott staggered then fell behind a tree. Blood spurted from the fresh wound as, on his back, he crawled, scrabbling at soil, fallen leaves, and roots with his hands and remaining good leg.

'Help. Oh please, no.' His cries were weak.

The big cat padded around the tree trunk. Teeth bared, it tensed to spring upon its victim. Overwhelmed by fear, Oakshott could only gargle incoherently.

The panther pounced but never completed its attack. Thwack. A golf club smacked into the side of the big cat's head. The panther tumbled aside.

'Leave the Honorary Vice Treasurer alone.'

Tommy stood between predator and prey. The black cat snarled and lunged at Oakshott's defender. Tommy jabbed the club at its face. With a snap of fang on wood, the cat bit off the club's head then retreated to gather itself for another assault. Tommy jabbed once more, and again. Crunch. Crunch. The panther munched its way up the shaft. The golf club was transformed, first into a stick, then a stump.

'Oakshott, old man,' Tommy said, 'I'm afraid—'

In the distance, a clamour of voices grew loud. With a roar of outrage, a mob of club-wielding golfers surged into the wood. As news spread of Tommy's lone mission, so had the indignation that is always so near to boiling point when a golfer's game is disturbed or cut short.

'We can't let Tommy face the filthy foreign beast alone,' shouted one patriot. 'Charge! Kill the blighter.'

The panther took in the astounding sights of the pastel-hued multitude in full cry then, in a silent, smooth motion, flitted into the shadows and was gone.

'What? Where did it go?' said Tommy.

The rescuers arrived in a tumult of strident voices and poor colour sense. Tommy knelt beside Oakshott who was conscious but still hysterical with fear.

'We'll get you seen to, don't worry,' Tommy said. He raised his voice. 'Is there a doctor here?'

Half a dozen consultant surgeons crowded forward.

As they set to work on him, Oakshott's bloodstained hand grabbed Tommy's arm. 'What did we do?' Oakshott said. 'What did I do to deserve this?'

Rosie, Faith, and Henry paused for breath inside the treeline. They surveyed the bounty hunters packed into the car park.

'We are safe here,' Henry said. 'I do not think that man will follow you again.'

Faith observed a large, obese hunter, assisted by four sweating mates, clamber to the roof of a white van. He tried unsuccessfully to gain the attention of the crowd milling around on the tarmac below him.

'What is he trying to say?' she said.

Rosie and Henry came to her side and watched the van's metal skin buckle and creak beneath the bounty hunter's weight. One of his sidekicks passed him a battery-powered megaphone and, as he stood upright, both huntsman and van swayed unsteadily. There was a burst of static as he switched on the megaphone then he held it to his lips.

'The panther—' But he was too quiet. He tweaked a dial on the side of the device and tried again. 'The panther's just been spotted.'

This time he was so loud that even the forensic technicians in the waiting room looked up from their work.

A hush settled on the car park.

The hunter raised his free hand high. In it, he held a mobile phone. This minor redistribution of his hefty bulk threatened his precarious balance and he staggered before steadying himself.

'The black panther,' boomed, his amplified voice, 'I've just heard, lads. It's at Hamley Golf Club. It's attacked someone on the course.'

With half a million pounds at stake, the bounty hunters did not wait to hear any more. Barbecues abandoned, they ran for their vehicles. Engines coughed into life.

'It was only minutes ago. Just minutes ago,' said the man with the megaphone. He looked around. Dozens of engines revved. 'Christ, they're all leaving. We gotta go, lads. Help me down.' A 4x4 tried to force it way past his white van but found its way blocked as other hunters pulled away from their parking places. The 4x4 pushed forward again and nudged the portly hunter's vehicle out of the way.

'Aargh!'

It was too much for his uncertain sense of balance. He tumbled off and landed on his four friends. Trucks and pickups swerved around their prostrate bodies to join the horn-honking gridlock at the exit to the car park.

Rosie snorted with derision.

'Should we follow them?' she said to Henry.

'Where is this place it has been seen?' Faith said.

Rosie calculated the distance before answering. 'It's the golf course near Lower Hamley Ten, maybe twelve miles as the crow flies from here, double by road.'

'Ah, I know this place. Then the *kyaani* will already be far away when these stupid men arrive,' said Henry.

'Oh.' said Rosie. 'So what should we do?'

'The *kyaani*, it was here last night. We will find its track and follow it. We search for its lair.'

'Just the two of you?' Unnerved by the Creswells' pursuit, Rosie's courage had become blunted.

'Just the three of us,' said Faith.

She placed her basket on the ground then unwrapped the long, thin linen-wrapped bundle. It contained two spears. One was identical to the short *assegai* carried by Henry. The other was twice the *assegai*'s length. Below the broad blade of its spearhead were two short metal cross-lugs. This was the spear Johnno had knocked over in the shed.

'For you.' Faith offered the long spear to Rosie. 'We need your help. It is not safe with two. Three is a good number.'

'Me? Oh no. This is crazy.'

'You have tracked dogs,' Henry said.

'Yes, sort of. But only... not to kill, not like this.' Rosie's pride would not let her mention the stretchy rubber pork sausages.

Henry took her right hand and wrapped her fingers around the spear's shaft.

'Now you track a big cat,' he said.

This is crazy, thought Rosie. I'm in Surrey, in the Twenty–First Century and I'm being talked into hunting a panther with a spear. But she did not take her hand from the shaft. She liked the feel of it.

'Er, I don't know how to use this,' she said.

'Then we will show you,' Faith said. 'Come.'

Brother and sister trotted into the dark woodland.

Rosie's decision-making capacity was paralysed by indecision. She looked back across the now deserted car park. The only people in sight were the police forensic team still hard at work around the waiting room. A dark cloud obscured the sun, and the scene, previously bright lit and tranquil, was transformed. It became bleak, empty and threatening, as if all the reassuring trappings of civilisation were no more than a mirage.

Rosie shivered. She glanced over her shoulder at the fast-disappearing Olembes then at the spear in her hand.

'Henry, Faith, wait for me,' she called out.

They had almost vanished from view.

Rosie ran after them.

'Wait for me.'

- 10 -

- Midday -

- Hamley Golf Club -

THE FAIRWAYS SWARMED WITH POLICE, PARAMEDICS, and over-excited golfers. At the First Tee, Coulston, dressed for the hunt, briefed a uniformed senior officer from the local force. 'I know it sounds crazy, sir, but that makes it three out of four partners in the Swanmere development attacked. We need to warn the fourth.'

'And who is that?' said Assistant Chief Constable Franklin.

'Alexei Zaharkin. The Russian oligarch. He has an estate only five miles away.'

Franklin winced. Last year, he'd had a brief, sharp, and ultimately losing dispute with Zaharkin over the legal status of the Russian's armed bodyguards.

'Prickly man,' he said, 'used to getting his own way, most unpleasant. I suppose it's what happens when you're worth more than two billion pounds.'

'Four billion, sir,' Coulston said. Since the encounter in the snow, he'd researched Zaharkin's background in detail.

'Really? What I remember most is the Foreign and Commonwealth Office briefing I received on his enemies.

The list was almost endless. There's the KGB or whatever they're called now—'

'FSB, sir.'

'Quite right, and the Russian mafia, Italian mafia, the Chinese, heaven only knows how many judicial inquires into corruption, pollution, extortion, and any other unpleasant noun ending in i-o-n. They all led nowhere. Good grief, the man's even got Greenpeace on his case. It's a wonder the Salvation Army isn't after him too. Worst of all are his ex-wives. We were told two have taken out contracts on him.'

'Welcome to Surrey's exclusive little piece of the Wild East, sir.'

'Are we sure this isn't something fanciful set up by one or other of those groups?'

Coulston had a brief, disturbing vision of the Salvation Army training killer big cats as a means of social justice and wealth redistribution. 'I think—'

'I mean, having these fellows on hand seems a little over-the-top.' The Assistant Chief Constable's gaze focused on a tableau in front of the clubhouse. Four pairs of Army marksmen sunned themselves beside a police incident trailer. Sipping mugs of tea and munching bacon sandwiches, they were a disconcerting and distressing sight for Franklin who had a deep-grained aversion to relinquishing any control to the military.

Coulston could feel a headache coming on. What was it about senior officers that meant so many of them became near-deranged when they achieved Franklin's rank? 'Sir, it is a big cat. Escaped or whatever, but it is out there. There's no doubt at all. It's killed twice and, in front of dozens of eyewitnesses, nearly made it three.'

'I know, I know. It's just so hard to come to grips with the reality of it. This is hardly a run-of-the-mill police operation, is it?'

'We need to find out which direction the panther's moving in. I'm just an advisor here, sir. You have operational command; I need your authorisation for those men to sweep these hills for tracks.'

'Just make sure they understand this isn't a free-fire battle zone. I want you to—'

Coulston never heard the rest of the order. It was cut short by the chewed stump of a golf club being waved under Franklin's nose. Tommy Belfast was very upset and keen to take out his anger on the uniform with the most gold braid on its shoulders.

'See this, my favourite hickory wedge?' he said. 'Had it more than fifty years. An antique. Look at it now. Look!'

'Mr. Belfast—' said Franklin.

Tommy was not prepared to be appeased. 'An attack like this, it's an outrage. It shouldn't happen on a golf course, it really shouldn't. Good God, you're a member here too. And another thing—'

A rising hubbub of hallooing voices came from beyond the clubhouse. There was a brief moment when all activity ceased. Police officers paused in their eyewitness interviews. The marksmen dropped their food to snatch up their sniper rifles. And Tommy Belfast's gaggle of followers swivelled almost in unison to face the source of the uproar.

Then, like a wave breaking around a lighthouse rock, the mob of bounty hunters surged past either wing of the building and towards the greens. Brandishing their shotguns, rifles and nets, they advanced on the fairway.

For Tommy, it was the final violation of what, less than an hour ago, had been shaping up to be a victorious round of golf. Waving his mangled club above his head, he charged off to intercept the intruders.

'Here, members only,' he yelled. 'Get off the fairways, you ruddy hooligans. Go on, be off with you. Members only, I say, members only.'

But his improvised cordon of golfers was swept aside by the determined charge of the money-crazed hunters.

Coulston dragged Franklin out of their path.

'Change of plan, sir,' he said. 'These idiots are going to be roaming the countryside for the rest of the day. So let's do our best to protect them from themselves.' The bang of an accidental shotgun discharge made everyone duck. 'And let's break out some high visibility jackets before these idiots accidentally kill us.'

'I'm jiggered,' said Rosie.

Hot, bothered, and tired, she sat slumped against the smooth silver bark of a beech tree. They were high on a hillside smothered in mixed-growth oak, ash, and beech. The woodland floor was blanketed with dry leaf debris, acorns, and nutshells, but the dense tree cover and slab-like sandstone outcrops kept fern and bramble to a minimum, and opened up long vistas between the trunks of the tall trees. Rosie had a clear view across the valley to the wooded slopes on the far side. Half a mile downstream, she could see cattle grazing in an open field. She frowned. Was that the rumble of heavy traffic she could hear?

Henry sat beside her.

'Is there a busy road near here?' Rosie said.

'Over there,' he pointed to the north. 'The motorway that circles London.'

'The M25?'

'Just so.'

Rosie stood to see if she could catch a glimpse of the familiar motorway. If they were close enough to the M25 to hear it, they had to be only a handful of miles from her mother's home. And the kids. A thought occurred to her. God, what if the big cat roamed in that direction? Into London?

'I can't see it,' she said. Despite the relatively clear view, there was no evidence of the presence of man, not even a pylon or telephone mast.

'It is over the hills,' Henry said. 'The noise travels far.'

Faith walked downslope and into a patch of sunlight. She began to pick the yellow five-petaled flowers that grew there, placing them in her basket. Abruptly, she stopped, stared up at the sky, one hand shading her eyes. 'Look,' she said and pointed.

Rosie saw a swirl of red above the ridge on the far side of the valley. They were birds, a whirring flock of about fifty or sixty, smallish in size, and making the most god-awful racket.

'What are they?' She was no expert but she had never seen British birds so vividly coloured.

Henry was watching them too. 'Ah, yes, they are, I think, from Australia. Little parrots.'

'Bollocks,' she said, too weary to be polite.

The flock swung in their direction. Almost before Rosie had time to take in their change of course, they were overhead. Scarlet and cacophonous, they wheeled to the north then were gone.

'Bloody hell, you're right, they're parakeets,' said Rosie. Her Aunt Sylvia kept a pair. And hadn't Bob Coulston mentioned them last night?

'Yes, just so,' said Henry. 'They nest on your Queen's land. Her castle, over there.' He gestured in the direction the flock had departed.

'Windsor Castle?' Rosie found it hard to reconcile the two things in her mind: the monarch's medieval weekend retreat, and the sight and sound of tropical birds in Surrey.

'Robert tells me the sight of them has caused many crashes on the M25. They surprise many people, not you alone.' Henry stood and stretched, back curved, arms wide. 'Come, we have a long way to go. We must find the cat before dark.'

Henry stalked the panther at a pace faster than Rosie had thought possible. She expected slow, uncertain progress; that the tracker would have to scour the ground for spoor, lose the trail, find it, lose it again, only to rediscover it after much searching for a fragmentary hint of a paw print or sliver of broken twig. Instead, he raced along, confident of the black panther's course.

'Henry, how do you do it?' Rosie said. 'How can you work so fast?'

'It is easy,' he said. 'I will show you.' He whistled low and sibilant to gain his sister's attention. 'Follow us when you are finished,' he called to her. 'I shall show friend Rosie how to track.'

'Go on, I will not be long.' Faith resumed her harvest.

He led Rosie along an indistinct trail that contoured the valley side.

'Many animals use this,' he said then glanced over his shoulder at Rosie, 'like your M25.'

'But how do you know which way the panther will go?' she said.

'I do not know where it will go, but I know where the *kyaani* wants to be and what it wants to do.'

'Vengeance.'

'Exactly. It wants go in this direction, and so it will not waste time. The *kyaani* will use the animal motorway and, hah, here, look!'

It was the faintest of pugmarks. Rosie would never have seen it, but for Henry sweeping leaves away from the soft indentation of the cat's paw in the mud. She noticed he first studied their surrounds with intensity before reaching behind to touch a woven-grass amulet attached to a thread that hung between his shoulders. Only then did he crouch.

He's worried and scared, thought Rosie. And that scared her. Even more than she was already.

'You can read so much. It is a male. Big,' said Henry. The tracker searched back and forth, until he found another paw print. 'Ah, here, just so. The stride is long; it travels faster than us. And it is still injured. This side,' he patted the pugmark, 'the stride is shorter than the left side.

It has not fully recovered.' Henry looked up and held Rosie's gaze. 'It is very dangerous.'

'Why?' Rosie said.

Faith joined them. 'Because it does not have so much strength and it cannot escape so easily,' she said.

'And so it becomes more angry,' said Henry. 'Instead of hiding, it will attack.'

Rosie scanned the slope they were on.

'Then surely we should be slower, more careful?'

'Trust in my brother,' said Faith. 'In the forests, the big cats have their favourite places to spring ambushes. Henry knows them all. He knows what to look for.'

'Sister, you are kind,' Henry said, 'but one thing puzzles me greatly.' He looked southwards. 'The golf course is over there, and we are here, nowhere near it.' Again, he patted the paw print. 'But this track is fresh, made after the rain last night. The *kyaani* came from the station. How can it be here this morning and over there at the same time. How is this possible?'

Rosie merely shrugged. More magic, no doubt. As long as they were behind the panther, not in front of it, she was content.

An hour later, Faith stopped them again. She had found more of the little five-petal flowers. The trio were in another woodland valley, in near identical terrain to where they'd seen the parakeets. Rosie could not care less why they'd halted. She was just glad of the break.

Henry squatted beside her. 'We cannot stay, when Faith has finished, we must move. It is not safe here,' he said in an agitated whisper.

Rosie lay on her back, eyes closed. 'Oh come on,' she said, 'we've been walking for hours and we've seen nothing.' She did not know which she disliked more: the sweaty hair stuck to her forehead, or the damp, slick circlets of perspiration beneath her armpits.

'But something has scented us. We are not safe.' Henry was nervous and on alert.

'So you keep saying,' Rosie pulled at her clammy t-shirt. 'But Faith over there is picking flowers, wild flowers, which, by the way, I am pretty certain is against the law.'

'What she does is important.'

'What's so—?'

Henry whirled around. Spear raised, he tensed.

Rosie reached for her weapon. So far, it had been of more use as a walking stick. 'Is it the panther?'

'Oh no, but this thing is dangerous. We have strayed into its territory.' Henry hissed to get Faith's attention. Seeing his stance, she placed her basket on the ground, retrieved her *assegai* then joined them.

Henry faced Rosie. 'Quick, I must show you how to use your spear. I should have done this before, but even now we may still have time.'

'Don't I just, y'know, yurgh?' Rosie made an unconvincing stabbing motion.

'No,' Henry said. 'Come, copy my actions. Stand like so.' He showed her how to ground and brace her spear. 'When it charges, you must not run. Be brave and take its attack on the point of the spear.'

'When what charges?' Rosie did not like the sound of this.

'If I told you, you would not believe me. You would not take this seriously. You must see this with your own eyes. And so we prepare. Now these—' Henry touched the cross-braces behind the spearhead, '—these will hold it away from you. My sister and I will attack from the side.'

'Hold it away from me?'

'If they did not, it would push itself along the shaft to attack you, kill you, even as it dies. It has no fear of humans.'

'But, I'm just a dog warden. I mean—'

Henry held his index finger to his lips and whispered, 'Hush, it is here.' He clicked his fingers. Faith was at his side, *assegai* ready. Henry pointed at a clump of holly bushes thirty paces away. 'It is there. Remember, you must hold it, hold it long enough for us to strike. Free, it is too quick. Wounded, too dangerous. And if you run—'

Right now, Rosie considered this by far the best option.

'It will kill you.' Henry's voice was the faintest of whispers.

And they were gone, hidden behind broad tree trunks.

Rosie stood alone.

'Where are you?' she whispered. 'Hey, you haven't told me what it is. This had better not be a joke. It's not very funny.'

There was a snort. The bushes rustled and shook then a hook-tusked wild boar emerged.

'It's just a pig,' Rosie said in a loud voice. 'Henry, Faith, it's only a...' Awareness dawned on Rosie that this beast was much larger than your average farmyard porker. 'Oh crap. Only a massive wild pig.'

The short-sighted boar made up in hearing and sense of smell what it lacked in vision. It grunted then moved with muscular solidity as it shifted its bulk to face Rosie. The boar pawed the ground. Dark bristles stood proud on its back as it shook its thick-muscled neck. The sunlight highlighted its pink-red eyes and the ivory white of its tusks.

It stamped once.

Twitched.

Stamped again.

Then, kicking back a plume of dry leaves, the boar charged Rosie.

She crouched low and grasped the spear just as Henry had shown her: the butt dug into the ground, her legs braced, hands wide apart on the shaft.

'Oh no, no, no.' It was almost on Rosie. The onrushing boar filled her field of vision.

Wham. Rosie staggered under the impact.

The hunting spear took the boar in the throat. Rosie tumbled onto her backside but kept her grip, kept the shaft steady. Just as Henry predicted, the impaled beast struggled to reach her, but was stopped by the spear's cross braces.

The Olembes leapt from cover and cast their spears. The two assegais struck the boar on either flank. It squealed then, to Rosie's immense surprise, died, suddenly, abruptly. She felt strangely cheated. Was that it? No agonised death throes? No final convulsive attack?

The boar's blood trickled down the spear shaft and onto her tight-clenched fingers.

'Yeuch!'

She released the spear, but the shaft stayed wedged between earth and boar. The beast twitched and Rosie jumped with fright.

The Olembes joined her. Faith put an arm around the shaken dog warden. 'You did well, Rosie.'

'A wild boar? Where did it come from?' Rosie said, her voice quavering. 'This is England, Britain, an island, we don't have wild boar. I mean, I can see that it is one, but—'

'But believe your eyes, sister,' Faith said. Then, as if nothing out of the ordinary had happened, she returned to picking the yellow flowers of the forest.

Henry knelt to examine the carcass. 'There are more than twenty of such beasts living in these hills, with babies, many babies,' he said. 'I have seen the tracks. And many hundreds more between here and the sea. Many bigger than this one.'

Rosie reckoned it must be at least twice her weight.

With a sucking noise, Henry wrenched his spear from the boar's flank. His throw had penetrated its rib cage to take it clean in the heart. The strong metallic smell of blood was mixed with the beast's malodorous scent, and it took several seconds for Rosie to overcome her gag reflex.

'Hundreds of them? Come off it,' she said.

'Help me,' said Henry. But she could only watch as Henry took her spear, pulled it from the boar's throat, and then recovered Faith's *assegai*. Rosie was certain the gristly sucking and tearing noises would live long in her memory. The tracker examined her spear's shaft with care, nodded his approval, and then, using some bracken leaves, wiped the blood from its blade.

'They are kept on farms,' Henry said. 'You did not know this?'

Rosie shook her head.

'No? Many have escaped. It is in their nature, they are very clever animals. This is a wild pig, not a farm pig. It can smell the wild, wants to be in the wild.' He knelt beside the dead beast.

'But there haven't been wild boar here since... since Robin Hood,' said Rosie.

'They are here now. They can survive as easily as the cat, the *kyaani*.' He took a playful tug of one tusk then looked towards Faith. 'Are you finished, sister?'

Faith waved; the basket was full. 'I have sufficient.'

'Then we go. The trail leads this way.' He set off with an energetic step. 'We shall return for the boar when this sad business is finished. There is very good meat on a boar. Many good meals.'

The limousine drove at reckless speed down the country lane. Valeri was at the wheel; Konstantin sat in the rear alongside Zaharkin. Through darkened windows the ghost-like images of sunlit hedgerows and fields flashed by. Valeri was tense, his shoulders hunched tight as he concentrated on the task of getting his boss back to the safety of the mansion as quickly as possible.

Dressed in a Savile Row suit, silk tie and handmade black leather shoes, Zaharkin talked into his mobile phone, his hands in constant impatient motion, chopping vertically to emphasize the positive and horizontally for the negative.

'*Da, da*, yes, yes. Oakshott, I understand. It makes no sense, but I understand. I will make preparations... *Nyet, nyet*, my friend, you are upset and hurt; what you say sounds insane, but I am a cautious man. I remember what you saw the day we hunted deer. I only wish I believed you then. So, I will make preparations. I have done so already but for different reasons. You know, in my homeland, my business rivals are, let us say, somewhat intense, and so I must always be ready to defend myself. And you, what do you do now? Maybe stay in hospital...? No? Then where will you go...? Swanmere? The mall? A good choice. It is like a fortress. You must lower the portcullis, yes...? Me?' He shrugged. 'I believe the best form of defence is attack. I have a plan. I will call you later. Okay, farewell.'

Zaharkin snapped shut the mobile phone, thought for a second then spoke to his bodyguards.

'I have jobs for you,' he said. 'Valeri, you must buy some portable spotlights and clean three hunting rifles.'

The sedan swung between steel gates and beneath a raised barrier. An armed security guard saluted from a sentry post. The gravel drive led to Zaharkin's elegant Jacobean manor hall in front of which a pair of guards, each holding two leashed Dobermans, patrolled on the lawn.

'Konstantin, you must find me a goat,' said Zaharkin.

'Boss?' The bodyguard twisted his substantial bulk to stare at his employer.

The billionaire sat in profile, his stare fixed on the trees beyond the mansion. 'A goat,' he said. 'Boys, we are going on a big cat hunt.'

- 11 -

- Late Afternoon -

- Heart of the Weald -

SUNSHINE FILTERED THROUGH THE LEAVES OF THE trees. The area between the clearing and the two mesh fences was devastated. Trampled. As if a marauding army had marched through. It had.

'Idiots,' Coulston said. He was stood in the middle of the Heart.

He sat on the grass and leant his back against the Queer Stone. In his hands was a posy of wild flowers identical to those collected by Faith.

'Morons,' he added with a degree of bitterness unusual for a copper inoculated against the worst excesses of human behaviour.

A twig snapped and, in a blur of movement, Coulston stood crouched, his rifle at the ready. The flowers tumbled to his feet. Henry, who had made sure to break the stick so as not to startle Coulston into hasty over-reaction, entered the glade from the far side.

'Robert, we are here,' he said.

Faith, her appearance still fresh and relaxed, was on the path behind him with Rosie, exhausted and unkempt, at the rear.

Coulston smiled as much at the trail-worn sight of Rosie as at the arrival of his two friends. Walking to greet them, he bent to scoop something from the mud then showed it to Faith. In his hand was one of her fragile woven cat's eyes. It was twisted, broken. He handed her the torn charm.

'The bounty hunters,' he said. 'Must have been a shotgun blast. They didn't even notice the damage, and wouldn't care if they had.'

'Did they find anything?' said Rosie. 'The cat, I mean. Did they kill it?'

'You must be joking.' Coulston said as he guided them back to the Carn Menyn bluestone. 'The one thing you can be sure of is the cat's nowhere near those fools.' Rifle slung across his back, he squatted on his haunches to reassemble his bouquet. 'We've arrested six for firearms offences, three for brawling, God knows how many for being drunk and disorderly, and four for public indecency. I sent them on their way. Under armed escort.' He handed the flowers to Faith. 'For you. Cymbeline. All I could find.'

'I fear we shall need every flower, every petal,' Faith said.

'Fear what? Why the flowers?' said Rosie.

Coulston ignored the question and spoke to Henry, 'The panther's trail led here?'

Henry nodded. 'Once more to the fence. It jumped over, only a hundred paces away.' He waved his spear in the direction they had come.

'Once more? Does it come here a lot?' said Rosie.

'Not here, not to the Heart, Faith has made sure of that,' Henry said.

'But to this general area for certain,' said Coulston.

The gentle wind shifted the trees' branches apart and allowed a shard of sunlight to strike the Queer Stone. Rosie, standing next to it, looked down and stifled a scream. For a passing moment, she saw a face carved in its surface: twisted and screaming in silent agony. Then the breeze weakened, the trees relaxed and the sunlight was gone. With it went the face.

'I saw it!' she said to Coulston. 'I saw the face you told me about.'

He walked to her side and listened as Rosie described what she had seen.

'You saw it too, didn't you?' Rosie said to the Olembes. 'You must have.'

From their appalled expressions she knew was right. Henry was pale with shock.

'The Heart, it cries,' said Faith.

'Must be one of those trick-of-the-light things,' said Rosie. 'Like the Face of Mars.'

'It appears you have a knack of seeing the things that I miss out on.' Coulston knelt and stroked the surface of the slab. He tilted his head to look along its surface. 'I've looked so many times, from every angle and never... Well, so the legend of the Queer Stone is true. I hope I get as lucky as you some day.'

Rosie decided it was the kind of luck she could do without. Reluctant to stand close to the stone, she walked over to the nearest of the mesh fences, hooked her fingers in its chain links and rattled them.

'I wonder why it comes here?' she said. 'Do you think it lives in there, somewhere in this estate?'

No one answered her; they were circling the rock, hoping to get another sight of the tormented face.

Still gripping the mesh with one hand, Rosie swung around to watch them.

'Did Henry tell you I killed a boar?' she called out to Coulston. 'A big one? With a spear.'

'Very big,' said Henry with mock-paternal pride.

'Oh my,' said Coulston his face still close to the stone. 'No, blast it, I can see nothing at all.'

Faith glanced up at the branches above their heads. They were bare of the charms that once hung from them.

'What has happened here?' she said. 'They have gone.

Every one of them is gone. This is not possible. No hunters could have done this.'

Dozens of the eyes, including the most ancient, lay torn and trampled into the ground.

'It is damn odd, they only loosed off one round here. Could it have been a wind?' Coulston said. 'But then there's been no gale, no storm, not recently.'

'This is no longer a place of sanctuary.' For the first time since Coulston had known her, he heard fear in Faith's voice. 'We are no longer protected here.'

He pulled out the charm she had woven for him. It was on a silver chain. 'I have mine.'

Faith surveyed the devastation. 'The beast has grown too powerful.'

'Bloody mumbo-jumbo,' Rosie muttered. 'It's just a bloody big cat.' She released her grip on the fence. 'Whose land is this?' she said to Coulston.

'Surely you remember? This is where we met. Over there is the Dawes' land, Faith and Henry's employers—'

'I'm just a dumb city girl, remember?'

'Once you've killed a wild boar you're not a city girl anymore,' he said.

Rosie felt a spark of pleasure at such praise then immediately felt embarrassed at the absurd idea of performing such a feat.

'And I'm surprised you haven't set off the alarms again,' Coulston continued, 'because the fence you've been pulling at belongs to Zaharkin, the fourth Swanmere partner.'

Four miles away, no one was in the security monitoring room. Valeri was lying prone on the lawn setting the sights of their hunting rifles, whilst Konstantin was having a little difficulty purchasing a goat at short notice. He'd learnt the hard way not to inform English animal-lovers that the goat they were selling would be used as live bait for a big cat.

The sky darkened as the cloud cover thickened. Rosie shivered. Without the sun on her back, the sweat chilled her. She resumed her hopeful inspection of the woodland beyond the fence. Daylight dimmed. Coulston peered up at what little of the sky he could see through the trees.

'Shouldn't be this dark,' he said. 'It's at least half an hour before sunset.'

'Inspector Coulston...' said Rosie.

He was still staring up at the clouds and did not notice how the other three stood frozen in their stances, eyes fixed on something beyond the fence. Nor did he notice the silence that fell across the glade as birds and forest animals fell quiet.

'Call me Bob, please,' he said.

'My brother, it is the *kyaani*!' In the stillness, Henry's whisper was as loud as a shout.

The panther faced Rosie. Only the chain link fence separated them. She had not noticed its arrival. One moment there were only the usual trees, ferns, bushes, and the next it stood there, not growling, not crouched ready to pounce, just there, watchful, as if waiting to see what they would do. And she was acutely aware that she no longer held her spear. When she had begun to tire, Henry offered to carry it for her and she had accepted gratefully.

'My God, it's even bigger than I thought.' Coulston unslung his rifle. 'Rosie, on a count of five—' he said then noticed how focused she was upon the cat's presence. 'Rosie, Rosie.' He dared not be too loud, too forceful, in case he triggered the panther's aggression. He tried again, 'Rosie Flinn.'

'What?' came the whisper. She was rigid, still as a statue.

Snick. Coulston eased off the safety catch. And that brought a reaction from the beast: a low, rumbling growl. Of course, thought Coulston, you recognise the sound, you know what could happen to you, what has happened to you. So why don't you run away? But the cat remained, standing four-square. It was a powerful, beautiful, yet terrible sight.

'What?' Rosie said again, still in a whisper, but this time with more emphasis.

Coulston jerked his attention back to her. 'On my count of five, I want you to run to your left, down the path between the fences, to the road. You know the way.'

He chanced a quick glance behind. Henry and Faith stood poised, *assegai* spears at the ready. The big cat continued to stare at Rosie, but its ears twitched as it tracked the careful, purposeful movements of the Olembes.

'One, two...' Coulston said.

Click, he eased home the hunting rifle's bolt. The panther hissed and bared its teeth.

Even more so than yesterday at Swanmere in the rain, Rosie felt her senses narrow down into a tight cone until all she could see, hear, smell was the big cat. And what a stink; how had she missed that? It was worse than the boar. Much worse.

'Henry and Faith will go with you.' Coulston said. 'Don't stop until you reach the road. I'll cover you. Three.'

He nodded at brother and sister. They nodded in return. They were ready. Coulston felt the darkness gather and deepen around the big cat. He aimed, knowing as he did, that one shot, not even from a high-calibre weapon like his could stop a predator of this size at this range. Despite their weapons and the fence between, they were in the panther's killing zone. A shot or a spear thrust might wound it fatally, but not before it would kill them all. His grandfather had drummed the lesson home. 'Why do you think the nabobs used to hunt tigers from atop elephants?' he'd say. 'Not because they liked the view, boy.'

'Four.'

The big cat's gaze switched to the man with the gun.

My God, thought Coulston, it's as if it knows what I said, and is counting along with me.

The panther growled again, but this time it built into a roar. They all felt its power. It made a physical impact on them, almost shaking them. This was something not even Coulston's grandfather had experienced.

Fear washed through Coulston's body. Both his resolve and aim wavered, but it was too late to change the plan.

'Five. Now, go, go!'

He pulled the trigger. The panther leapt. Rosie and the Olembes sprinted for the path.

Coulston's shot went wide. The predator crashed into the chain link fence and began to climb.

'I didn't miss, I know I didn't. I'm sure I didn't.' Coulston swore long and loud as he reloaded then fired again. The muzzle flash penetrated the gloom and he saw the big cat twist then leap aside. For a moment he thought he'd hit his quarry but, again, the bullet flew wide and into the woods. In evading the gunshot, the cat tumbled back from the fence. Its stare was fixed on the hunter as it rolled on its paws and gathered itself for another leap. The fear-induced fog of darkness spread to envelop Coulston. All he could see were two yellow-green eyes as the man-eater moved towards him.

'Oh shit,' he said.

Panic overwhelmed him; he ripped Faith's charm free from its chain, flung it at the panther. It flinched. He ran.

As the terror-induced adrenaline spike hit Coulston's bloodstream, events became a blur of motion interspersed with strobe-like snapshot images of sprinting feet; of Rosie, Faith, Henry, their eyes wide in fear; of the panther loping alongside but still beyond Zaharkin's fence. Coulston reloaded as he ran. He shot again, but, unable to steady his nerves, his aim was wild and he missed.

Rosie burst from the overgrown path and onto an empty stretch of road. The Olembes were right behind her.

'Sister, the circle, be swift,' Henry said. 'Rosie, come stand with me.' He grabbed Rosie by the elbow; thrust the long spear into her hands.

Faith strewed her yellow-petaled flowers on the black tarmac, sketching out the circumference of a wide circle around them.

Coulston backed out of the woods, raised the rifle, fired, and missed once more. Unhurt, the panther glided into sight, lunged forward, and leapt the fence.

The ring of flowers completed, Faith fell to her knees. Arms upraised, she chanted in Ghanaian.

Coulston took another shot but, with nothing more than a shift of its shoulders, the panther again dodged his aim. Now silent, it padded into the cover provided by the thick growth of bushes that sprouted between boundary fence and road.

'Rosie, Henry, your spears,' Coulston said. 'I think I'm out of ammo.'

'What? Oh, sure.' Rosie looked uncertainly at the spear in her hand then braced it as she was taught. 'I'm not certain what good this will do.'

Coulston entered the circle. He began to pat his pockets in search of extra rounds. 'I keep shooting. Shooting and missing. What the hell is going on?'

'You cannot rid us of this *kyaani*,' said Henry, 'not until it is ready to sleep again. We must trust in Faith to help us now.'

The panther was an indistinct shape prowling thorough the undergrowth alongside the road.

The chanting stopped.

Faith knelt, head bowed.

'Look,' said Rosie.

The big cat stood on the road. It glared at them, the personification of a killer. Its deep, rumbling roar began to grow once more.

They all froze in their stances: Rosie and Henry with spears ready, Faith kneeling, and Coulston awkwardly posed with his right hand dug deep in the trouser pocket of his left leg.

Henry gasped. 'So big, so strong. I have never seen a leopard like this.'

'We must also be strong, my friends,' said Faith. 'Do not flee. It will not, cannot, cross the circle.'

Despite the bizarre improbability of Faith's words, Rosie found herself believing the Ghanaian. 'Don't worry,' she said, 'I'm not planning on going anywhere.'

Light from the setting sun broke through the cloud and illuminated them. The darkness lifted and, as suddenly as when it first appeared, the panther was gone.

'Hey, where did it vanish to?' Rosie said.

Henry placed a hand on her forearm. 'Your spear will not be needed. The circle has broken the darkness.'

'Certainly seems to have done the trick,' said Coulston. 'Thank you, Faith.' He stood on tiptoe, looking down the long, straight road. 'There's a car coming, we'd better get out of the way.'

'Oh, come on, flowers?' Rosie said. 'A circle of flowers scared that monster away? How do you know it wasn't this car's engine noise?' She pointed at the distant vehicle. 'Bob, surely you don't believe this.'

'Honestly, I don't know what to believe apart from what I've seen with my own eyes,' he said.

Rosie snorted in disgust. Yet, notwithstanding her scepticism, she was reluctant to step outside the ring.

Faith handed her a single flower.

'Cymbeline has power. Like the Heart of the Forest. It tames the restless spirits,' she said.

'It's just a bloody big cat,' muttered Rosie, but she accepted the flower.

'One that can dodge bullets,' Coulston said.

'Or maybe you're just a lousy shot.' Henry and Faith laughed. Infuriated, Rosie turned on them. 'If this *kyaani* is as you say, then why did it attack us? We've done it no harm.'

The onrushing car, a silver Range Rover, saw them and honked its horn.

Henry shrugged. 'It is wild, untamed, and we hunt it.'

'My brother, the hour is getting late; the light fades,' said Faith. 'We cannot stay here.'

Aha, thought Rosie, underneath all that supernatural charisma, she agrees with me.

'My car got left behind at Swanmere when all hell let loose at the golf club,' Coulston said. 'I need to get back there, get my spare ammunition.'

The big car was almost upon them. Its headlights came on, full beam, dazzling. Coulston moved to the side of the road opposite the fence. The Olembes did the same. Rosie followed them. She was certain the big cat lurked over there, waiting for the car to pass.

'Swanmere? That's miles away,' she said.

'Indeed it is. You coming or staying?'

And with the self-confidence of a police officer who had never failed to force a vehicle to stop for him, he walked into the middle of the road, right palm raised in the international signal to halt used by all coppers.

The Range Rover braked.

Just.

In.

Time.

'Bloody show-off,' muttered Rosie who suspected the threat of the rifle cradled in Coulston's left arm had as much to do with anything as his assertion of natural authority.

Johnno Dawes loved driving his brute of a car. It allowed him time to meditate, to relax. Right now, he felt in need of some tranquillity because his vision of an idyllic life in the country had faded fast. First, there were the intractable Olembes. Polite and efficient, definitely so, but it was impossible to force them to do something if they didn't want to do it. The discovery of the spears had shaken him more than it should have, he now admitted to himself. He had over-reacted. But the Olembes were definitely tangled up in this outlandish man-eater business. Then there were this morning's events at the golf club. He and Naomi had been expecting a stately introduction to the social scene, perhaps even membership invitations over lunchtime gin and tonics in the bar. Instead, they'd experienced the terror of a monster stalking the greens, an invasion by the gun-wielding, sweaty hoi polloi, followed by the army, the police, and the media. Johnno missed London so much the homesickness twisted in his gut. He missed the grit, the stench of diesel fumes, the drinking water recycled through six human bladders, the crush on the Underground, the rancid smell of deep-fried fast food, and the ever-present background rumble of traffic. He missed it all.

Naomi watched the countryside flash past. A 'Deer Crossing' sign appeared up ahead.

'Darling, have you ever wondered how they train the deer to cross at the signs?' she said.

Johnno slowed the Range Rover. 'It is a puzzle, isn't it? Bloody council, wasting precious—'

'Resources on animals, I agree. I say, let them cross where they want.'

The sign behind them, Johnno accelerated. They sat in silence for a few minutes more.

'Nao,' he said as they rounded a bend in the road, 'have you thought about moving back to London?'

'Of course,' she said. Naomi had been wallowing in her own fantasy: a therapeutic tour of the fashion boutiques of Paris, Milan, and New York. 'This has been a disastrous experience. We need to get away; we need time to think. We shall be at the house soon. If you like we could pack some clothes quickly and be in—'

Johnno stared forward. In the distance, he could see movement on the road. He honked the horn. A frown creased his forehead. 'Isn't that the Olembes? What are they doing here, standing in the middle of the road?'

'Quick, speed up. We don't want to—'

'Pick them up. Quite.' Johnno gunned the engine and accelerated. He flicked on the headlights then, after a moment's thought, switched them to full beam. 'That should do the trick.'

'Well done.' Naomi smiled as the Olembes plus two others, white people, how strange, hurried to the side of the road. 'Look at them, they're nothing more than peasants.'

Before Johnno could reply, a tall man, armed with a rifle, one hand raised high to stop them, stepped into the road.

Johnno stomped hard on the brakes.

Rosie leant forward. 'It really is terribly kind of you to give us a lift.' She had to shout. In order that they fit their weapons into the vehicle, the rear door was jammed wide open. Once again, it proved difficult to fit spears into a car, even one as large as the Range Rover. The blade of Rosie's long spear now protruded from the rear hatch door, whilst its butt tapped against the inside of the windscreen. With the door ajar, the road noise made light conversation difficult.

Neither Naomi nor Johnno answered her.

She tried again, but the impulse to challenge their snootiness meant the tone of her voice came across more like one of her kids boasting about what they'd done at school. 'I killed a wild boar today,' she said. 'It was really big. Look, I've got its blood on my sleeve.' She thrust her arm between driver and passenger seat.

Johnno concentrated on the road. Swanmere Mall could not appear fast enough. Naomi edged away from the gruesome evidence of Rosie's hunting ability.

'And, hey, you can still see some blood on the spear, right here.' Rosie tapped the shaft. It was about three inches from Johnno's face. Henry's cleaning had been imperfect, a few flakes of dried blood landed on Johnno's shoulder.

In an effort to get Rosie to shut up, Coulston attempted to jab her in the ribs with an elbow, but even the broad rear seat in a Range Rover has its limits. The four trackers were crammed in so tight that Coulston's movement accidentally jerked his gun's muzzle upwards and into the soft fabric of the roof interior. He attempted a surreptitious wipe of the dark gunpowder residue left behind, but only smeared it further. As he did so, Coulston caught Johnno watching him in the reflection of the rear view mirror. He sighed and glanced across at Faith and Henry. They'd sat there, silent and stoic, ever since they'd climbed in and discovered from whom they'd hitchhiked a lift.

'Er, sorry about all this,' he said. 'It's vital police business.' In an attempt to bolster the Olembes' status in the eyes of their employers, he added, 'Faith and Henry have been wonderfully helpful. They can track the panther better than anyone.'

Naomi's temperament, always brittle, snapped.

Her scream of incoherent anger, thwarted entitlement, and general sense of injustice was as drawn out as the time it took Johnno to, once again, slam on the brakes and stop the car. She leapt out of the Range Rover and yanked open the passenger door on the Olembes' side.

'Out, out, all of you,' she shrieked. 'I don't know who you think you are, or what you're doing here, but just leave us alone.'

Henry and Faith climbed out.

'With your, your stupid good manners and your, your...' Naomi stalked to the rear, pulled Rosie's long spear free, flung it on the road, slammed the door shut then turned on her unwanted passengers. 'Why don't you just go back to Africa and leave decent, white people like us in peace,' she said then added for emphasis; 'This is a Christian country, you're not wanted here.'

Henry and Faith were more than a little puzzled by her last statement. They might not be white, but, unlike the Dawes, they did actually go to church.

'And you, chasing your bloody strays—' Naomi pivoted around to face Rosie as she clambered out and then leant back inside to begin the task of extracting the *assegais* from the car. 'Wearing your stupid dog person uniform, thinking you're as good as us. Well, you're not.'

Rosie made sure the spear tips cut two parallel grooves in the roof fabric.

On the far side of the car, Coulston stepped onto the road and opened his mouth to speak, but Naomi got there first. 'You're a policeman; you're what's wrong with this country. Just look at you: scruffy, no respect for your betters, scaring people with your guns. There was a time in this country when a policeman maintained the social order, but not you. No, you'd rather chase some mythical big cat. Well, I think you should go live with your black friends, go back to Africa, see how you like it there.' She climbed back into her seat. 'Take your bloody panther with you. And get a shave whilst you're about it.'

She slammed shut the door.

It was the longest uninterrupted speech either Naomi or Johnno had made in the presence of the other since the couple had met.

Coulston watched the Range Rover swing around and speed away. 'Actually, it's a probably a jaguar,' he said to no one in particular. 'From South America. So it'd be bloody stupid to take it to Africa.' He rubbed the coarse bristles on his chin. There'd been no time to shave this morning. 'Mind you, she's right about the shave,' he said. 'I could do with one.'

Rosie said, in the best impersonation of Naomi she could muster. 'What perfectly awful—'

'People,' said Coulston. He tried to but could not keep a straight face. His fingers dug into his jacket's breast pocket as he resumed his hunt for another rifle round.

Henry retrieved Rosie's spear. He handed it to her.

'Where exactly are we?' she said. In the gathering gloom, Rosie could see they were on an isolated stretch of road near identical to the spot they'd been picked up from but no other landmarks were visible.

'Still a fair few miles to go,' Coulston said. 'Come on, it's a warm night, it'll only take a couple of hours or so to get there.'

'Henry, what will you and Faith do?' Coulston felt the lining of his hunting jacket but found nothing. 'It sounds like you don't have jobs anymore.'

Henry smiled and his sister did too.

'What can we do in the face of such anger? If we walk in grace, we will find a path,' said Faith.

They began their trek towards the shopping mall. Rosie kept glancing behind. She would have preferred a greater separation between themselves and the black panther. Preferably an entire continent. Or two.

Henry noticed her agitation.

'Rosie, you must wear this,' he said. He reached behind his neck, tugged at the thread of his charm, and tore free the cat's eye amulet.

They stopped walking to allow Henry to tie it around her neck.

'What is it?' she said.

'It protects you from the panther,' said Faith. 'They like to attack from behind; when you are not looking. The eye makes them think you have seen them. Have you noticed Robert wears one too?'

'No longer. Sorry, Faith.' Coulston pivoted his shoulders to show its absence. 'I threw it at the panther. Back there in the woods. Stupid, I know. I panicked and I'm not proud of it.'

Faith said nothing. She hugged him.

'I know you probably think wearing this charm is more craziness, but it does work,' Coulston said to Rosie. 'I looked it up after Faith gave me mine. Foresters in India use the same trick to ward off tigers.'

Rosie liked the light touch of the charm on her back. It was reassuring, she decided.

'But what about you, Henry?' she said. 'Don't you need it as much as me?'

He laughed and took her by the elbow. 'Come, we shall walk together and share its protection. Besides, you have done very well today—'

'Your star pupil,' said Faith.

'Indeed, this is so. Rosie has earned it.'

After a minute of silence save for the tread of their shoes on the road, a thought occurred to Rosie. 'Bob, I know I'm a beginner at this sort of thing, but shouldn't we let the Army guys know where the panther was. I mean it can't be fifteen minutes since we last saw it.'

'Good idea, I'll call it in,' he said, 'but there's not much point. It's already dark, only complete madmen would hunt a black panther at night.'

- 12 -

- Night -

- The Zaharkin Estate, Upper Hamley -

'BLEEEAH,' SAID THE GOAT.

'This was a bad idea,' said Valeri.

He had grounds for his complaint. The goat made its plaintive cry once every twenty seconds, as regular as clockwork, and, Valeri checked the luminous face of his wristwatch, it had done so in each of the one hundred and thirty–four minutes since sunset. Whether there was food in its mouth at the time made no difference to the animal, it still bleated. By Valeri's reckoning that made it four hundred and two times since he'd climbed, very reluctantly, into this bloody tree. He shifted in his perch. There was a very uncomfortable stub of a small twig positioned where it had no right to be. Right cheek, left cheek, or the gap in-between, he could not find a pain-free position on the oak tree's branch.

'Bleeah.' The goat did it again.

Four hundred and thee.

The creature had started to become annoying after the first four skull-penetrating cries, but, although Valeri prided himself on his patience, it was now getting downright aggravating. He glanced to his right where, beyond Zaharkin, Konstantin sat on the thick branch. Each man wore a harness secured to the tree by karabiners and slings. Valeri blamed his friend for the racket. He felt he should have checked to see how noisy the goat was before he bought it, but, even in the weak, backscattered light from the arc lamps, he could see Konstantin did not share his agitation. Eyes closed, the big man sat in tranquillity, back braced against the thick webbing of the slings that held him safe.

Valeri stroked the stock of his rifle. 'A bad idea,' he repeated.

'*Tchush sobach'ya*,' Zaharkin said. 'Bullshit. Valeri, you sound like that goat. Like a goat that wants to have sex with that goat.'

Right on cue, the goat bleated.

'All I mean, boss, is that we are too static. It makes us vulnerable.'

Konstantin stretched, yawned, and took out the earplugs he'd been using. 'What's up, boss? What are you two arguing about this time?'

Valeri went rigid with rage. Why hadn't he thought of earplugs too?

'He thinks you getting the goat was a waste of time,' said Zaharkin, never one to refuse an opportunity to practice his divide-and-rule technique.

'That so?' Konstantin leant forward to glare at his partner. He was proud of his achievement. He'd definitely been given the toughest of the tasks. Unable to find anyone willing to sell him a goat, he had waited for a petting zoo in Woking to close before making a raid on its goat pen.

Valeri gave him the fig-sign, the Russian equivalent of the finger. 'No, I mean why are we up here?' he said. 'We should stay tactical. In war, static means death. Konstantin knows this, yes?'

With reluctance, the other bodyguard nodded.

Zaharkin attempted to master his impatience. He needed these two, despite their squabbling. Anyway, he knew that staking the goat here in his woods was a perfectly legitimate tactic. 'You were *Spesnatz*, yes? Both of you. You know how to hunt, how to kill a man.'

'This is a man-killer, not a man,' Konstantin said.

'You have hunted bears with me. This is no different,' said his boss. 'All big beasts have to be shown respect. You tempt them. You give them what they want. The cat cannot resist the goat. It will come. Then we shoot.'

Bleat, went the goat.

'Whatever you say boss,' said Konstantin.

'*Zhopa*,' muttered Valeri. 'Asshole.' Then a new thought occurred to him. 'But, boss, what if we're the staked goats?'

Zaharkin frowned. Konstantin nodded agreement. And, as if on cue, they heard the chonking sound of a power unit cutting out. A spotlight went out. Chonk. Chonk. Two more of the lamps shut down.

'What the hell?' said Zaharkin.

Chonk. Chonk. The last two were out. Startled by the sudden dark, the goat made an especially long bleat. In the distance, the diesel generator continued to chug.

Three torches clicked on.

'Someone's got to go down and fix those lights,' Zaharkin said.

'Boss, I suggest we stay up here. Until dawn, until it is safe.' Valeri knew better than to volunteer.

'What if the damn cat comes when lights are off?' said Zaharkin. 'Then we waste a night. And a goat.'

'*Passhol v'tchorte*,' said Konstantin. 'Go to hell. What if it comes when we are on the ground?'

'So you are not going to go down?'

'*Nyet*.'

'No way.'

'Pass the ladder to me, you cowards.' Zaharkin pointed behind Konstantin to where it was wedged in the branches.

Thirty seconds later, the lightweight aluminium ladder clattered down. Zaharkin slid down its struts to the ground. Swiftly, he unslung his rifle, holding it ready in one hand. A torch was in the other. He looked up at the now invisible branch. 'You two assholes are out of a job in the morning,' he muttered.

The ladder was yanked up.

'We heard that,' said Valeri.

The two bodyguards watched the beam of Zaharkin's torch as it played over the goat then moved towards the first of the light stands they had placed between the trees.

Konstantin shifted in his perch. 'Give me Mujahedeen *Dukhs* any time.'

'Do you think this cat will pounce on him?' said Valeri.

'Hope so,' said Konstantin. He mimicked Zaharkin's voice; 'you mean you pathetic weaklings are not going to go down there? Must I do it?'

Valeri sniggered then sniffed the night air.

'What is that smell? Konstantin, my friend, you need a bath.'

The darkness between the two men shifted.

Two golden cat's eyes appeared.

The panther growled.

And ivory yellow claws slashed.

Zaharkin flicked the spotlight's switch on and off. Nothing happened. He shone his torch at the lamp's element. 'Shit, not blown. Must be the cable between here and the generator.'

Konstantin shouted an incoherent alarm.

Valeri screamed. And was cut off abruptly.

Zaharkin dropped his torch in fright. 'Hell.'

A rifle shot slashed the night, its flash illuminating what? Zaharkin got the briefest impression of a man struggling with a shadow. Now Konstantin screamed. Zaharkin picked up the torch and ran.

'Hold on boys, I'm coming.' He blundered into the terrified goat, tumbled to the ground, staggered to his feet then stumbled hard against the tree's trunk.

There was silence but for a steady creaking, a noise Zaharkin half-recognised but could not identify.

Holding torch against rifle barrel, he shone its beam up at the branch he had been sitting on. It was empty.

Creak, creak. There was that noise again. His gaze swept across the undergrowth. Three–sixty degrees. Nothing.

Creak, creak.

Zaharkin took a step backwards and bumped into something. Gasping in terror, he whirled around.

Valeri hung upside down from his creaking harness, his throat ripped out.

Whumph. Something brushed his back.

Alongside Valeri was Konstantin. Again upside-down. Again dead. Bloody and dead.

'*Tchyort voz'mi!* Oh shit.'

Zaharkin did the only sensible thing anyone could do. He hurtled through the trees and towards the safety of home. As he sprinted faster than he had run in thirty years, he pulled a walkie-talkie from his belt.

'Release the dogs! Release them now!'

Panting, Zaharkin emerged from the wood. His bright-lit home was in sight. Only the lily-covered ornamental lake lay between him and safety.

Zaharkin slowed his pace as he watched his four Doberman Pinschers bound across the lawn on the far side of the water. Relief washed over him, he was nearly home. Fierce, loyal protection was at hand.

With what little breath remained, Zaharkin shouted to them, 'To me, boys, to me.'

To his delight, the dogs swerved towards him, skirting the pond as they ran. Their vocal chords severed when they were puppies, they made no noise save for the thump of their paws on the ground and the wheezing of their breath.

Thirty paces away, the panther prowled from the trees and met them head on. Zaharkin gasped, he had no idea it was so close to him. The fight was short, brutal, and silent. The big cat twisted sinuously between lunging jaws. Despite their size and lean aggression, the Dobermans were outmatched in speed, strength, and ferocity. In a blur of claws and fangs, the dogs were tossed aside.

Zaharkin watched the panther break the neck of the last living Doberman. The slaughter completed, the cat turned to stare at him then slipped back into the woods. Its intent was clear to the Russian. It was going to come at him out of the darkness. He looked right then left. In either direction it was at least a hundred paces before he could clear the pond's border and take a direct route to his mansion.

'No, either way is death,' he said.

A long-forgotten memory came to him. Something he'd done many times as a child to hide from friends. He waded into the water, his legs brushing the reeds that fringed the pond. Zaharkin grasped a stalk.

'Ha, yes, this will work.'

He broke off a length of the reed and blew through the hollow stem.

'Cats don't swim,' said Zaharkin with satisfaction.

Reed in mouth, he waded deeper into the pond and ducked beneath the surface. Only the top third of the reed was above water. His breath rasped in then out of the tip.

But although he might be wily in the ways of hunting in Russia's *taiga* forests, and certainly knowledgeable about the bathing preferences of domestic cats, like Jervis, Zaharkin was sadly mistaken about panthers.

A black shadow slid into the water. Head held clear, ears erect, the big cat glided towards the reed bed.

Zaharkin breathed. In. Out.

The panther's snout, eyes, and ears glistened in the bright, distant lights.

In. Out.

The cat's head dipped below the surface.

In. Out.

Then...

Silence.

Blood spurted from the reed tip, a great cherry red fountain. The stalk was yanked down and the water churned turbulent red then subsided into stillness.

In the distance, the goat bleated again.

- 13 -

- Night -

- Outside Swanmere Mall -

COULSTON'S CAR, A BMW SERIES 5, SAT IN THE MIDDLE
of the vast deserted parking lot. Whilst he took another
call on his mobile phone, Rosie leant against the car's
bonnet to examine the blisters on her feet. The Olembes
rested upright in stoic silence, supported by the shafts of
their cloth-wrapped spears. After their experience with the
Dawes, Coulston insisted everyone make an effort to
camouflage their weapons.

'I have never felt so tired.' said Rosie.

Coulston snicked shut the mobile phone.

'Turns out Mr. Oakshott has surfaced,' he said. 'He just
called Mid-Surrey Police and, surprise, surprise, he's holed
up here.' He nodded at the gleaming white ramparts of
Swanmere's walls. 'The idiot only just let them know; he
discharged himself from hospital hours ago. Apparently he
arrived about three o'clock, kicked out the shoppers,
locked down the mall, and called in extra security.'

Rosie switched her foot examination from left to right
and began to unlace the boot. 'Let me guess. You're going
in there to talk to him.'

'I am. You coming? Wouldn't you like to meet the man who started all this?'

'You promised me a lift home.'

'Offer remains, only—'

'After you've comforted that blood-sucking—'

'Member of the public who happened to be attacked by a black panther only this morning.' Coulston said. They both grinned at yet another echo of the Johnno-Naomi double act. Once started it was very hard to stop. 'You can wait here if you prefer,' he added. 'The cat appears to like hanging around you.'

Rosie grimaced as she pulled off her sock and saw the size of the blister on her heel. Wincing at the pain, she pushed herself away from the car, placed her full weight on both bare feet, then straightened her stiff back. She gazed across the deserted car park and to the dark woods beyond. Despite the relatively early hour, what few vehicles remained sat like far-flung islands in a sea of black tarmac. She shivered. It reminded her of the car park at Whitecombe Station.

She had called home, an hour ago. Her mother, supremely unimpressed by Rosie's boar killing exploits, made her daughter promise not to go anywhere else outdoors tonight. In contrast, Lizzie asked if Rosie would teach her how to kill pigs too. Peter wanted to know if boar blood was the same colour as his and, when told it was, lost all interest. Where was the excitement in that? Slaying wild beasts became merely another of the things his Mum did. And whatever Mums do is, as all children know instinctively, not very interesting.

'Well? You're welcome to sit it out in the car if you're not coming,' said Coulston.

'No thanks. I think I'll tag along, just out of curiosity,' she said.

'Henry, Faith, you coming with us?'

'Of course, friend Robert.'

Coulston opened the boot of his car and retrieved a box of rifle ammunition.

'Hmm, not much left, there're only four cartridges in here.' With those few rounds stored safely in a jacket pocket, he locked the BMW.

A distant car horn sounded and they were illuminated by headlights as, one behind the other, two vehicles swept into the parking lot. Accelerating fast, they drove straight towards the four trackers, the roar of their engines disrupting the stillness of the night. Dazzled by the headlight's glare, Rosie could not make out who or what these newcomers were. It was only when they pulled up alongside that she could recognise them as a police 4x4 followed by an Army Landrover. Then she saw a familiar face and stepped behind the Olembes. With luck, she'll never notice me, thought Rosie.

Suze Derrington wound down the driver's side window of the lead vehicle. 'Sir, it's all kicked off over at Zaharkin's estate.'

'What's happened?'

'Reports of shots and screams. The call came from one of the staff but there's no sign of Zaharkin, they wasted at least an hour looking for him, before they called it in. Idiots. Apparently, he and his bodyguards went hunting the big cat. Sniper Team One's already there. Team Two's with me.' She pointed at the Landrover. 'And we've been detailed to join the search. We were just passing here when I got the call. I thought I'd better give you a head's up.'

Coulston's phone rang. 'Thanks,' he said to Derrington then answered it. 'Yes, sir, I've just heard—' He walked out of earshot.

The detective sergeant placed Rosie under her fierce scrutiny. 'I can see you, dog warden,' she said. 'There's no point hiding.'

Rosie felt like she had reverted to the age of six and was being scolded by a strict headmistress.

'Our friend has shown great ability,' said Henry.

Oh, God, no, thought Rosie. You're a kind man, but please don't make this worse.

'Oh, yeah?'

'Yes, she has faced the *kyaani* twice and has not flinched.'

Derrington's glare switched from Rosie to Henry. 'This keyanny, is it the panther?'

'It is,' said Henry.

Those dreadful eyes returned to Rosie's face. 'So you saw it twice but did not kill it once? Brilliant.'

Faith intervened. 'But she has also killed a great boar of the forest.'

'A wild pig? Oh, it gets better and better. Just wait 'til I tell Steve about this.'

Mercifully, in the darkness no one could see Rosie's face flush red with embarrassment.

Phone call finished, Coulston strode back. 'Sergeant, you'd better get going. Assistant Chief Franklin will call ahead to the security people here; get them to open up for me. And I've asked for backup. We need to give this Oakshott man more protection.'

'Sir, are these people strictly necessary?' Derrington jerked her head at the Olembes and Rosie. Her tone of voice made clear her disapproval. 'I mean, we've got all the manpower we need.'

Coulston turned to smile at his three friends. 'Oh, you'll be amazed at what they can do,' he said.

'I'd be amazed if that were true,' said Derrington than, as an insolent afterthought, added, 'Sir.'

Before Coulston could answer, she revved the engine, released the hand brake, and wrenched the police vehicle into a sharp U-turn. With a double-toot of their horn, the Army snipers followed.

'Right, let's get this over with,' said Coulston.

They walked towards the distant loading bays at the rear of the mall.

After a minute, Coulston spoke again. 'She really doesn't like you,' he said.

Rosie ignored him. She looked to her right and towards the black outline of the hills.

'It seems so unreal,' she said.

'What does, sister Rosie?' said Faith.

'All this: wild boars, black panthers in rural Surrey; you casting spells; Henry casting spears. Me. With a spear. Unreal. I mean why here? Why now? Why Swanmere?'

'The *kyaani*—' began Henry.

'I know, I know, here for vengeance. And that stupid Oakshott man wounded it. And big cats are big on revenge. It might make sense to you lot, but not to me.'

With a sweep of his arm, Coulston encompassed the wide expanse of empty car park. 'Even here, when the cars go and the people go, the animals take over the emptiness. It's like your wild boar. Thy escaped and discovered the unoccupied spaces: the places we've abandoned. And so did the panther; the pumas; the jungle cat, all of them.'

His words reminded Rosie of the wondrous red swirl of the parakeets in the sky.

'We've become urban creatures,' Coulston added. 'Most of us experience the world about us through tinted car windows. All those people like the Dawes, there's so many of them. They say they live in the countryside but they don't, not really, all they do is drive through it. Hardly anyone goes into the wild. It's on their doorstep; they just don't encounter it. But nature's a powerful force, always full of surprises. And, well, if a wild animal's injured it still needs to eat, it needs easy prey.'

'My missing dogs and cats.' The idea no longer shocked her.

'Then we notice a predator's there, then it enters our world, but not on our terms. And now it's too late. This big cat won't go back to the hidden places. I wish it wasn't so, but we have to kill it. And soon.' He kicked at a pebble. It skittered away into the darkness.

They arrived at the first of the goods bays. A wide steel shutter sealed the entrance to its loading dock.

'So how do we get in?' said Rosie.

'Won't take long.' Coulston inspected the mall's high wall. 'Ah, okay, there's one.' He waved at a bracket-mounted camera. 'By now, they'll know we're coming. Someone will be here soon.'

'At least the panther can't get in this place, not with all these cameras and lights.'

'Christ, lights and cameras won't stop it, Rosie,' said Coulston as he continued his examination of the enormous building, 'but these walls might.'

'There are many dark places for it to hide, to watch, to move; more than we can ever imagine, or see,' said Faith. 'Look for the *kyaani* in the shadows between.'

Rosie and Coulston stared at her. One was a sceptic, the other agnostic, but both were chilled by her words.

'Full of grim thoughts, aren't you? And I thought you were the cheerful one around here,' said Rosie.

The bay's steel shutter began to clank up. Surprised by the sudden noise, the startled hunters jumped with fright then laughed at their reaction. Bright light spilled across the forecourt and, as the opening grew, they could see the backlit movement of legs and feet inside. When the shutter screeched past waist height, one of the figures bent at the knees, head ducked low. A security guard, a man in his forties, stocky and uniformed, grinned at them.

'Inspector Coulston? Baz Bishop, Head of Security,' he said. They shook hands. 'Am I glad to see you, mate. The boss, Mr. Oakshott, has gone all... well, let's just say his internal satnav needs a re-boot. Come on in.'

Four guards accompanied Bishop, all armed with shotguns. They eyed Coulston's rifle with suspicion, and he reciprocated the feeling. After his encounter with the bounty hunters, he did not like the idea of gun-toting civilians, leastways ones he did not know.

'I hope you fellers have been trained how to use those things,' he said.

'We're all ex-Army if that's what you mean,' said Bishop. He took in Rosie and the Olembes. And their cloth-wrapped spears. 'You lot some kind of police undercover squad?'

'I'm a dog warden,' said Rosie.

Bishop stared at her grimy, bloodstained clothing, wild hair, and the inexpertly concealed long spear.

'Riiight. Well, the boss wants to meet you anyhow,' he said to Coulston 'He's in Security Control.'

Bishop inserted a key into a wall-mounted steel box beside the door and turned it. With a shriek of sliding metal, the shutter began its slow journey back down.

They climbed the steps that led up from the pit of the dock. Once in the main body of the mall's warehouse, Rosie gawked at the scale of it. Each loading bay was partitioned from the others by a concrete wall, but they all opened into one vast stockroom. Many hundreds of yards long, the warehouse ran the length of the building. It was crammed high to the ceiling with shelving containing the mall's merchandise. Even though Swanmere was closed, there was the constant hum and whirr of machinery. Its architects had installed a computer-controlled, robot-driven goods system that unified freight delivery for the myriad of stores in the mall, ensuring swift and efficient restocking.

'Step back, people,' said Bishop.

Beeping loudly, a driverless forklift truck rounded one of the wide aisles between the shelves. It towed four cartloads of boxes. Reading the information printed on them, Rosie could make out they contained assorted footwear, the property of a national chain of shoe shops.

Behind their backs, the black panther stole beneath the still-closing shutter and slunk unnoticed into the pit's darkest corner.

The forklift with its little train of goods pushed through the wide, opaque plastic sheets stretched across one of the exits.

'Follow me. The Security Office is this way.' Bishop led them through the maze of crates and shelving.

Clunk. The winding motor cut out. The shutter was down. And the mall was, once again, sealed from the outside world.

At the control desk of the security control room sat the sole surviving Swanmere partner. Only he didn't know he was the last, not yet. Underneath a brown leather jacket, Oakshott still wore the loose hospital pyjamas he'd been issued before fleeing Accident and Emergency. Stitched up, pumped full of broad-range antibiotics and painkillers, he felt little physical discomfort despite the bandages on his arms, chest, and right leg, but blood seeped through those dressings that were visible.

One wall of the windowless room held banks of CCTV monitors in a layout similar to, but much more extensive than, the installation at Zaharkin's mansion.

'Inspector Coulston, sir,' said Bishop.

Oakshott kept his full concentration on the screens, his eyes in constant motion, searching for danger. One hand rested on the camera joystick, jerking it again and again as he changed the camera image displayed on the large central monitor. He switched camera every second, so fast that Rosie could not bear to watch. The stroboscopic effect made her feel ill.

'It's here, I'm sure of it,' said Oakshott.

'Have you seen it?' said Coulston.

'What?' Oakshott temporarily scrutinised the gaunt policeman then, just as swiftly, his eyes returned to the TV monitors. 'You're that man, the Surrey Panther man, the one who said it was out there all those years. They should have listened to you.'

'Have you seen it? Is the panther here?' said Coulston, alarmed by Oakshott's behaviour. There was now a hard, urgent edge to his voice.

Henry began unwrapping the spears.

'No one believed me either,' said Oakshott. 'I shot it, but no one believed me.'

'Sir, have you actually seen the big cat in the mall? On the cameras?' Coulston said, his jaws muscles locked tight with annoyance.

'What? No, of course not, not yet. But it could have got in. It must be here. It follows me everywhere I go. If we keep looking, we'll see it.'

Out of Oakshott's eye-line, Bishop shook his head in silent despair at his boss' erratic behaviour. 'We've been locked down since mid-afternoon,' he said to Coulston. 'Guards on every exit beforehand, the loading bays, everywhere. No-one's seen a thing.'

'But it is here, I know it,' said Oakshott. Everyone in the room understood that this was a man teetering on the edge of sanity, and everyone sympathised. His pain, trauma, and stress were visible to all.

'Me and my boys'll go do another sweep, sir,' said Bishop, desperate to escape the tense, fevered atmosphere. 'You'll be safe with Inspector Coulston and his, er, team.'

Oakshott's gaze never left the wall of screens. 'Right, thank you, Bishop.'

'And more armed police will soon be here.'

'Thank you, Bishop.'

The security chief left the room.

'No one believed me,' said Oakshott once more.

Coulston pulled a chair alongside the property developer. 'I was there, four months ago,' he said as he sat down. 'The day you shot at the panther. I heard you fire your rifle.'

That got Oakshott's attention. He finally made eye contact. 'You were in Zaharkin's woods? What were you doing there?'

'Tracking the cat. You know you wounded it? Right rear leg.'

'I did? Is that why it did this to me?' Oakshott touched his own bloodied right leg and gasped with the pain. The agony bent him double. The medication was wearing off.

When he looked up, he noticed Coulston's companions. 'Who are you?'

Coulston leant back in the chair. 'Rosie has faced the panther twice, just like you. Face-to-face. And Henry has tracked and killed many leopards.'

'How many?' Oakshott said eagerly.

'My brother has been hunting them since he was child. He saved many lives,' said Faith. There was fierce pride in her voice.

'Is it... is it going to kill me?' Oakshott said to the Olembes.

Unhappy that his attempt to calm the man had become diverted so quickly, and dreading what Henry would say, Coulston cut in hard. 'I've ordered protection for yourself and Mr. Zaharkin, who is apparently missing.' He glanced at the red numerals of a digital clock set high above the monitors. 'They should be here in the next twenty minutes. You really should have told us much earlier exactly where—'

But Oakshott was relentless. 'Why does it want to kill me? I mean, how does it know? And why did it attack Jervis and Beacon? How did it find them?'

Coulston's phone rang. He flipped it open. 'Excuse me,' he said as he walked to the far corner of the room.

'It does not seek revenge for your bullet,' said Faith.

'You awoke the sleeping hills, you filled the silver lake, burned the woods,' Henry said. 'It is a matter of vengeance.'

Oakshott shook his head.

'It's just a bloody big cat,' he said.

'That's what I used to say,' said Rosie, 'but the more I learn, the less sure I am.'

'You're no hunter, not like these three.' Oakshott's old arrogance had resurfaced. 'And the policeman said you've faced the cat twice?' There was incredulity in his voice. 'Who are you exactly?'

Rosie bristled at his words; she most definitely was a hunter. 'I'm Rosie Flinn, County Dog Warden.'

'What? But—' Oakshott got no further. Coulston stood over him, his face grim.

'I'm afraid Alexei Zaharkin's dead,' he said. 'Killed by the panther. Along with his two bodyguards.' His words came out in a brutal rush and he regretted it immediately. 'I'm sorry,' he said, his voice trailing away.

Oakshott slumped in his seat. His hand resumed its manic flicking through the security camera feeds.

'Don't be, he was a bastard,' he said. 'An absolute bastard.' He looked up at Coulston. 'And now there's only me left from that day. Only me.'

'ETA for the armed backup is confirmed as twenty minutes, sir. It won't be long.' Coulston said. He placed his hand over Oakshott's and stilled the wrenching of the joystick. 'And there's one good thing, if you can call it good, that is.'

'What's that?' Oakshott said.

'We estimate Mister Zaharkin was killed approximately three hours ago. Long after dark, and long after Mister Bishop secured the mall. There's no way it can be here.'

Behind Oakshott's back, Henry opened his mouth to speak. Coulston caught his eye and made an almost imperceptible shake of his head. Oh shit, thought Rosie, they think it could have moved fast enough to get here. To be here already.

'Just relax, sir,' said Coulston. 'Like I said, there's no way it's inside the mall.'

No energy-saving measures were taken that night. Shop fronts might be darkened or shuttered, but every walkway, every atrium, and all the food courts were bright-lit.

Baz Bishop and his four men: Wicksy, Robbo, Terry and Tam, patrolled the upmarket mezzanine level, past jewellers, designer shoe shops, and fashion outlets. The mall was silent save for the squeak of their boots on the polished marble and the distant gushing of the fountain in the central concourse.

'This is bloody stupid,' Robbo said. 'What good's a double-barrelled shotgun going to be against a man-eater?

You see the size of the gun that copper was carrying? I reckon it's the kind of firepower we need.'

'Didn't see you objecting when the boss offered us a week's wage for a night's work,' Bishop said.

'Two barrels mightn't do the trick, but our ten together will,' said Terry.

'Amen to that,' said Bishop. 'Tam, Terry, Wicksy: you check the galleria opposite. Me and Robbo will take this 'un. Then all of us'll do a sweep of the ground—'

A shotgun boomed. Baz spun around and saw the nearest shop's plate glass window disintegrate in the blast. A burglar alarm wailed.

Robbo stood, feet apart, smoking shotgun levelled.

'I saw it, Baz. In the window,' he said. 'I saw it.'

Bishop clicked off his safety catch.

'Cover me, boys,' he said.

All former infantrymen, they fanned out in the approved fashion. Bishop approached the window.

'I hit it, Baz. I'm sure of it,' Robbo said urgently.

Bishop kicked away the upright shards of plate glass that remained. He stepped cautiously inside, boots crunching on clothing coated in fractured glass.

'I saw it; saw the spots,' said Robbo.

'Spots?' said Terry. Puzzled, he looked sidelong at his mate.

'Robbo?' Bishop's calm voice came from the darkness of the shop's interior.

'Boss?'

Baz poked his head out from between the shredded gauze curtains of the display. 'You want to remind us what a panther looks like?'

'Well...' Robbo was never comfortable being the centre of attention.

'Take your time.'

'It's big,' he ventured. 'Bigger than a pet cat.'

'Good. Keep going,' Bishop said.

'Er, and this one was yellow, with black spots. What? What did I say?'

The other guards gave him looks. Old-fashioned looks.

Robbo's shotgun blast had strewn display mannequins across the floor. With his gun barrel, Baz lifted the tattered remnants of a leopard-skin patterned coat from the wreckage.

'Repeat after me, you moron; a panther is black, it has not got any spots,' he said as he pulled a walkie-talkie from his belt. 'And will someone please switch off that bloody alarm?'

'Roger that, better a false alarm than the real thing. Out.' Coulston replaced the handset and turned from the control panel.

'Well, as you heard, it was a false alarm. Seems one of the guards decided to take a stand against the fur trade.' He faced Oakshott. 'Sir, I'm going to find out where those marksmen have got to and I need to let them know where to rendezvous? Is Goods Bay No.1 a suitable place, it's where we came in?' Coulston wanted to get him thinking positively. The wounded man's face had turned pale when they heard the distant, but unmistakeable reverberating boom of the shotgun. He nodded. Coulston made the call, leaving Oakshott to resume his crash course in West African mythology.

'So, if, as you say, I, with my partners, awoke a forest spirit, how can I appease it?' he said.

'Oh, please,' said Rosie.

'Hold on a moment,' Oakshott said to her. 'You're the one who said it's more than just a big cat, I heard you.'

Rosie did not answer. She no longer knew what to make of it all. It seemed a foolish idea to be certain about anything.

Oakshott swivelled back to face the Olembes. 'And how come, if it is so implacable, you're hunting it? I mean, what are you doing here, if all this death is so inevitable?'

Wow, a good question, thought Rosie. He might be a dumbass, but he's a smart dumbass. Wish I'd come up with that.

'It cares not for people,' Henry said. 'We do what we can for the innocent.'

'So I don't stand a chance?'

There was no reply.

Terry, Wicksy, and Tam as they emerged from a dark side gallery. They were illuminated by light reflected from the polished white marble tiles of the main gallery. The trio walked onto the cross-bridge that formed the mezzanine's central area and approached the escalators linking their level to the ground floor.

'Baz, we're done. All clear,' Tam shouted.

'Don't think he's listening, mate,' said Terry.

Thirty–odd paces away, Baz gesticulated furiously at the forlorn Robbo. The three men stopped to watch.

'You got to feel for him,' said Wicksy. 'We're all so jumpy it could've been any one of us.'

'You reckon?' Tam said.

'Nah, it had to be Robbo, but—'

One of the three 'up' escalators behind them whirred into life.

'Christ!'

The three guards all started with fright.

'See? Jumpy,' Wicksy said.

'God, it nearly made me heart stop,' said Tam. 'Thought I'd wet meself.'

Terry frowned. 'Weird though. They don't activate unless someone steps onto them.' He walked across to the top of the escalator to look down its length.

'Bloody hell,' he said.

The panther was crouched on the metal treads.

It glared up at him. And sprang at his throat.

In the security control room, the first they heard were more distant shotgun blasts. Then the screaming began.

'Look!' yelled Rosie. On the black and white monitor screen, the panther coiled, leapt, twisted, in a killing frenzy.

'Oh for—' Coulston was still on the phone to Franklin. 'It's here, sir, inside Swanmere. We need those lads right now, and we need ambulances.'

'It's coming for me, oh God, it's coming for me,' Oakshott curled into a foetal ball, his stare fixed on the gruesome one-sided slaughter as it played out on the monitor before him.

Bishop was the last man standing. He tried to club the big cat with his shotgun, but could not withstand the ferocious efficiency of the attack. He died with the panther's jaws clamped to his broken neck. But the big cat did not stay to feast. No sooner was Bishop dead than, in one leap, it disappeared from the camera's field of view.

Oakshott uncurled. He punched up camera after camera. 'Where is it? It's vanished.' They all scanned the wall of monitors. The big cat was gone. 'What shall I do?'

'Bob, we have to help them,' Rosie said.

'It's too late for those poor sods.'

'It'll come here. After me.' Oakshott began to sob.

'Maybe we should barricade the door?' said Rosie.

Coulston made a quick survey of the room. 'As long as a panther can't turn door knobs I think we're safe in here. We just need to sit tight and wait for reinforcements.'

'Brother Robert, the cat is between us and your policemen,' Henry said.

'Damn, you're right. We're stuck inside and they're going to be stuck outside.' He crouched beside Oakshott. 'How do we open the doors, sir?'

'The loading bays?'

'Any door that will let the marksmen in and us out.'

Oakshott pointed at the CCTV monitors. 'Bishop has the... had the keys.'

'Can't you open any from here?' said Rosie.

'No, only at the doors themselves. It's policy.' He looked eagerly at the four of them. 'Listen, you're the trackers, the experts; suppose I double the bounty, make it a full million, will you go out there and kill it?'

'I'm a policeman, I, I can't—' said Coulston.

'I can write a cheque. Right now.'

He pulled a chequebook from his jacket pocket. As he wrote, he smudged blood on the paper. Coulston placed his hand on Oakshott's arm, and stopped him from writing further.

'Double it again,' he said. 'You can afford it.'

'Two million? I don't think—'

'Exactly how much is your life worth, Mr. Oakshott?'

Oakshott amended the amount and signed the cheque.

'Are you crazy?' said Rosie to him. 'I don't want any part of this.'

He looked at Rosie. 'You could do with the money, right? You can't be making much as a dog warden, not judging by the state of your car.' He glanced towards Faith and Henry. 'All of you. Am I right?'

As the others hesitated, Coulston stepped in. 'Listen, the important thing is to get a door, any door, open. We have to get those keys. Mr. Oakshott can stay here where he'll be safe.' He frowned at the wounded man. 'You're not going to leave are you?'

'Absolutely not.'

The policeman picked up the cheque and read it. 'Like I said, I can't take any money. Clearing up this fiasco is all part of my job, but it's not theirs.' He returned it to Oakshott. 'If we kill the panther, they can share your cash. Agreed?'

Coulston plucked the bunch of keys from Bishop's belt.

'Covered in blood,' he said. 'Story of my week.'

Rosie, Faith, and Henry guarded the approaches to the site of the killing.

'I feel awfully exposed,' Rosie said. 'It may not look very far to those main doors but I'd rather walk over a bed of hot coals.'

'You're right. We could do with some protection.' Coulston studied the various shop fronts, then slung his rifle, picked up Baz's shotgun, checked its load, walked to the windows of a sporting goods store, and hammered the shotgun butt against the glass.

'Bob! What the hell are you doing?' shouted Rosie.

Coulston cracked the glass and smashed his way in. The alarm sounded loud and strident until he blasted it with the shotgun.

'You wanted protection?' he shouted at them. 'Well, it's in here.'

- 14 -

- Night -

- Sporting goods store -

THE ACTIVATION OF THE BURGLAR ALARM TRIGGERED spotlights set high in each corner of the hanger-like sporting goods superstore. They cast brilliant white light across the interior. The four trackers split up to investigate. Rosie hefted a hockey stick, compared it to her spear then tossed the stick aside.

'What are we looking for?' she said.

Coulston's reply came from the rear of the shop, 'Over here.'

The back wall was devoted to American football gear: helmets, shoulder pads, and shirts. Coulston unhooked a NFL helmet from a rack and gave it to Rosie. 'Jacksonville Jaguars for you,' he said. 'I'm saving the Carolina Panthers for myself.'

Rosie inspected the jaguar decal on her helmet.

'Bob, earlier, back when the Dawes kicked us out of their Range Rover, you said you thought the big cat is a jaguar, not a leopard.'

'I did.' Coulston was clearly reluctant to go further.

He's hiding something from us, thought Rosie.

'And does it matter? Aren't they the same thing? Just as bad?' she said.

'Oh, it matters.' Coulston took his time. Rosie, Henry, and Faith stood still, waiting for his answer. He strapped on the Panthers helmet before he spoke again, 'A jaguar is to a leopard what a homicidal maniac is to a street mugger. It's in an altogether different league. You saw it today. It's bigger, stronger, meaner.'

Rosie looked again at the decal. It no longer seemed such a good joke.

'Finally, I understand why this *kyaani* is so big,' said Henry. 'I have never seen a jaguar before.'

'They have the most powerful bite of all the big cats,' said Coulston. 'In the wild, they crack open turtle shells and hunt caiman alligators.' He hesitated then said, 'Um, when Dawlish Beacon was killed, his skull was cracked open. In one bite.' He rapped his helmet. 'Leopards don't do that.'

'That's horrible,' said Rosie, her face ashen.

Coulston equipped Henry with Detroit Lions headgear and Faith with a Cincinnati Bengals helmet. 'Remember, big cats often go for the throat and neck, so keep your chin down and watch each other's back.'

In an adjacent section of rugby clothing, Coulston found a rack of chest impact protectors. 'Ah, okay, there's some more useful kit over here.' He tossed the padded undershirts to the others. 'This isn't exactly Kevlar, but it'll help.'

Rosie tried to pull it on, but the ultra-snug design was not meant to be worn by females. 'Haven't they got any women's sizes?' She rootled through the shelves. Hmm, all of a sudden I can see the attraction of looting, she thought, and immediately felt guilty. 'Shouldn't we pay for all this?'

The Olembes nodded their silent agreement.

'Look, don't worry, nobody's going to complain about us protecting ourselves,' said Coulston. 'I'll get it all sorted out tomorrow. I'm a policeman, remember?'

Rosie dug out an undershirt that fitted, but it was far from comfortable across the chest and she fought for breath as she struggled into it. 'Why...' she said between pants, 'do... we... need this... padding?'

Coulston put on some plates of American football armour. He pulled tight the straps of an over-sized shoulder protector. 'Er, for when it knocks you on your back and tries to disembowel you with its rear claws.'

'Charming.'

'Let's hope it won't come to that. If I can get just one clear shot from my rifle—'

'Yeah, just like earlier,' said Rosie.

Faith interrupted their squabble.

'Robert!' she said in an urgent whisper. 'Brother Robert!'

The panther stood outside the smashed window.

It growled its deep bass rumble. It was a sound Rosie now knew meant certain trouble. Hisses meant 'keep away'; a growl meant you were in for a fight. The man-eater padded inside. Pieces of broken glass cracked under its weight, but failed to cut the thick soles of its paws.

Coulston reacted quickly; he raised his rifle and took a snapshot. The panther's reactions were faster. It streaked forward and the shot flew high over its head. Then the big cat was on him, rearing up to rake with its fore claws. He clubbed at it with his rifle and had as little success as Baz Bishop. The gun was swatted aside. They crashed backwards into a rack of clothes. Coulston's hands were clamped around the cat's neck as he fought to keep its jaws from his throat.

Rosie gripped her spear's thick shaft and charged.

The big cat saw her coming. It dodged the spear tip and disappeared between the disordered racks of football shirts.

'Where is it? I can't see it,' she said.

Coulston was unconscious, having lost his helmet in the struggle and then hitting his head on the steel leg of the clothes rack. One cheek was gashed bloody and raw, and the panther's claws had ripped away the shoulder guards, scoring deep wounds in his chest.

'We need to get him somewhere safe,' Rosie said.

With Faith standing guard, they dragged Coulston behind a counter displaying golfing accessories. They stayed low, cramming themselves into the narrow space between the display and a pillar. There was barely room for them all. Rosie had to squat awkwardly to avoid kneeling on Coulston. Faith cradled his head in her lap as she tried to staunch the wounds.

Henry raised his head to search for the panther.

'It must be near to us, but where?' he said.

He had to shade his eyes with a hand to cut out the harsh glare of the emergency lights. The shadows they cast were as dark as the panther's coat. He could see no sign of it.

But two unblinking amber eyes watched the humans jam themselves into the tiny space.

Rosie stuck up her head, 'It has to be out there.' Treading on her spear's shaft, she nearly lost her balance. 'Oh damn, sorry, got to get this blasted thing sorted out.' Their three spears were so entangled it felt a little like being caught up in a life-size game of *Kerplunk*.

The panther gathered itself.

It leapt.

Oblivious to the attack, Rosie was bent over, her back to the cat. 'If I just do this,' she said, turning as she tugged her spear's tip from the shelf it was stuck into. It jerked up, over the lip of the counter.

The spearhead took the still-airborne cat in the throat. Rosie sobbed with fear, but kept a tight hold on the shaft. Under the weight of the pinioned big cat, she slipped and fell backwards until she was lying on top of Coulston. The panther's rear claws scrabbled for purchases on the glass counter top, but the spear's crossbars held it firm. The Olembes were huddled beneath the cat's exposed underbelly and they stabbed upwards with their short spears. Stabbed again. And again. Blood gushed from its wounds in hot, salty spurts. Then the panther went limp. With an almighty shove, Rosie levered the carcass over the countertop. It thudded to the floor.

Her legs trembling with shock, Rosie stood, leant on the blood-smeared glass counter, and drew breath.

'Oh, that was horrible, just horrible,' she said.

Henry and Faith helped each other to their feet. Like Rosie, they were spattered head to toe in blood.

Faith embraced her.

'Rosie, you have saved us,' she said.

'But it was a fluke. I just—'

'You are a fine hunter,' said Henry.

Embarrassed by the praise, Rosie leant over the counter to look at the dead panther.

'That's strange,' she said. 'It looks so much smaller now it's dead.' Under the bleak lighting, the dead predator's fur, now matted with blood, had lost its lustre. It seemed impossible that this could have been the large, ferocious creature that attacked them. Her forearms slipped on the bloody surface. 'Oh, yeuch!'

She looked beneath the countertop for tissues but found none.

Still unconscious, Coulston groaned. Rosie scrambled over to him. Searched his pockets. Pulled out the key ring.

'Henry, can you give that Oakshott man these keys, they're for the door we came in? Tell him the big cat is dead but we need an ambulance for Bob.'

'Of course. I will be fast, for brother Robert's sake.'

A thought occurred to Rosie and she called after him. 'And don't forget to get our cheque before the scumbag changes his mind.'

A cluster of police vehicles was drawn up at the rear of Swanmere Mall. Their flashing blue lights reflected off the building's white wall like the flicker from a giant TV screen. Whilst a vanload of police marksmen prepped their weapons, Assistant Chief Constable Franklin talked over his radio to his boss.

'Roger that, sir, I've just spoken to Mr. Oakshott, the surviving partner. He's on his way down to let us in. I'll keep you informed. Out.' He watched a council dog van pull up.

Don got out and walked over to Franklin.

'Don Burgess, Chief Dog Warden,' he said as they shook hands. 'I've got those nets you requested.'

'I'm afraid it's going to have been a wasted trip. Sorry to have dragged you over here unnecessarily.'

'Wasted?' Whoopee, thought Don, no paperwork, no inter-departmental dispute over who pays for the gear, it's a win-win, but he kept his face straight and said, 'How come? Have you caught it?'

'It seems the panther got inside the mall, killed five guards but was itself killed by a team of hunters including one of your people.'

'One of my people? You don't mean Rosie Flinn?' Damn, there was going to be a shit-load of paperwork for this.

Oakshott limped along an aisle between high-stacked shelves of merchandise. The bleak warehouse was illuminated sparsely; the computer-controlled robots didn't need much light to work. He smiled as he jangled the keys, then stopped, looked behind and saw... what?

Nothing moved, but he was certain something was there.

He waited a handful of seconds but all he heard was the clatter and whine of a pilotless forklift as it sped along a parallel aisle. Oakshott knew he was safe, knew the big cat was dead, and yet something familiar niggled at the edge of his senses, something that signalled danger. Head erect, he sniffed the air, unwittingly imitating the deer shot by Zaharkin so many months ago. He didn't know what was wrong, but it scared him.

Thoroughly spooked, Oakshott resumed his trek to the

loading bay but, fighting the pain, he walked faster.

And he no longer played with the keys.

Or smiled.

Henry returned to the sports shop to find Coulston sitting upright, a towel held to his cheek. Rosie had found a first aid kit in the shop's staff room and Faith used its bandages to bind dressings against Coulston's ripped chest. Grinning as he entered, Henry held aloft Oakshott's cheque then saw the grim faces of his friends and faltered.

'What is wrong? Brother Robert, are your injuries serious?'

'No, no, nothing like that. I've got one hell of a headache and I'll need a lot of stitches but I can walk, after a fashion.' Coulston waved him closer, pointing at the dead panther. 'Henry, what do you make of this? What did we miss?'

The Ghanaian knelt beside the dead big cat.

He carefully examined the carcass and it did not take long for his breath to catch in surprise. 'But this is not the panther we hunted, the one from the woods today. This is too small and see here...' He ran his hand through the fur of the black panther's right-side haunch. 'It is not wounded.' He looked in wonder at Coulston. 'It was never wounded.'

Coulston glanced up at Faith and Rosie. 'See? I said Henry would agree with me. It's the wrong panther.'

Rosie felt crushed and confused. After the elation of their escape, it seemed cruel that such a simple and complete end to the affair could become so complicated.

'So,' she said, 'let me get this straight. If I killed the wrong panther then where's the right one? How can there be two?'

'There must be an adult pair. This is a female. The one that chased us today, that was much bigger; a male,' Coulston said.

Rosie looked at the dead cat. It did seem small-ish. She just wished it were bigger. And alone.

'Two of them,' she said with a sigh as she cast around for her spear, found it, picked it up. 'I guess I'm going to need this again.'

'The *kyaani* lives,' Faith said to her brother.

'It hunts,' he agreed.

A terrible thought occurred to Rosie. 'Oakshott's in the warehouse,' she said, 'and on his own. What if the other cat's here? You thought it could have caught up with us, I could tell you did. Come on, we've got to find him.'

'Help me up,' said Coulston.

It took all three of them to get him to his feet.

'Bob, it might be best for you to wait here.'

'God no, we should stick together.' He gasped in pain as Faith helped pull his jacket on over his bare chest. 'You'd better go check the coast is clear. Just give me a sec, I need to alert our backup.' Wincing with the effort, he pulled his phone from his trouser pocket. 'Could someone find my rifle?'

The call to Franklin was brief, curt, and disbelieving, but Coulston did not care what a senior officer thought of him, he was used to it. 'Just assume there's always been two of them and act accordingly,' he said then disconnected the call.

The others had exited the store. He stood still, waiting for the pain to ease, steeling himself for the effort he knew he had to make. He gazed at the dead panther, admiring the heft of its long, smooth musculature. He'd been right about one thing, this was certainly no leopard; it was a melanistic jaguar. He examined the wounds, the stabs to its belly, as he tried to visualise its last moments.

'Bob, come on!' shouted Rosie from outside. 'All's clear.'

But Coulston saw something new. Gasping in pain, he knelt beside the body.

'Oh, dear God, it can't be true,' he said.

Oakshott stopped again. He was halfway to the loading bay door, halfway to safety. He knew he should keep moving, but fear triggers strange impulses: instincts reaching back to humanity's caveman roots, perhaps even further. Oakshott did not choose it, if his injuries could have let him run, he would have, but something deep inside made him first turn to look for a threat. Better to know what it is and how far away, said his inner caveman.

He stood in the middle one of the wide roadways that divided the high shelving into terrace street-sized blocks; his feet were on the metal control strip placed there to guide the robots. Panting to get air to his anxiety-stressed body, Oakshott looked right and left, ahead and behind, but saw nothing to alarm him. The only movement came from another distant forklift stacking pallets on carts.

But there's still one place left to check, his instinct warned. He looked up and saw it: the shadow of a panther cast high onto the far wall as it leapt from aisle to aisle, swiftly closing the gap between them. Run, his inner caveman warned, it has the high ground; it has the advantage over you. Even at this distance, Oakshott could see the big cat's stare: intent, focused solely on him. It leapt another aisle. Run, run, run, said his primeval self.

Wounds forgotten, fuelled by adrenaline, Oakshott ran for his life.

- 15 -

- Night -

- The Rear of Swanmere Mall -

'Get a move on!' Franklin bellowed.

A police van reversed at high speed into the steel shutter. It hit with a clang that echoed across the vastness of the car park, but did no damage to the loading bay door that, as the Assistant Chief Constable had recently discovered, was designed to resist ram-raiders. The van, however, was less sturdy. It was now several inches shorter.

'Christ, this place is a bloody fortress,' said Don.

Franklin waved at the driver. 'Again! Don't stop. Again!'

But, when the policeman behind the steering wheel shifted into first gear, the rear axle refused to move. The last impact had fractured the vehicle's transmission.

Rosie thought they'd been lucky, very lucky and she did not like the idea of fighting the odds much longer. The memory of watching the female panther slaughtering five armed guards churned her guts. She knew the big male would be an even tougher opponent. As the four trackers approached the plastic-curtained entrance to the warehouse, another forklift exited. It towed three heavily laden cargo wagons. They stepped aside to let the diminutive goods train past.

An idea occurred to her.

'You know,' she said, stepping onto the footplate of the little truck and grasping the steel roll bar above the seat, 'it might be faster if we rode in one of these.'

'Rosie, do you actually know how to drive it?' said Coulston as he watched the robot slowly trundle her back in the opposite direction.

'I used to work in a mail-order warehouse,' she shouted. 'I can drive one of these in my sleep.' She sat in the driver's seat. 'There must be some way to switch off the autopilot? Aha.' She knocked a lever from 'A' to 'M'.

'I really don't think this is a good idea,' shouted the now-distant Coulston.

The forklift began to accelerate.

Rosie called over her shoulder to her friends. 'It's fine. I won't be a mo'.' She bent her head to look closer at the controls. 'So where's the brake?' She hunted for a foot pedal, a lever, anything.

The rate of acceleration increased. The hijacked forklift and its little train of goods wagons were moving too fast for her to dismount without risking injury.

Faith shouted a warning. 'Sister Rosie!'

Henry was sprinting in pursuit. Behind him, Coulston leant against the breezeblock wall; laughing so hard he feared his wounds would re-open.

Rosie looked up. A concrete wall loomed ahead and a low-speed, mini-train wreck ensued. She wrenched the steering wheel hard over to the right. The forklift skidded and hit the wall sideways on. Its carts tipped over, one after the other. They spilled a mixture of dried fruit, vitamin supplements, herbal remedies, assorted children's clothes, and some scuba regulators.

Henry pulled Rosie free of the debris.

'You are not hurt?' he said.

Rosie examined the wreckage. So much for that idea. 'Thanks. I'm fine. Um, shall we walk?'

Despairing of out-pacing the big cat, Oakshott hauled himself up a metal staircase and into the cramped office cabin that overlooked the goods floor. Scrabbling amongst the keys on the ring for the correct one, he locked its steel door. The window in the door's upper half was made of wire-embedded security glass and Oakshott peered through, looking for the panther. What he saw made his heart thump loud and erratic in his chest. The man-eater was at eye level. It crouched on the top of a teetering stack of crates, only a short distance away. The big jaguar glared at Oakshott then sprang across the divide, paws outstretched, directly at the face it could see in the window.

'Aaah!' Oakshott staggered backwards.

The glass starred but did not break and the big cat landed on the metal platform outside. Intent on using its body weight to batter open the door, the panther lunged again. The glass weakened. Oakshott heard the crack and groaned. He was boxed into a trap of his own making.

'How the hell am I going to get out of here?' he wailed.

The tiny office had only one exit and the bloody cat that it covered. He hunted around for a weapon and found nothing. Was there a hiding place? What could he do with a filing cabinet, a desk, and two chairs? Nothing. Escape? There must be a way. He spied a ventilation duct and climbed on the desk to reach it.

Crash, went the panther. Crack, went the window.

Oakshott attempted to pull free the grille that masked the vent. He jumped, but failed to get a grip and landed with his weight on his bad leg. The searing pain nearly made him lose his balance. Fighting the agony, he steadied himself. His legs trembled with the effort and his breath came fast and shallow. He took a deep gulp of air. It was important to be calm, to save his strength for another attempt.

'Come on, Oakers, less haste, more speed,' he said.

Crash. Crack, crack.

The window was not going to hold much longer.

He keened with fear and leapt, punched, pulled then wrenched the grille free. Key ring in mouth, he jumped again and forced his arms inside the vent's opening. Using the friction of skin against bare metal he squirmed in a little further. He was inside. Delight replaced fear, and Oakshott crowed with joy until he thrashed his still-exposed legs and discovered that, although his head and torso might be in the duct, his trousers were snagged on the vent's sharp metal lip. He was stuck.

Crash. Crack, crack, crack.

The window was about to break.

Those terrible sounds gave him all the motivation he needed. He took one great breath and heaved. The trousers tore, as, behind and below him, there came the tremendous noise of breaking glass. The force of the big cat's attack punched the window inwards and sheared it from its frame. Crying with fear and pain, Oakshott surged forward, wriggled his way to safety. His feet disappeared into the duct just as the big cat forced its way into the room. The panther leapt at the horizontal flue, but the shaft's dimensions were too small, and it could not claw its way into it. The big cat tumbled inelegantly to the office floor.

Panting for breath but elated that, once again, he had escaped his partners' nemesis; Oakshott elbowed his way along the metal duct.

'Come on, come on,' he said between clenched teeth that still held the key ring. He repeated the mantra with every successful forward heave. Oakshott knew he was already clear of the office and currently somewhere high above the warehouse floor. He had a vague idea that, up ahead, this shaft would meet a T-junction. If he took the right turn, he could crawl all the way to the loading bay. Then Oakshott heard a long metallic creak. The aluminium trunking was swaying. He stopped crawling as he recalled the flimsy construction of the brackets that suspended the duct from the ceiling. Could he go back? No, definitely not. He realised he had no choice but to press on as fast as possible. But he was too late. With a twang of parting metal, the joint beneath his face gave way as the combined effect of his motion and extra weight sheared it apart. Light spilled in and through the gap. Oakshott could see the concrete warehouse floor far below. The keys dropped from his mouth as, panting with terror, he tried to wriggle forward and escape. 'Oh no, it can't end like this. Not after everything else,' he moaned.

But the creaks and groans grew louder. The flue swayed, spasmed, then buckled.

'It can't... oh no. Oh—' gibbered Oakshott.

Ptang. The vent lurched downwards as a bracket tore free from the ceiling. Like an eggshell being cracked open, the ducting spilled its contents.

The panther, which had been listening with interest to the noises coming from the ventilation shaft, caught a glimpse of Oakshott, arms and legs flailing, as he fell past the office window.

There was a thud and the crunch of splintered bone as he hit the concrete floor.

Oakshott lay dead, but he had achieved a victory of sorts. For the third time he had thwarted the big cat.

The man-eater padded down the steps. It sniffed the blood spreading from Oakshott's shattered corpse then, no longer interested now the hunt was over, ambled away. An apparently effortless leap took it up and to the top of a stack of crates. A second jump returned the panther to the uppermost level of shelving. A third leap took it across an aisle and it was lost from view.

Sixty feet above Oakshott's body dangled the keys to the mall's exits. The key ring was hooked on the jagged metal of the ruptured ducting.

Rosie, Coulston, and the Olembes entered the warehouse. The policeman's wounds forced them to move slowly and they halted many times to let his pain ease. He used Rosie's spear as a staff to lean on and she now carried his rifle. They trod warily through the aisles; concerned that Oakshott did not answer their shouts.

'Robert,' said Henry as the loading bays drew near, 'I...' He hesitated. 'Something... something is here.'

'The panther?' Coulston stopped and reached for his rifle. Rosie exchanged weapons with him.

Henry nodded.

Without anyone suggesting they do so, they formed a square, back-to-back, spears and rifle pointing outwards.

Rosie watched the high stacks for movement.

'Henry, how can you tell?' she said.

'I do not know. I just feel it.' He sniffed the air. 'Maybe something I smell, something I hear.'

'What can you smell?' said Coulston.

'Only blood and fear. Our fear; other people's blood.'

Rosie strained her senses, hoping to catch some clue, but all she could hear was the repeated beeping of a nearby forklift.

'Shouldn't we try to find Oakshott?' she said. 'If the doors are just over there he should be nearby.'

'Oakshott, Mr. Oakshott!' shouted Coulston.

His voice echoed through the vast warehouse but, save for the persistent sound of the forklift, there was silence.

Coulston's phone rang. 'Sir...? No, we're looking, no sign of him. And Henry thinks the panther is here, inside... Yes, the second one.'

'Oakshott, where are you?' Rosie yelled. 'Are you hurt?'

Faith had a go. 'Mr. Oakshott!'

Indicating they should move towards the docking bay, Coulston carried on talking to Franklin; 'We're just approaching the door now, sir. Have you has any luck getting in?' He stopped by Loading Bay No.1's unopened door. 'Oh, yeah, I can see that for myself. Well, we need

Oakshott and his keys... No, still no sightings of him and I'll update you as soon as... Okay, will do.'

He ended the call then bent to examine the locked switch for the shutter. He grunted with pain as the movement stretched the gashes on his chest.

'Not much point in forcing it,' he said. 'Might jam it shut forever if we tried.' He looked up. 'Where the hell is that beeping coming from?'

It was starting to annoy them all.

And that was when they found Oakshott's body.

'Oh crap,' said Coulston.

'Precisely,' said Rosie. 'I guess Faith and Henry told us this would happen.'

'I wish it were not so,' said Faith. 'In the end, he was a generous man. He should not have died like this.'

Rosie said nothing. In her opinion, his actions had nothing to do with generosity and everything to do with self-interest. He died a greedy man, she thought.

Oakshott's death-fall had ended with his body spread-eagled across one the guide tracks for the robots. A forklift with its little train of goods had blundered into the corpse. Safety protocols then cut in. The robot had stopped, reversed, advanced again, detected the obstacle, stopped again, reversed again and so on, and all the while its alarm sounded continuously.

'Poor man. Was it the panther?' said Rosie.

'He fell from there.' Henry pointed up at the ruptured trunking high overhead. They all looked up.

'Couldn't take his weight,' Coulston said. 'Bruce Willis has a lot to answer for.'

Something glinted and caught Rosie's eye. 'Are those the keys up there?' she said, squinting upwards.

'Bloody marvellous,' said Coulston.

'How the hell are we going to get them?' said Rosie.

Coulston cast around for a ladder. 'Somewhere there must be a—'

The black panther attacked. It leapt from its hiding

place between two stacks of crates and onto Henry's back. His helmet was in its jaws, and the cat's head wrenched from right to left as it tried to crush both NFL headgear and his skull. But the sturdy Detroit Lions helmet withstood the bite, and the panther's teeth were deflected.

Shocked by the speed and aggression of the attack and slowed by his wounds, Coulston worked the bolt of his rifle. He'd forgotten to load a fresh round.

'Brother!' Faith threw her *assegai* and hit the panther in the flank.

Rosie launched herself forward and jabbed with her spear. She missed, but, as in the sports store, her attack forced the big cat to release Henry. His head bounced once, twice, on the concrete and he lay still. Leaping away, the panther turned towards them and snarled. Coulston aimed and fired, but the panther was too fast. In one sinuous motion, it bounded back into the cover of the shelving and evaded the shot. Faith's spear clattered free as the cat was lost from sight, hidden the confusion of barrels, boxes and assorted equipment stacked beneath the office stairs.

Faith rushed to her brother.

'He lives,' she said.

'Where the bloody hell has it gone?' said Rosie.

'Over here, quick,' Coulston said.

Ignoring the pain of his wounds, he grabbed the unconscious Henry by the collar and dragged him towards a metal enclosure that bore the sign:

PAINT STORE - INFLAMMABLE MATERIALS

Its wooden shelves were crammed with tins of paint and solvents. The available standing room was tiny, but it had the priceless assets of a wire mesh frame and a metal door with a sliding bolt that locked it shut. Coulston hauled Henry inside. Rosie was next and held the door open for Faith to squeeze in. It was tight fit.

'Faith, we need Henry's spear,' said Coulston as he reloaded. 'And yours too.'

Eyes wide with fear, Faith raced back to Oakshott's body, picked up the *assegais* and ran back, all in less than five seconds. To Rosie it felt more like five nerve-jangling minutes. Her shaking fingers fumbled the bolt several times before she rammed it home.

- 16 -

- Night -

- Outside Swanmere Mall -

'GUN SHOT,' DON SAID, 'THAT WAS A GUN SHOT.'

'I know. Must be Bob Coulston's rifle,' said Franklin. He stood with hands on hips and watched the continuing debacle of the attempt to break into the mall. 'This just isn't working. We're the police, we're meant to be good at things like this.'

A second police van's rear end was now crumpled by their failed attempts at ramming the door. Two police marksmen, their weapons laid on the ground, knelt, and attempted to wedge the van's jack under the shutter.

'Waste of time,' said Don. 'We need something bigger and heavier. And quick.'

He walked away from the throng and surveyed the terrain behind them. Beyond the goods delivery zone was the overspill car park and beyond that... Don's heart leapt; he'd seen something that might work. He ran to the dog van, started the engine then reversed backwards. Policemen scattered right and left as the van's squealing brakes brought it to a halt alongside Franklin. Don threw open the passenger door.

'Get in,' he said to the Assistant Chief Constable.

'What? Why?'

'Swanmere Phase Two: the building site. Don't argue. If you want to save them, get in. I need your help.'

The panther charged the paint store, forcing the entire enclosure to shudder and shift. The cage was not secured to the floor and the impact distorted the metal frame so much that the bolt-locked door bounced open. The big predator sprang for the entrance.

'Bob! Faith!' yelled Rosie.

She jabbed with her spear. The panther seized the shaft in its teeth and snapped it in half. In those powerful jaws, it might as well have been a toothpick.

Faith pushed past Rosie, stabbed with her *assegai*, and scored the man-eater's ribs.

Coulston took a shot at point-blank range.

'I hit it!' he said.

Finally, thought Rosie.

But the big cat appeared unaffected. Once more, it attacked through the open doorway, the claws of one paw hooked into the mesh as it raked Faith on the arm with the other.

A metal rack containing variously coloured fire extinguishers was screwed to the side of the wooden shelving. In desperation, Rosie grabbed a CO_2 cylinder, pulled the pin then blasted the black panther with it. The freezing cloud of white gas stopped the man-eater in its tracks. Shocked by this new threat, it retreated out of range.

Pfffft. Its supply discharged, the extinguisher hissed into silence.

White clouds of gas rose from between the black panther's shoulders as its body heat evaporated the snowy crust covering it. The beast roared at Rosie and gathered itself to leap again. She used the only weapon at hand and hurled the extinguisher at their attacker. With a resonating clang, it struck the panther's skull a hefty blow. The big cat yowled with pain and retreated to the shadows.

Coulston slammed the door shut then used his belt to secure it tight.

'Faith, Rosie, you did well,' he said.

'I am hurt,' said Faith.

The wound was worse than the claw marks across Coulston's chest. The panther's savage assault had ripped away the muscle in Faith's forearm to expose white bone. Rosie tried to staunch the bleeding with bandages torn from Faith's skirt and her own shirt.

'You may be hurt,' she said to Faith as she worked to bind the lacerated flesh, 'but so is the cat.'

'Enraged, more like,' said Coulston. He stood inside the door, rifle at the ready. Every movement was agony for him. Raising the rifle to sight along the barrel was so painful his breath came fast and shallow. 'It just seems unstoppable. Nothing damages it. We've got to get out of here.' It was obvious they could not resist many more assaults like the last. In the hope that inspiration might strike, he scanned their surrounds.

Rosie plucked a second foam extinguisher from the rack. 'Maybe we could use this?'

'To do what? Foam it to death?'

'No. I could wedge it in its mouth and you shoot the canister. Boom! One headless cat. Problem solved.'

'It isn't a bloody great white shark out there. Crap ideas like that only work in the movies. Just ask Oakshott. Oh no, that's right, you can't.'

'All right. No need to get sarcastic.' Rosie turned to Faith. 'Now's a good time to come up with some magic flower, a spell, something.'

Faith smiled and took Rosie's hand. 'My sister, now we can only trust in ourselves.'

Rosie's jaws clenched. So much for magic, she thought.

Coulston searched frantically in the pockets of his hunting jacket.

'Bloody hell.'

'Now what?' said Rosie.

He held up a single rifle cartridge. 'I'm out of ammo. This is my last round. Definitely.'

The panther attacked once more. This time the big cat threw its weight against the side of the cage. The whole enclosure rocked, nearly toppled over, but fell finally back into place. Tins of paint clattered to the floor.

'It's trying to push over the cage,' said Rosie as she attempted to use her arms, legs, and torso to stop the cans from spilling everywhere.

'This thing moves?' Coulston kicked the base of the cage with a boot. The action had been so frenzied that only now did he recognise the fact. 'Come on, help me.'

Wincing with the effort, he smashed the shelving apart with his rifle butt. The last of the paint pots fell to the ground. Faith crouched over her brother to shield him from the splashes of paint.

'Bob, what are we doing?' said Rosie.

'We're going to shove this thing over to the loading bay door. Grab Henry's spear and look after it. I need you to push at the front,' he said. 'Faith you'll have to drag Henry. Can you manage it with one good hand?'

'It is not far.'

Coulston lifted the rear of the cage.

'Push,' he said.

Rosie obeyed and the paint store screeched forwards. Sobbing with the agony and the effort, Coulston lifted the rear end higher, up and over the jumble of paint tins, but then was forced to let go. He did not have the strength to clear all the debris. Inch by inch, they slowly forced the enclosure across the floor.

Goods Bay No.1 was in sight.

They rested.

Coulston forced his words out between pants. 'If we can... get to the corner... by the door then we can try... to force the lock... on the shutter.'

'Okay, but you save your breath, I'll do this one' said Rosie. 'Let's go again, on three. Faith, Bob are you ready?' They nodded. 'One, two, three, up.' With a screech of metal on concrete, the cage shifted again. 'And down.' The metal frame banged onto the floor.

They stretched to ease their pain-stricken bodies, but the respite was short. The big cat charged. The paint store tipped up as the jaguar's solid bulk struck its side. The entire structure was about to fall over. Coulston leapt for the roof and hooked fingers through the mesh. His body weight stabilised the cage and it settled to the ground, but the pain from his tight-stretched wounds was so intense he thought he might pass out.

Rosie thrust at the panther with the *assegai*, its narrow blade perfectly suited to jabbing between the wires of the mesh. Realising it could not get at its prey, the big cat paced out of spear range and returned to the dark spaces between the giant racks of shelves.

'That was close,' Rosie said.

Coulston collapsed to his knees. He knelt alongside Henry, arms hugged across his chest.

After a minute passed, he said, 'Christ, it hurts, but at least we're nearly clear of these bloody paint cans.' Despite their efforts, a lot of containers, timber, and tins remained inside the cage. 'One more heave over this lot and it'll be easier.'

The panther leapt onto the paint store's roof and the cage rocked under the force of its landing. Coulston grabbed one side to quell the motion, but did not have enough strength to stabilise it. It began to keel over. Rosie rammed her *assegai* upwards. The big cat saw the spear and, conscious of how exposed were its belly and chest, sprang to safety. The departing shove from its hind legs corrected the enclosure's teetering motion and, after rocking back-and-forth violently a couple of times, it steadied and settled itself.

'We'll never make it at this rate,' Rosie said.

'But we've got to try,' said Coulston. He stood and readied himself for another effort. 'Come on, all together, on three again. One, two—'

'Brother Robert!' shouted Faith.

The panther threw itself at the rear of the paint store where Coulston stood ready to lift, his back to the attack. The metal frame shuddered and was shoved forwards several paces by the predator's impact. Desperate to keep away from the big cat's claws, he stumbled towards the front, tripped over Henry, and fell to the floor.

'Why doesn't the bloody thing die?' he said as Rosie and Faith helped him to his feet. 'We've hurt it enough.'

'Fire cleanses all; only fire can drive the *kyaani* away,' said Faith.

'If only we had a flame thrower,' Rosie said.

And that gave Coulston an idea. 'Maybe we do,' he said. Thrusting paint cans aside; he hunted through the shelf debris. 'These might do it.' He selected a small white plastic drum and a plain two-litre bottle. Both were nearly full.

He unscrewed the bottle's cap. Sniffed it. 'Good,' he said. 'It's white spirit.'

The panther charged again. The cage see-sawed.

They held their breath until it thunked back down.

'Paint thinner,' continued Coulston. 'Highly inflammable.' He removed the screw top from the bottle. 'Rosie, next time the cat attacks, pour this on its fur.' He held it out to her. 'Come on, I can't hold onto this forever.'

Rosie was sceptical both of this new tactic and of her ability to pull it off. Nevertheless, she took the bottle.

'Why? How?' she said.

Coulston removed the drum's cap.

'Just do it, please.'

The big cat noticed no one held a spear anymore. Claws extended and fangs exposed, it lunged from the shadows. The enclosure swayed onto one side as the man-eater stood on its hind legs and pushed. Rosie screamed with fright and involuntarily squeezed the plastic bottle she held. A jet of white spirit splashed the cat's underbelly.

Faith and Coulston grabbed the mesh beneath the panther's claws and pulled down. Again, disaster was averted, but the effort took its toll. Both were weakening.

The panther no longer hid, it dropped to its paws and paced around the cage, out of range of the spears, but eager to close again with its prey.

'Good, well done,' said Coulston as he watched the jaguar. 'Now quick, let's move. Faith, you've got Henry. Rosie, lift with me. One, two—' Coulston kicked over the drum of white spirit. Its contents glugged onto the floor. 'Three. And up!'

He heaved the paint store over the last of the wrecked shelving. They shoved the enclosure across the floor. Coulston straightened his back to lift the rear of the paint store clear of the still-emptying drum. Rosie's right arm strained with the effort as she pushed. In her left hand, she clutched both the white spirit bottle and Henry's spear against her chest.

The big cat attacked from behind, but Coulston dropped the cage to prevent it crawling under, and the panther's impact only succeeded in propelling the mesh enclosure further towards the pit of the loading bay.

'Rosie, the bottle,' shouted Coulston. 'On its head. Pour it on its head.'

She let go of the mesh and jetted the rest of the white spirit into the cat's eyes. With a roar of anger and pain, it spun away, shaking its head to rid itself of the stinging liquid.

'We're almost—' But Coulston didn't get a chance to finish the sentence.

Enraged, the cat leapt at them. The structure rocked sideway. Coulston, arms stretched high, teeth bared in silent agony, jumped, and hung from the roof once more. The paint store crashed back down, and the policeman dropped to the floor and staggered backwards into Rosie.

The pair of them tumbled over Faith and Henry. His face almost level with the concrete floor, Coulston could see, reflected in the overhead light, the growing pool of inflammable paint thinner. It now lapped against the nearest storage racks.

'It's spreading fast,' he said. 'Get up, quick, we need to push.'

They reached the lip of the pit.

'How do we get down those?' said Rosie.

A flight of concrete steps led to the door mechanism. It was clear to her that it would be impossible to slide the enclosure down them without it toppling over or, if it got stuck half-way, its exposed underside would be open to attack from the panther.

'Doesn't matter,' Coulston said. 'We've got to kill the cat first. We need to spin the cage about. The door has to face the other way, towards the white spirit.'

They rotated the paint store.

Frustrated by its failure to get inside the cage, the beast launched another assault. Rosie was ready with the spear, but it attacked with such speed that, before she could react, the enclosure was forced to the pit's edge. She dropped the *assegai* and rushed to help Faith and Coulston push back against the mesh. They held it steady, but Rosie's left hand was too close to the big cat. It moved so fast she barely registered what happened. One second the panther was at a safe distance, the next her fingers were in its jaws. Rosie tried to pull back but was too slow. Its great incisors snapped shut.

The pain was searing, more intense than anything she'd ever experienced. Her entire forefinger and half the index were gone. Stunned by the savage attack, she stood still, left wrist clutched by right hand, and stared at the blood, her blood, spouting from the wounds. It seemed so unreal. She was nauseous to the very pit of her stomach, but felt detached from what had occurred. Tears started in her eyes. It can't be happening; it shouldn't have happened, she thought, not to me.

'Rosie, Rosie stay with us,' Coulston tore strips of grubby cloth from Henry's shirt. 'Faith, talk to her, she's about to faint.'

'Sister Rosie, we will help, this will help,' Faith said as, one-handed, she began to bind Rosie's wounds.

Coulston took her face in his hands, turning her eyes away from the bloody stumps of her fingers. 'We're almost there. The pain will pass. We can't stop now, no matter what happens. Understood?'

She nodded then said; 'Now I know what Big Mo's rubber sausages felt like.'

'Pardon?'

'Sorry. Just a bad joke.'

He lowered his hands, smiled, and said; 'Bloody hell, you know between the four of us, we could just about make one fully fit person.' Coulston stepped across the unconscious Henry to the door, and unstrapped the belt from the lock. 'Until we find a way to open the shutter, we're cornered,' he said, 'but at least we can make sure there's only one direction from which the panther can attack.' He jerked his chin towards the maze of crates. The still-spreading pool of liquid glistened under the floodlights.

'Ah, I understand,' said Faith. 'If we offer it the open door, it must come at us through fire and flame.'

Rosie put it more simply. 'A fireball?'

Coulston nodded.

He unslung his rifle.

Loaded his last round.

'No matter how many times I shoot at the beast, it seems to have no effect. So we'll make sure my bullet hits something I can't miss. A ricochet off the floor should create the spark we need.' he said. 'Faith, on 'three' you open the door. Rosie, if that monster makes it across the flames, can you throw your spear? Faith, you too?'

'I can try,' Rosie said. Left hand held tight against her waist she bent and picked up Henry's *assegai*.

Faith did not speak, just nodded.

Fighting the pain from his chest wounds, Coulston raised the rifle, steadied it, holding it snug and firm against his shoulder. 'Okay, one, two—'

Rosie tried to straighten upright, but the throbbing pain was too intense. The best she could manage was a half-crouch stance, with spear held at rest on her right shoulder.

'Three.'

Buckled by the paint store's tormented journey across the warehouse floor, the door screeched as Faith pushed it open.

Rosie readied the spear.

Coulston's finger tightened on the trigger.

No big cat appeared from the behind the crates.

They waited, wondering how long they could stand ready to use their weapons before pain overwhelmed them.

The building was silent save for the now-distant beeping of the robot forklift thwarted by Oakshott's death fall.

Rosie was the first to speak. 'Bob, maybe it's—'

The black panther padded into the open and advanced towards the cage door. Blood glistened on its wounds. It growled, the sound building from deep in its chest, low and rolling until it culminated in a roar. At the pool of white spirit, the big cat paused. It bent its head to sniff the volatile liquid.

Rosie's heart sank. 'Shit, it's not going to—'

The man-eater leapt for the doorway, stretching full-length to clear the evil-smelling paint thinner.

Coulston took his shot. The bullet hit the centre of the pool. Sparks flew and ignited the vaporised fluid above the liquid in an explosive whoof of expanding flame.

The panther, much of its fur already drenched in paint thinner, was engulfed mid-air by the fireball. Its coat caught fire. Ablaze and writhing, the big cat landed in front of the cage. Eyes the same colour as the flames glowered from amidst the inferno as, utterly implacable, it gathered itself for one final attack.

'Your spears!' shouted Coulston.

The blazing cat charged.

Faith threw her spear but the panther batted it aside.

With a scream, Rosie cast the *assegai*. It flew straight, hard, and true. The spearhead sliced into the panther's throat. The big cat reared up, and toppled back into the fire. It twitched once, twice, and then lay still.

There was no time to celebrate, a second drum of inflammable liquid exploded and sprayed fire across the warehouse. Wooden pallets, cardboard boxes, and the goods they contained tumbled onto the dead male jaguar. Its pyre began to burn at a ferocious pace. Tongues of flame licked the ceiling.

'It is done, the *kyaani* will sleep again' said Faith. 'Henry will be happy.'

It occurred to Rosie that the odds of Henry ever regaining consciousness and hearing the happy news were slim to none. The fire would consume them first.

The engine turned over, spluttered, and died. Don pushed the throttle back in.

'Never thought I'd get a chance to put all those weekend visits to Digger World to good use,' he said as he pressed the starter to clear the excess fuel. 'The trick is not to pull the throttle out too far.'

Tyre iron in hand, Franklin watched from the rear of the cabin. Since they were stealing a vehicle, Don has insisted the Assistant Chief Constable do the actual breaking and entering. It left the Chief Dog Warden to the taking without consent part of the crime.

Don tried again. This time the engine caught. It coughed into life. A blue-black cloud of acrid exhaust fumes swept in through the window Franklin had smashed.

'Of course,' said Don. 'Driving JCBs is very different from handling this monstrous beast.'

He forced the stick-shift into first gear, pulled out the throttle, and they ground forwards.

With a whoosh of water, the fire sprinklers kicked in, but the flames had spread to combustible goods sheltered from the downpour by the shelves above. The three hunters watched the conflagration grow.

'Bob,' said Rosie.

'What?'

'I left the fire extinguishers on the far side—'

Coulston finished the sentence for her. 'Of the fire.'

They all ducked as a distant explosion toppled one of the storage rows.

'Oh dear, they were right where that just happened. Sorry.'

'Never mind. At least we got the cat.'

The flaming liquid lapped against the cage door.

Rosie unstrapped her Jaguars helmet. 'Looks like it got us too.'

They abandoned the paint store, heaving the steel frame onto its side and, carrying Henry between them, staggered down the steps.

Using the butt of his rifle, Coulston hammered at the locked steel casing of the shutter switch.

'If I could only get this open.'

A gout of black smoke made him duck low. They all began to cough.

'Got to keep trying.'

Now sitting, Coulston hammered again.

'This is stupid,' said Rosie.

'Well, what do you suggest?'

She assessed the scene. The fire was growing fast, but they were not cut off from the warehouse. A narrow strip of concrete alongside the nearest wall was still clear of flame.

'There's the forklift by Oakshott's body,' she said. 'If I go now, I could reach it.'

'There's no way it can open this thing. The shutter's way too heavy and this pit's in the way too.'

'Not what I was thinking.'

'Anyway, you couldn't even work out how to use the brakes last time,' said Coulston.

'Exactly, but I could steer it.'

Whoomph. Another barrel of inflammable liquid exploded. Red embers danced in the air as the flames spread.

Rosie acted before she had time to consider the recklessness of her action. She sprinted up the steps, skirted the conflagration then ran towards Oakshott's corpse.

The forklift was still there, still patiently waiting for the blockage to be removed. Rosie disconnected the little truck from its carts, clambered into the driver's seat then knocked off the autopilot.

Reaching backwards, she found the safety harness strapped behind the seat, undid it, and clicked it into place across her waist. She then nudged the forklift forwards and manoeuvred it around Oakshott's corpse. As before, it began to accelerate. Steering one-handed, she aimed for the loading bay. A wall of fire blocked the way, but she could not stop. Arms raised to shield her face, Rosie and the forklift arrowed through the flames. They reached the lip of the pit and launched into space. To Rosie's disappointment, they fell a long way short of the door. The truck landed but then bounced into the air. Still airborne, its two prongs punched at waist height into the giant shutter and pierced the steel slats. The forklift's chassis slammed up against the shutter and stopped.

Both Rosie and machine were suspended above the ground. Very slowly, the forklift toppled sideways. Steel screeched as the two prongs pried apart the shutters then, with a crash, the machine slid backwards and freed itself from the door. It came to rest on its rear end, twin forks pointing upwards. Helped by Coulston and Faith, she clambered free.

'Who said becoming a dog warden was a safe career option?' Rosie said. She limped to the gash created by her giant can-opener. 'I think we can get Henry through here.' Savouring the sweet-smelling air that poured in from outside, she looked through the hole. Two giant, dazzling headlights raced towards her. She recoiled in alarm. 'Watch out!' she yelled. 'Those bloody idiots don't know we're coming out.'

Kerrang. The steel shutter bent and buckled.

'Quick, my friends, against the wall,' said Faith.

She shoved Coulston and Rosie towards where Henry lay in the pit's corner.

Rosie could hear a throbbing diesel engine reverse then roar as it accelerated forwards again. With a deafening crash, the shutters ripped free from their guide track. The giant yellow earthmover from the construction site trundled into the loading bay. 'I hope you're not expecting me to sign an overtime slip for this,' Don shouted to Rosie from its cabin window.

Swanmere mall was aflame. Hoses from a dozen fire tenders attempted to stem the blaze. Rosie, Faith, and Coulston watched the conflagration whilst paramedics attended to Henry.

'So two panthers did all this, huh? Quite a couple.' said Rosie.

'Just so,' said Coulston. He tried, but failed, to keep the satisfaction out of his voice.

Rosie glanced at Faith. 'And we did good, killing the big bad *kyaani*.'

'It is not good or bad, light or dark,' Faith said, 'it just is.'

Yeah, right, thought Rosie, I saw it die. Saw both of them die. Made sure both of them died. There didn't seem to be anything spiritual about that process.

One of Swanmere's citadel-like concrete walls collapsed into the inferno. It was clear to everyone watching that this was a fight the fire brigade was going to lose.

'And so the *kyaani* has vengeance,' Faith added.

'And so it does,' said Coulston.

Another section of wall slumped. Two great gouts of flame and embers shot high into the sky. For a brief moment, they created the indistinct illusion of a pair of yellow cat's eyes.

Nah, said Rosie to herself, it's just a trick of the light.

- 17 -

- Two days later -

- Forestry trailhead, The North Downs -

'YOU'RE LUCKY WE COULD USE THE SLOPE,' SAID Coulston, 'we'd never have got it down here otherwise. Not in the state we're in.' He glanced at his watch. 'Look at the time, it's taken us three hours.' Gasping for breath, he leant against the side of Rosie's car.

'Well, I couldn't leave it up there. What a waste that would have been,' she said.

They were both pale and sweating. Coulston looked ill. He should still be in hospital, under observation, thought Rosie.

'Thanks,' she said. 'I couldn't have done it without you.'

'No problem, I had to get up here anyhow, get outdoors, get some fresh air. I can't stand hospitals.'

Rosie lifted the car's rear hatch, slid out two metal snow tracks, and then positioned them angled down between car boot and the ground.

'You're kidding,' said Coulston, 'we'll never get it up those. It's too heavy.'

The painkillers prescribed for Rosie's wounds made her cheerful and optimistic about their prospects. 'Come on, we can roll it across and inside. It's almost downhill, just like you said, and look!' She brandished a small block and tackle. 'I don't know how to use this, but I'm told they work really well.'

Coulston groaned. 'Just so long as I don't open up any wounds. I've still got miles to walk.'

'Are you sure you don't want to come to the butchers with us? I just need to pick up the kids then head over to Bankstone. I can drop you off anywhere you like.'

'No thanks, I bought some meat this morning, and I've seen enough slaughter in the past week to last a lifetime, I don't need to watch any more.' He pushed himself away from the car. 'Right then, let's give this a go.' He took the block and tackle from her. 'Let me show you how this works. You're a hunter now. If you kill a boar, you need to be able to get it home afterwards.'

The Olembes stood on the steps of the manor house in Lower Hamley. Henry leant on a pair of crutches.

'Goodbye, sir, madam,' he called.

'Farewell, I hope you find happiness,' said Faith.

She raised her unbandaged arm and waved at the Dawes' 4x4 as it departed down the drive, preceded by two removal trucks.

Inside the Range Rover, Naomi refused to acknowledge the Olembes, but stared straight ahead. With any luck, she thought, this will be the last time we ever have to travel along these claustrophobic, tree-infested lanes. It gave her little consolation. Desperate for a quick sale, they had found only a single buyer in the post-panther house price slump.

'The humiliation of it, Johnno,' she said. 'The humiliation.'

'To sell to one's own—'

'Servants. We'll never live it down.'

Nigel Peckworth scratched his head. 'It's quite a beast, I've never had to work with one of these before so I'm not too sure.'

Rosie tried again. 'Come on, Nigel, how many sausages?'

He hummed and hawed, crouched to inspect the carcass where it lay on the stainless steel trolley. He'd never before seen a pig of this size, farm-bred or wild.

'Okay, if you insist, about two hundred. At least. But it's a waste of the better cuts.'

'Hear that everyone? At least two hundred bangers!' shouted Rosie.

There were cheers and woofs from inside her car.

Lizzie leant on the back seat and called out to Nigel through the open boot. 'My mum killed it!'

Peter joined in, 'She killed a panther too!'

'And it ate two of her fingers,' added Lizzie with pride.

Embarrassed, Rosie held up her bandaged left hand.

Nigel whistled, 'So the stories were true. I never know what to believe in the papers. Well, I suppose we'd better get started,' he said. 'If there's as many wild boars in these parts as you tell me, this won't be last one I'll butcher. I need to get practising.'

From inside the car there came the frantic sound of scrabbling claws and Big Mo shot out of the boot as if rocket-propelled. His target was the open entrance to the butcher's meat store.

'Oh no, not him,' cried Nigel. He slammed shut the door before the dog reached it.

Big Mo stood defiant.

He growled at Nigel.

The rear doors of Rosie's car were shoved open. Out spilled the children and Little Mo. But the German Shepherd did not come to the aid of his pack leader. Peter's arm was draped across his shoulders and he looked with adoration at the little boy, content to follow anyone who had proved himself willing to defend Little Mo's food bowl from the voracious terrier.

Rosie stood with hands on hips.

Big Mo saw her and growled.

'Sit!' said Rosie, 'Big Mo, sit.'

Big Mo looked at Nigel, the children, Little Mo, then again at Rosie.

He dared not hold her stare.

He sat.

On the woodland slope high above the hollow where Zaharkin shot the stag and Oakshott wounded the panther, Coulston trod softly around large man-sized boulders fallen from a sandstone outcrop. He paused, listened, and knew he had been right when he examined the dead female panther back in the sports store.

'Getting close now,' he said.

He eased the daypack from his back. From it, he removed a soft but heavy package wrapped in white greaseproof paper. Even those simple motions were painful. Hauling the boar to Rosie's car had been a feat of agony-filled endurance. He was exhausted. Only an urgent sense of obligation had brought him here.

Once he steadied himself, Coulston listened again and, for the first time, could clearly hear the mewing. Up and to the right, he thought. He clambered over a rock outcrop, his boots scraping flakes of weathered sandstone from its surface. The mewing stopped. Coulston had been heard, but it no longer mattered, he now knew where to look. From inside a deep, dark hollow beneath a house-sized boulder, three small pairs of eyes watched him with suspicion. Hunched together for warmth and security, the cubs hissed. Framed by black fur, small white fangs were bared against this frightening intruder.

Coulston kept his voice low and friendly. 'Hey, little ones, there you are, missing your mother. Sorry it took so long, I had to wait for the fuss to die down. I bet you're hungry.'

He opened the packet. Inside were some strips of beef and an unskinned rabbit. He tossed the meat down the hole, and heard chewing and contented purring. The rabbit followed, fur and all. Coulston rested his head against the cool, dry surface of the boulder and smiled as he listened to the cubs crunch the bones.

THE END

ABOUT THE AUTHOR

Jack Churchill is the pen name adopted by Martin Belderson to avoid confusion between his fiction and non-fiction books.

Trained at the BBC as a director, he has made more than thirty full-length documentary films, mostly in the fields of natural history, science and adventure sport. During that time, he has been charged by rhinos, chased by elephants, been caught up in sea-battles, filmed in the Hot Zone of an Ebola Fever outbreak, fallen off mountains, and once trod on a sleeping bushmaster viper. He regards himself as very lucky to be alive.

Along the way, Martin has also won quite a few awards and nominations for his films, screenplays, and short stories. He is attempting to use the recent digital convergence of the creative arts to weave writing, graphic design, film-making, and drama production into a single career. It's horribly complicated. If it fails, he plans to go back to one of his first jobs: selling potatoes door-to-door. It might be easier.

For more information about the author's encounters with big cats, plus videos, details of the cover art, information on possible big cat sightings in Britain, and much more, go to the Big Cat web page (www.4winds-productions.com/big-cat).

IF YOU ENJOYED READING *BIG CAT*, PLEASE RATE, SHARE & REVIEW THE BOOK

Books need readers. As an independent publishing imprint, we rely upon the goodwill of readers who enjoyed this book to help spread the word. It would be immensely helpful if you could take the time to do so. You could post a review on Amazon, Goodreads, or other review sites. Recommending the book on Facebook or Twitter would also be very useful in helping this book find readers. Thank you.

The book also available on Kindle and other eBook retail outlets.

— *MORE FICTION FROM JACK CHURCHILL* —

COMING SOON IN 2014

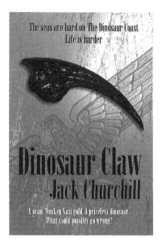

Dinosaur Claw

by Jack Churchill.

Publication August 2014.

Available from The Aeolian Press
in eBook (Kindle, Nook, Kobo, &
iBook) and in paperback.

Price: tbc.

A comedy thriller (August 2014). 70,000 words.
Price TBC

The hunt for a priceless dinosaur. Salvaging sunken Nazi gold. What could possibly go wrong?

Kath and Jim 'Deano' Deane struggle to make a living. She has to hold down three jobs to make ends meet; he's a remarkably unsuccessful inventor. To escape their poverty trap, they fake the search for an invaluable dinosaur fossil. The scam is meant to provide cover while they pursue their real objective: the secret salvage of gold from a sunken wreck. When the fossil attracts the unwelcome interest of two ruthless and powerful collectors, these rivals' determination to secure the claw threatens to unravel the whole plot.

**The seas are hard on Yorkshire's Dinosaur Coast.
Life is harder.**

Read Before Filming Book #1

The Art of the Documentary Interview

by Martin Belderson

Available on Kindle, Nook, Kobo & iBook in May 2014. Published in paperback in June 2014.

Read Before Filming Book #1: The Art of the Documentary Interview by Martin Belderson

Published in eBook (May 2014)
Price TBC
How to conduct effective film and radio interviews
Hints and tips from experienced pros in easy steps

The first in a series of low-budget field guides containing practical advice and tips about advanced aspects of film-making that every aspiring professional should know. Using dozens of interviews with veteran documentary-makers, crews and editors from the film, radio and TV industries, these books delivers entertaining anecdotes, cautionary disaster stories, and improbable tales of victory over adversity. The books contain quick reference checklists at the back of each chapter.

Made in the USA
Charleston, SC
07 February 2014